PENGUIN CRIME FICTION

GRAVES IN ACADEME

Susan Kenney won the Quality Paperback Book
Club "New Voices" Award for the best first novel
of 1984 for *In Another Country* (also available in
Penguin). She is also the author of one previous
mystery featuring Roz Howard, *Garden of Malice*.
She teaches writing at Colby College in Maine,
where she lives with her husband and children.

GRAVES
—IN—
ACADEME

SUSAN KENNEY

PENGUIN BOOKS

PENGUIN BOOKS
Published by the Penguin Group
Penguin Books USA Inc.,
375 Hudson Street, New York, New York 10014, U.S.A.
Penguin Books Ltd, Harmondsworth,
Middlesex, England
Penguin Books Australia Ltd, Ringwood,
Victoria, Australia
Penguin Books Canada Ltd, 10 Alcorn Avenue,
Toronto, Ontario, Canada M4V 3B2
Penguin Books (N.Z.) Ltd, 182–190 Wairau Road,
Auckland 10, New Zealand

First published in the United States of America by
Viking Penguin Inc. 1985
Published in Penguin Books 1986

7   9   10   8   6

LIBRARY OF CONGRESS CATALOGING IN PUBLICATION DATA
Kenney, Susan, 1941–
Graves in academe.
(Penguin crime fiction)
I. Title.
PS3561.E445G7   1986b   813'.54   86-4953
ISBN 0 140 1.3349 6

Printed in the United States of America
Set in Times Roman

For Punch Grow, Loel Kline,
Pat Onion, and Barbara Sweney,
*Neighbors, colleagues, friends—
and indefatigable readers
of rough drafts*

My special thanks to Jessica Munns for bringing to my attention the splendid possibilities of Aphra Behn's *The Rover*, the text of which I have altered slightly in my production, and to Edwin B. Barrett for the loan of a phiz.

This work was completed with the help of a grant from the National Endowment for the Arts.

GRAVES
IN
ACADEME

PROLOGUE

If you had been watching College Hill at dusk that night in early November, you would have seen the mist rising out of the damp ground and blanketing the college in ever-thickening layers, until only the lighted spires of the Library and the Chapel are visible above it, and the last streetlight casts an ever-decreasing cone of yellow light across the street and sidewalk. A fine rain floats down, visible only in the arc of the glowing street lamp, and slicks the sidewalk, the stiff grass, the street.

A person watching would have seen people walking by in pairs, in groups, singly, students returning up the hill from town to their dormitories, professors walking down the hill to their homes in town, all hurrying past, their voices muffled, huddled together in the fog, and cars creeping up or down the street, their headlights boring into the dense fog no more than a dozen feet ahead.

Sometime later, a man so tall it seems his head might poke through the fog into clearer air above walks by, hands in his pockets, looking from side to side as though searching for something. As he passes under the last streetlight his head is momentarily visible, but his face is obscured by the pulled-down visor of a baseball cap. There is the sound of

*a jet plane passing overhead, its noise muffled by the fog.
The fog settles in even closer, thicker, until the pale round
glow of the last streetlight looks like a giant dandelion gone
to seed.*

*Not long after, a pickup truck emerges briefly from the
fog into the circle of light, moves slowly through it, then
disappears. Nearby a car door slams, slams again, a motor
coughs and roars. The pickup reemerges going the other
way, disappears again, the purr of its engine cut off as
abruptly as its visibility.*

*By dawn the fog has lifted, and the air is cold and clear,
so that from the street the girl is clearly visible, sitting in
the small stone gazebo at the edge of the woods, not far
from the last streetlight, her bright red jacket like a beacon
in the early morning light. But she is not wearing the jacket,
only jeans and a flannel shirt, the down jacket flung across
the back of the stone bench next to her shoulder. There is
a thick book open in her lap, but she is not reading it. She
stares with half-open eyes off into space, contemplative. An
early jogger pads by, and, his eye caught first by the bright
red jacket, cranes his neck around to look at her, but does
not stop.*

*The girl stares on, unmoving. When the jogger comes
back the other way a half hour later, she is still sitting there
exactly as she was. This time the jogger stops, his breath
panting out a ragged stream of vapor in the chilly morning
air. There is no such stream emanating from the girl. He
stands on the sidewalk for a moment, looking at her, then
picks his way over the frozen hillside to where she sits stiffly
propped on the stone bench in the little shelter. Bending
over with his hands on his hips, he stares at her face, then
down at her hand resting lightly on the book as though to
hold her place. After a moment he turns and hurries back
to the sidewalk, stands there looking up and down the road.
He hops up and down several times, flapping his arms and*

blowing, and then starts back down the hill at a pace much faster than a jog.

This is what someone watching that foggy night and bright November morning might have seen.

But there was no one watching.

Was there?

CHAPTER

1

*R*oz Howard watched as the young man behind the counter laboriously wrote out her ticket. She glanced upward idly at the sign overhead. MOOSEHEAD AIRLINES. She'd asked for a reservation, of course, called from the International Terminal in Boston after flying in from Edinburgh, but the young man who answered explained that since they were really a small commuter airline, hardly more than a shuttle service between Boston and Maine, they never made reservations in advance. But there would be no problem getting a seat, he assured her, so she had ridden over on the airport jitney. And here she was, waiting while he made out the one-way ticket. Evidently they did sell round-trip tickets, even little monthly packets of them, advertised behind the counter at a substantial discount, just like a train, but she'd hardly be needing those. She could make her return reservation when she saw how things worked out at the college and had a better idea of how long she was going to stay.

Not only when, but where as well. Not back to Poughkeepsie, of course; in the middle of the summer, forwarded all the way to the tiny cottage she was sharing with Alan in the Highlands, she had received a polite but firm letter from the chairman of her department indicating her contract as an assistant professor of English had not been renewed. Just as she had suspected; no second book or series of major articles, no tenure, hence no job. She could have gone back after her leave was up for the remaining year of her contract, but who wanted to hang around when it was common knowledge you'd been, as they put it, terminated? No, it was time to take stock of where she was, and not just in her career, either. There had been entirely too much career of late, and the tragedy she still felt, obscurely, that she might have prevented if she hadn't been so pigheaded about furthering her academic career, and so naive about people's intentions. Alan had done his best to disabuse her of this notion, when he wasn't distracted by other more immediate and less abstract activities involving the two of them.

And of course Alan himself, the whole long, lovely summer stretching into fall in the Highlands—what was she going to do about him? Or, rather, us, she thought, for she had gotten into the habit of thinking of the two of them as inseparable, parts of a whole. But feeling as she did at times uncertain, even panicky, about the prospect of marriage— or any other long-term arrangement, for that matter—when she had been unexpectedly offered the one-year emergency replacement position at Canterbury College two weeks ago, she had agonized for a while, then decided to take it. Give the two of them time to cool off, to take stock. They were neither adolescents nor first lovers, but even after four months together, with no end in sight, it was clear there was plenty of passion still unspent. And passion clouded judgment. Could it possibly work? She thought so, hoped so, but hadn't she thought and hoped that about her so painfully concluded affair with Tony? She still had the belief, gleaned from her mother, the old-fashioned romantic, that if it was right, it would survive any difficulty, any test, even separation.

Besides, there was her career to think about. Should she

give it up to stay with Alan? Would she have to? She didn't know. Anyway, the job was for only nine months, one of which had already passed, with a month off in January—Alan might fly over then—and she could be back in Scotland by June. And it was a favor to a friend of an old friend.

She hoped she wouldn't regret it. It had been barely eight hours since she left Alan in the bleakly modern airline terminal improbably set on an old clan marching ground in Edinburgh, and already she felt as though it had been a lifetime. She remembered his look, the tousled mahogany hair, the ironic triangular grin that had once seemed puckish, even faunlike, and now was simply Alan's, the light odor of turpentine emanating from his jacket as he enveloped her in a last bear hug, hand luggage and all, lifting her off the ground in the process.

Plopping her back down on her feet, but not letting her go just yet, he said in the deep, husky voice that had gained back considerably more of its Scottish burr in the last few months: "I do wish you weren't going, you know."

Roz, who was experiencing similar misgivings, nevertheless pulled away and, frowning at him in a feeble attempt to simulate exasperation, replied: "Don't worry; I can take care of myself."

"Oh, I don't doubt that," Alan said, bringing his hands up to adjust the collar of her raincoat. "If ever there was a maiden—metaphorically speaking, of course—who could manage her own rescues, it's you, fair Rosamund," he said, resting his hands on her shoulders. "While I, in the best tradition of the White Knight, do little more than tumble off my horse at your feet." He grinned, the two wide circumflexes bracketing his smile. "After the fact, of course."

"Better late than never," Roz murmured. Overcome by a pang of loneliness, she had buried her face in his sweater—it was quite brisk for the first week in October—and was standing there with his arms wrapped around her when the

loudspeaker burred an announcement, and the other occu-
pants of the small lounge began to mill toward the exit
ramp. "There's your flight, my dear." Kissing her once more
lightly on the top of the head, he had said simply, "Take
care of yourself," then with a ghost of the familiar pointed
grin, added that odd medieval catchphrase, "For the nonce."
Then he had turned, stuffed his hands in his trouser pockets,
his rumpled trench coat fanning out behind him like the tail
of a large bird, and walked away.

Roz sighed. So now, thanks to her old classmate Judy Laster,
formerly a junior professor at Canterbury College, now at
Brandeis, here she was in the Boston airport, on her way
to Southwark, pronounced South-werk, Maine (or, as the
young man had said it, Suth-wahk), four weeks into fall
term, to pick up the threads of the courses suddenly vacated
by one P. (for Peveril) Clark Parsons, senior professor and
department chair, who had died in some sort of freak accident a little over two weeks ago. Roz was still not certain
of the details. But the acting chairman, at great expense and
very long distance, had begged and pleaded with her to fill
in. They needed someone who could teach *Beowulf* and
Chaucer as well as modern literature; their other medieval
person was on leave in Yugoslavia, and the others had tried
filling in, but it hadn't worked out; the students were com-
plaining, even asking for their money back. It was only a
half-time appointment, but the salary was very good; they
were desperate. And it wasn't as if she didn't need the
money; she had a little income from her parents' legacy—
they had died in an accident two years ago—but it was
hardly enough to get by on for long. Anyway, loose ends
were loose ends. She fit the bill, so here she was.

"Here you are, miss. Gate C," the young man said, handing over her ticket. He came around the counter and picked
up her bag, plunked it on the scale, then, somewhat to her

surprise, picked it up again and started lugging it down the long terminal corridor. She followed him as far as a small lounge with a few plastic chairs and a counter the size of a lectern. The young man put down her bag, stepped behind the lectern, and looked expectantly at her, holding out his hand. She stood there, perplexed. What did he want now?

"Ticket, please," he said politely. "The other passengers are already on board," he added as he tore her ticket off the backing. "The plane's about to leave."

Worried, Roz peered through the open door leading to the runway. This was the last scheduled daily flight to Maine. "I hope they're not going to leave without us," she said to the young man. She still couldn't see the plane.

"Can't do that," the young man said as he lifted her bag and started through the gate. "I'm the pilot."

Ten minutes later Roz, the eleven other passengers, the pilot and copilot, were back in the lounge. They had been revving up for takeoff in the smallest commercial plane Roz had ever seen in real life when the pilot, calmly listening to the crackling of his earphones, suddenly stood up (as far as he was able) in the front of the plane, and walked back down the tiny aisle, stooping over even further to tell each passenger to please leave the plane, there was a slight technical difficulty, and they wouldn't be taking off right away.

There was a flurry of activity at the gate, and Roz turned away, uninterested in technical difficulties, wishing only that she were closer to completing her long journey from Scotland. It was bad enough having to leave Alan in the first place (even though he had scrupulously left the decision up to her) and now not to be able to get there from here seemed the last straw. She folded her arms and glowered out the observation window at the little plane squatting on the ground, noticing for the first time the dark brown moose face painted over the nose, with cockpit windows for eyes,

and what she had at first taken to be blotches of tan paint
carelessly splashed on clearly meant to be antlers spreading
back over the wings and fuselage. Moosehead Airlines
indeed. She stared thoughtfully at the plane, wondering what
the problem was.

"Doesn't look like the kind of plane someone would bother
to put a bomb on, now does it?" a deep masculine voice
drawled directly behind her. Roz whirled, confronting a tall,
craggy-faced, broad-shouldered man in a fringed leather
jacket, tight Western-cut twill pants, a battered wide-brimmed
hat—no, a cowboy hat, but in Logan Airport on its way
to Maine?—and wait a minute—she looked down at his
feet—yes indeed, embossed square-tipped, high-heeled dress
cowboy boots. Suppressing a snort of laughter, she thought,
Oh, boy, Buffalo Bill rides again, and then, rather belatedly,
a *bomb*? She gave the cowboy a look of utter disbelief, and
shook her head, feeling dazed.

He bowed slightly. "I acknowledge your skepticism,
ma'am, but would I lie to you? Sad but true. We've all been
bumped from our cozy little airplane out there because of
a bomb threat—first ever, no less—to our very own Moosehead Airlines not ten minutes ago." The cowboy shook his
head, scuffed a boot across the linoleum. "It'll just turn out
to be a student prank, I'm sure; they're pretty mad at us
right now, what with the uproar over fraternities and what-
not. The college has just had its annual fall Trustees' round-
up, and this bunch here"—he gestured broadly toward several dour-looking gray-suited and blue-blazered ladies and
gentlemen gathered at one side of the lounge—"is the trav-
eling dog-and-pony show—the administration, that is,
myself included—of Canterbury College, Southwark, pronounced Suth-wahk, Maine. Luke Runyon at your service.
I'm the Dean." He swooped the cowboy hat off his head
and bowed formally, holding the hat in front of his chest
like a swashbuckling cavalier.

Roz stared at him blankly, completely at a loss for words. The Dean? Canterbury College? But really, she told herself, it wasn't that much of a coincidence, was it? With an airline that small, it was more than likely most of the people on it would be going the same place. But could this old cowhand from the Rio Grande, with his tousled sandy-brown hair and bushy frontiersman's mustache, standing there in front of her looking like a cross between General Custer and the Marlboro Man, be the Dean of the College, for all intents and purposes her boss? Would anybody make up a thing like that? He must be new since Judy's time; she would certainly have had something to say about *him*.

"Uh, how do you do," she said quickly, trying to recover herself. At least he didn't sound funny; there was only the barest trace of Western drawl in his low, rather pleasant voice. "I'm Rosamund Howard, and I happen to be going to Canterbury too...."

"Oh, sure. P. Clark's replacement. I've just sent you a contract letter." He paused to grin at her, showing teeth as large and white and even as piano keys. "But you won't have gotten it yet; problem with your address, pretty remote place. Pittenweem, Scotland, was it? No one had ever heard of it." He looked at her curiously, as if to say, What was a nice girl like you doing in a place like that? "So, to make a long story short, it's waiting for you in the English office." He paused again, contemplating her. "Didn't think you'd be so young. Or good-looking. Somehow medieval and women's studies don't quite seem to fit...." He squinted at her, crinkling up the bronzed weather-beaten face in an appraising look.

Roz drew herself up to her full height of five feet seven and a half inches, not about to be treated as an attractive fluffhead, particularly by this macho man in a cowboy getup. It was the old hairy-legs theory of feminism again. In the course of her fifteen-year—if you counted undergraduate—

career in academia she'd run into his kind countless times, the patronizing, condescending, woman-preacher-dog-on-its-hind-feet,what's-a-pretty-girl-like-you-doing in-a-job-like-this, the dyed-in-the-wool male chauvinist, always staring at your legs to see if your seams were straight, or worse, now that the world was into the era of visible panty lines. Oh, she'd definitely seen his kind before. But not in cowboy boots, never mind the hat. That made it even worse, somehow. She glared at him.

Luke Runyon looked down at the floor and shuffled his boots, then gave her a disarming grin. "Aw, shucks," he said in the tone of a hayseed whose bluff has been called, "I'm just jealous. I used to be an English professor myself. Still am, when I'm at home—back in the classroom. Which, unfortunately, is not nearly often enough."

"Then you should know," Roz replied crisply, still not willing to let him get away with it, even if he was just kidding, "that antifeminism—discrimination against women—has its roots and much of its purest expression in the literature of the Middle Ages. The patristic fathers, St. Jerome in particular..."

Luke shut his eyes and held up his hand in the tribal gesture of peace. "I give up," he said in his normal voice. "I stand corrected. I wish I could say I was just checking, but I can't. My field is nineteenth-century American. You know, *The Scarlet Letter, Moby-Dick,* the James brothers. Hank and Willy, not Frank and Jesse," he added unnecessarily. "Anyway, I meant it as a compliment." He extended a callused, strong hand, looking properly abashed. "Friends?"

Roz hesitated, but only briefly. After all, she was going to have to work for him. And he seemed sincerely apologetic. She held out her hand.

Luke grasped it, held it warmly for a moment. "Now that's settled, would you join me for a drink? There should be just enough time while they search the plane and all our baggage. I'd be honored."

Roz found herself nodding. He smiled again, not so broadly this time, and inclined his head toward the exit. "After you, Miss Howard," he said politely. As they left the lounge area, he tossed the cowboy hat into one of the pink plastic chairs. "Just a prop," he said as soon as they were out of earshot of the others. "I only wear it for Board meetings; it drives the Chairman crazy."

Chuckling amiably, he took Roz's arm in a mildly proprietary fashion and escorted her down the long corridor that led into the terminal lobby and into the airport bar.

CHAPTER

2

*R*oz started up the stairs of Tabard Hall, the ancient ivy-covered building that housed the offices of the Canterbury English department. The stairs were metal and rickety, seemingly suspended in the middle of the large lobby like a dinosaur skeleton hastily assembled and then strung up on end. Her clogs made a bonging noise that echoed throughout the building with each step. She winced and tried to tiptoe. Obviously the stairs—and the building—had been constructed before the advent of clogs. Very possibly, Roz thought crossly, they had been constructed before the advent of women as well, at least in these hallowed halls of one of the oldest men's colleges in the country, open to women only in the last few years. And obviously still in the process of being dragged kicking and screaming into the twentieth century; she had not been able to locate a women's bathroom anywhere on the first floor, only offices with the names of various senior members of the English department, all of whom seemed to be men. At least so far.

Her calves were beginning to ache. Oh, the hell with it, she said to herself as she bonged her way up the remaining flights of stairs and tramped down the corridor, peering at names and numbers on the series of pebble-glass door panels.

She was looking for the Third-Floor Conference Room, and already late, she saw by her watch, for her first department meeting. Not theirs, of course, some four weeks into the semester; at least she supposed not. From behind the door at the end of the hall she heard faint murmurings. She pushed the door open and went inside.

It was very warm in the top-floor room, and Roz found herself nodding drowsily as Mr. Parfit Knight, acting chairman, droned on about curriculum changes. Ten minutes, including introductions, and already her mind was wandering. But she didn't really have to listen to this; it all concerned course requirements for next year, and next year she wouldn't be here, or so she assumed. Not that they didn't seem to be an amiable enough group; Knight had introduced her to everyone as soon as she had entered the room. Luke Runyon had been right. It was a large department for so small a college; besides her there were at least seventeen bodies, not all of them full-time — she herself was officially only part-time, since Parsons, as chairman, had had just three courses, one this semester, two second — but all of them full votes, as Luke had informed her last night in the airport bar. A substantial bloc. She looked around the table, trying to sort out names and faces. Iris LeBeau — that was easy, the lone woman, sitting ramrod straight in the nonsmokers' corner, glowering at her colleagues from under gray unplucked eyebrows, her steel-wool-colored hair arranged in a precise, metallic-looking braid around her head that made Roz's loosely pinned up dark brown hair (she had gotten into the habit of wearing it down when she was with Alan, but now that she was back in harness she had knotted it up at the back of her head for a more professional look) seem positively Pre-Raphaelite. Iris was taking notes, not even looking down at the paper, reminding Roz of some very expert knitters she had known. She must have very controlled handwriting, Roz thought, not even to have to check

even once in a while whether or not she was writing over previous lines.

Next to Iris sat a man named Manciple. Roz had done a
double take when she first saw him; the slightly wavy dark
hair combed back in rigid furrows from the pronounced
widow's peak, the gimlet eyes glinting suspiciously around
the room, the ski-jump nose swooping down over thin lips
set in a grim line, the five-o'clock shadow that made the
rest of his face look ashen. But no, it couldn't be. What
would a disgraced ex-president of the United States be doing
here? Why, he hadn't even been an English major, had he?
She looked again briefly, trying not to stare. Of course it
wasn't; she could see that now, but this man looked enough
like him to win a celebrity look-alike contest, peevish, dis-
contented expression and all.

On his right was an amiable-looking, rosy-featured older
man named Franklin, with a neatly trimmed snow-white beard,
and next to him two younger bearded persons Roz had already
gotten confused; was it Feeney and Kelley, or Keeney and
Feeley? Anyway, Feeney was the one with the beard like a
ruffle around his rather elflike face, whereas Kelley's was
slightly more pointed and Edwardian. Then Knight, the acting chair, a middle-aged personage with a scraggly Yassar
Arafat beard at odds with his mild demeanor, and an assortment of junior professors and instructors whose names Roz
had lost track of completely. Eight full professors, not counting the deceased Professor Parsons; not bad for a department
of eighteen. Not a bad quota of beards, either.

Unable to dredge up any more names as a mnemonic exercise, Roz let her mind wander back to last night, and her conversation over drinks with Luke Runyon. He was really much
nicer than she had first imagined, his mountain man imper-
sonation aside, and he had in the hour before they were finally
allowed to depart (of course there had been no bomb, a student
prank after all, but you couldn't be too careful. Even in this

quiet day and age lunacy or terrorism could strike anywhere, college campuses included; think of the Cornell takeover years back, the Kent State massacre; it had happened before; it could happen again) filled her in on numerous aspects of life at Canterbury.

"Well, Clark Parsons's death was a terrible shock, of course," he had said, shaking his head over the double martini he had ordered, straight up, no olive, just a peel of lemon, while Roz sipped her vodka and tonic. "I felt pretty bad; we'd just had a blowup, name-calling in the halls and everything, over the Freshman English issue—rotten mess, and still unresolved, though Knight isn't quite so recalcitrant—and then he turns up dead. Between that and all the uproar over getting rid of the fraternities, the faculty and students are all split six ways to Sunday, and every one of 'em is mad at me." Luke gave her a rueful smile. "It's been quite a semester so far, with worse to come."

"What exactly happened to Professor Parsons?" Roz inquired, more curious about her predecessor in the class she was going to pick up tomorrow than she was about the seemingly ubiquitous campus question of whether to eliminate fraternities, the fashionable issue of the 80's as the Vietnam War had been to the 60's. And what a falling off was there. But back to Parsons. She felt she ought to know as much as had been revealed publicly about his unfortunate demise; her students, if they were like the students anywhere else, certainly would.

Runyon stirred his drink with his little finger, flicked the drip aside. "It's pretty gruesome. He was out in the woods cutting firewood—a favorite hobby of his, heated his whole house with wood, hot water, the works, saved thousands of bucks a winter, he claimed—with a wood splitter he'd rented, not an hydraulic one, but the old-fashioned kind, one with a giant screw that splits the really big logs by drilling into the center until they crack apart." Luke paused, looking at

Roz as if to see whether he should go on to the gory details. She nodded impassively, indicating interest. "Anyway, something went wrong, and..." He stopped abruptly, reached down and gulped a substantial portion of his drink, his bronzed face suddenly gone pale.

"That's all right," Roz interrupted quickly. "You don't need to go on. I get the idea."

"Actually he bled to death," Luke finished after a moment. "His eighty-year-old mother found him, but by the time the ambulance got there he was a goner. Poor bastard."

"Sudden deaths are always a shock, aren't they?" Roz remarked, trying to move the conversation onto a more abstract, less graphic level without completely changing the subject. Luke was still looking a little wan around the edges. "Particularly in these isolated college communities," she rattled on, "where everyone is so close. You just don't think of that sort of thing happening to someone you know."

"That's true. And this is the second one in less than a year. It's going to ruin our reputation as a sylvan idyll and clean-air country club among the pines. Not to mention one of the ten best small liberal arts colleges in the country."

There was an odd note in Luke's voice. Roz stared at him. The second one in less than a year?

Luke stirred his drink again, looking abstracted. Now that she thought about it, Judy had mentioned something in one of her letters. A girl found dead not far from campus, an accident, apparently drug-related—or had it turned out to be suicide? She wondered whether that had ever been settled. "I remember something about that," she said. "I was at Vassar at the time, but a friend of mine who used to work at Canterbury..."

"Yes, well..." Luke began. He was interrupted by the crackle of an intercom.

"All passengers waiting to board Moosehead Airlines Flight 207 please proceed to the airport lounge, Gate C.

Your flight is ready to depart." Luke drained his drink, reached over and picked up her jacket, held it up for her to put on. Roz thanked him and moved toward the exit while Luke stopped to pay the bill. She was just about to push the door open when Luke nudged her aside, reaching for it at the same moment; their arms crossed, tangled momentarily. Startled, she disengaged herself, feeling awkward. It had been a long time since she had had to fight anyone over who was going to open the door; as far as she was concerned, it was whoever got there first.

"Allow me." Luke motioned her through, grinning his lopsided, boyish smile. "I'm a gent of the old school."

Roz, who had always felt like a fool going up to a door and halting like a balky horse while her date opened it, nevertheless stood back and let him hold the door for her. What was she supposed to do, elbow him in the solar plexus and knock him to the floor with a karate chop? A gentleman of the old school, huh? No doubt he also did car doors and lit cigarettes, not that she smoked. But surely it was harmless enough, this *politesse*, certainly not worth making a scene over. Let him open the doors if he wanted to. As long as he got there first.

Roz jumped as the intercom boomed again. "All passengers for Moosehead Flight 207 please proceed immediately to the departure lounge."

"We'd better step along," Luke said, taking her arm as they walked down the corridor toward Gate C. "Or they'll go without us. Then we'd be stuck here overnight." He paused briefly. "So how're your nerves?"

Oddly enough, Roz had not been nervous. It had been comforting somehow to be able to see lights on the ground, shadowy outlines of houses, buildings, the coastline winding in and out, the silver line of a highway angling north. "That's how they navigate," Luke had told her casually. "They just follow the Interstate right up the line. Can't miss

it, and if the plane breaks down, they just put it down right
on the median strip." Roz laughed, wondering if it were
true. They talked for a while about Maine, about life at the
college, her plans for the course she was taking over, a
survey of English literature.

"Now there's something I've always wanted to get
my teeth into," Luke had said with interest. "Oh, well,
maybe someday..." Not long after that somewhat wistful-
sounding statement he had excused himself, tilted the wide-
brimmed cowboy hat over his face, and gone to sleep, leaning
back in the aisle seat next to her with his long legs stretched
out, fancy cowboy boots crossed at the ankles. Looking at
him, she had been reminded of Alan; the same sturdy, wide-
shouldered six-foot frame, the heavy, unruly head of hair
(though Luke's was lighter, without the auburn tinge), the
crinkled, ironic eyes. But really they were not at all alike.
Unlike Alan, who was so direct and matter-of-fact, Luke
seemed to have a touch of the tall-tale artist about him. Flying
up the Interstate indeed. Of course the leather jacket and wide-
brimmed hat didn't help much, never mind the boots. He must
have been joking. But every time she had looked out the tiny
window, there was the highway just below, heading north, a
strip of satin ribbon winding through a seemingly endless
expanse of forest. And he had thought Pittenweem was remote.

Finally Roz had fallen asleep herself, slept most of the
way to Southwark, lulled by the rocking, vibrating, humming motion of the little plane. The acting chairman and
his wife had been there to meet her, fluttering and solicitous.
Luke, seeing that she did not need a ride, had gotten into
a high-sprung brown four-wheel-drive Ford pickup with
racing stripes and a bucking bronco on the tailgate, tipped
his hat to all, and driven away into the dark. The Knights,
at her request, had taken Roz straight to the faculty apartment in one of the dormitories that was to be her home for
the duration.

* * *

Roz jerked alert, her recollections suddenly interrupted by the abrupt change in the tone of the meeting in the Conference Room.

Manciple was speaking through teeth clenched so hard his lips seemed to writhe with every word, and his words, spoken in a low voice so controlled and well-modulated it was almost an insult, hissed over the gathering like a spume of acid. "With all due respect to my esteemed colleagues, how can you all be so naive? I beg you to think of the political implications of this issue. Clearly"—he paused for emphasis, and when he resumed, his voice was fairly dripping with contempt—"*clearly* this can be seen as a plot on the part of the administration and the Dean, purely and simply to destroy our power base. If we even *think* of giving up or in any way compromising the Freshman English requirement, it will cost us half our numbers. At least half. And I warn you, this man may well be the next president of Canterbury." He snapped his mouth shut and leaned back in his chair, drumming impatient fingers on the tabletop, and nodded with exaggerated, even sarcastic, politeness to Roz and several of the younger and no doubt untenured members huddled together at the far side of the table. Roz hoped she did not look quite so bewildered as they; she'd been involved in her share of department wrangles, and had a fair idea what to expect: an hour or two of fruitless debate, a vote, no decision, the motion tabled until the next time, and endless corridor and telephone lobbying to bring recalcitrant colleagues around. Whoever persisted longest finally prevailed, with bad blood all around. In a department this large, she couldn't imagine that a majority could ever agree on anything.

Roz quickly scanned the other faces around the table. Parry Knight was blandly tapping the eraser end of a pencil on his yellow pad, as though used to this kind of outburst. Iris LeBeau sat as ramrod-straight as ever, glaring at Manciple with the same severe but inscrutable expression she had been wearing since Roz came in. Kelley (or was it Feeney, she wondered, trying to remember which beard was which) was sitting quietly with his head in his hands, while Feeney tipped back in his chair, his hair and beard a curly gray-black aureole, arms folded across a trim, blue-denim-clad midriff. Of the rest, only one of the full professors—Pierce, she thought his name was—betrayed any reaction. Thin and gray as a monk, with a narrow fringe of beard along his jaw, he was quietly swinging his head from side to side, his cavernous eyes rolled up to the ceiling in an attitude of patient martyrdom. No one else seemed particularly perturbed by Manciple's harangue, much less his tone; they all regarded the speaker, if they were looking at him at all, with quiet impassivity.

"I'm sure we all understand your concern, Winston," Franklin intoned in a voice considerably more mellifluous and oratorical than Manciple's, "but I think someone should probably fill in the newcomers on what's at stake." Obviously that someone, he began to drone on about the history of the English major at Canterbury College from the vantage point of a twenty-year veteran in the trenches. Shoes began to shuffle across the floor, clothes rustle, bodies squirm. It was like watching a freshly dug bed of worms.

Finally Manciple broke in, slamming his hands down flat on the table, his eyes flashing, his voice a lash.

"This is ludicrous. It's perfectly clear what we have to do, but if the rest of you are too naive, or perhaps too pusillanimous, to keep this conspiracy of philistines—"

"That sucks," said a voice behind Roz. She turned—everyone turned—to stare at the frowsy-haired, sleepy-eyed young man with the sharp profile of a hawk, sitting against the wall near the door, his chair tipped back on two legs. He was tossing his head; his eyelids fluttered as though he were about to go into a trance. Or have a fit. Then, to Roz's relief, he opened his eyes wide and let the chair fall forward, clearly alert. "Spare us the dark predictions, Winston; we've heard them all before," he said in a tone of weary resignation. There was a faint murmur of appreciative assent. But this served only to infuriate Manciple further.

"Idiots!" he bawled. "Naive and insufficient cretinous degenerates!" he snarled, waving a clenched fist across the table. "It's up to us to take up the cudgels now Parsons is gone, and if you're all too namby-pamby..."

"Now just a minute," a mild voice interrupted. "Can we hold it right there?" Feeney had rocked forward and was resting his elbows on the table. Next to him, Kelley had put his head down on his folded arms, his shoulders shaking, but whether he was sobbing or laughing Roz couldn't tell. Feeney looked all around the table, smiling amiably, obviously the voice of sweet reason. "I'm sure we all know what's at stake with this proposal. You do away with the full-year requirement, and as far as staffing is concerned, our ass is grass."

"And the Dean's the mower," Kelley added in a muffled voice.

"Toro, Toro, Toro!" someone muttered in a stage whisper. Several of the junior professors began to snort, and, much to Roz's relief, people began to laugh. The tension appeared to be broken.

"So let's just forget our differences and give the Dean our answer," Feeney ended reasonably, and suddenly everyone began to talk at once, across the table, shouting down the length of the room, gesticulating, arms waving like distress flags on shipwreck. "Order, order please!" Knight said, pounding his own fist now.

"Show of strength, show of strength!" spoke up a wavy-haired man who might have been extremely handsome if he hadn't so closely resembled a disgruntled satyr. He stood up, to a sibilant chorus of catcalls and "Hear, hear"s.

"We're the largest and most powerful department in the college," he boomed, waggling terrier eyebrows that stood out above his eyes like half-furled awnings, curled into such an elegant crest that Roz wondered if he had a special tool to comb them. "The last bastion of Western culture as it should be passed on to our heirs. We understand this better than any of *them*...." He paused to fling his head in the direction of what Roz took to be the administration building; his amazing eyebrows lifted, floated gently in the air. Roz stared, fascinated; she couldn't tell whether he was serious or not. "If we give in on this issue, it will be only the beginning. Don't forget the fraternities, and where we stand on that! We must never give in! We will fight them on the beaches ... we will fight them on the ...."

"Question," Kelley said quietly, drumming his fingers on the table. Traces of tears were still visible, glistening in the small hairs of his beard.

"Second," someone said immediately.

Knight spoke up hastily, sweating with relief. "The question has been called—no, please sit down, Huberd," he remarked to the disgruntled satyr, "and thank you for your thoughts on the matter—all in favor of rejecting the proposal of the Dean to reduce the Freshman composition requirement to one semester raise your right hand."

Seventeen hands went up. Roz stared around the table.

"Miss Howard?"

"Er ... yes?" Roz looked at the chairman, startled at being individually addressed.

"Thank you; that makes it unanimous," Knight said crisply, and banged his yellow pad on the table. "I will convey our decision to the Dean immediately. Thank you, ladies and gentlemen. Until next week, when we shall take up the question of other departments being allowed to offer courses to fulfill our literature requirement."

"Well done, Parry!" Professor Franklin intoned amiably, coming to his feet. "That'll show 'em. He may be a marathon man, but it'll take more than he's got to go the distance with us." He shook a raised fist in the air. "The fraternities are next!" he orated roundly, and was just as roundly ignored. The English department was on the move.

Chairs scraped back, feet shuffled, voices chattered, mumbled, chortled, murmured. Roz watched, bemused, as hands were shaken, congratulations given. Isn't that just something, she thought. This wasn't at all what she expected, either from experience or from what she had learned in talking to Luke Runyon over drinks. In spite of all the strife and division, the name-calling and insults, the department had closed ranks, and handed down a unanimous rebuff to the Dean's demand. Remembering his casual remark about getting the department into line and on track with the rest of the college, she wondered how he would react. It would be interesting, though she wasn't sure she approved of what appeared to be a garrison mentality among her colleagues, with Luke as the enemy. Too bad; she really rather liked Luke. Not that it mattered; none of this concerned her anyway. She was just a temporary replacement, she could be friends with everybody. Each issue had to be argued on its merits, didn't it? And you should never vote if you were uninformed. Speaking of which, she had to see about her course, get the class list, the syllabus Parsons had been working from.

She was halfway down the second flight of stairs before it occurred to her that one of the votes inadvertently recorded in that unanimous rebuff was hers.

CHAPTER

3

Roz shuffled the pages from Parsons's class folder and took out the syllabus. English 21a, Survey of English Literature, A.D. 800–1666, MWF 11:30–12:30, Mus 211. So the course met Monday, Wednesday, and Friday for an hour in Room 211 of the Music building, just across the way. And lunch hour at that; not the greatest time in the world—she could hear the stomachs growling already, the restless scuffing of soles, the surreptitious glancing at watches, of students longing for lunch, not literature. She would have preferred either earlier or later, but coming *in medias res*, as it were, she had to take everything as read. In fact she had rather prided herself on this; they had offered to let her change the reading list, but she had said no, of course not, the students would already have bought the book, and so forth. She had been relieved to find that the book was *The Norton Anthology of English Literature*, Volume One, the same one she used in her own survey courses—Caedmon to Cowper, always available and up to date, not to mention the free desk copies— so she could just step in with no trouble. It wasn't that all knowledge was her province, certainly not, but the fact was—she looked down at the familiar, fondly recollected names—this had been her specialty in graduate school, before the development of her interest in women's studies and twentieth-century biography. *Beowulf* to Milton, with a little Chaucer—actually rather a lot of Chaucer, and the more the merrier—Marlowe and Shakespeare, some miscellaneous poets thrown in here and there, and of course Milton.

She looked more closely at Parsons's syllabus. There were twelve weeks of classes, and Parsons had scheduled almost two weeks on *Beowulf*, just over two on Chaucer—so little?—then one on Marlowe's *Dr. Faustus*, two on Shakespeare's *King Lear*. Then a week on *The Duchess of Malfi*, part of a week on Bacon, and—wait a minute—only two weeks on *Paradise Lost*?

Roz sat back in her chair. It looked like she was going to have to change some things after all. It was a real killer of a syllabus, and already over two weeks behind. She counted up on her fingers; only eight weeks left, and *Beowulf* still to finish. It was a hefty semester's work, and she would have to crowd things up even more if she wanted to get everyone in. And of course she had her own ideas about these writers, themes in their work, their relation to one another and English intellectual history. It was too late to start over. Or was it? If she was going to have to change things . . . She stared at the syllabus. She could pick up with *Beowulf* this morning, spend today and Monday redirecting the course by summarizing her own view of the work as religious propaganda—a Christian author's record and moderately sympathetic indictment of a dark and vindictive pagan culture where ignorant armies clashed by night and even the best of heroes failed, a world not entirely vanquished even in his own time—and go on from there. With a few cuts, one or two additions and some simplification . . .

She picked up a ballpoint pen and began to cross out lines, scribble others in. She had to have more time on

Chaucer—imagine doing *The Canterbury Tales* and leaving
out the Wife of Bath—and on *Paradise Lost.* That didn't
leave much time in the middle; even if she substituted *Othello* for *King Lear,* both *The Duchess of Malfi* and Francis
Bacon would have to go. She crossed out more lines, added
a few, then sat back and perused the result. Yes, it would
all fit, and allow her to touch on some of the women's issues
so sadly neglected in most introductory English literature
courses. Rape versus romance, the subjugation of women,
the backgrounds of antifeminism—it all went very well with
this reading list. She smiled briefly, remembering her conversation with Luke. Since *Othello* was not in the *Norton,*
the students would have to buy another book, but it was a
small book in the Pelican Shakespeare series, and not expen-
sive. They could probably afford it. She could announce all
the changes today. They were a little behind, but they could
catch up.

The syllabus, on the other hand, was pretty raggedy-
looking. Impossible to follow, as a matter of fact. She'd
better have it retyped. George could do it for her in no time;
George, short for Georgianna, was the departmental secretary, always eager to help, willing, able, and a dynamite
typist, with the most amazing wardrobe Roz had ever seen
outside a disco, and bright red hair swirling down to her
shoulder blades.

She turned to the class list. A bell rang somewhere; she
looked at her watch—time to head over. She grabbed up
her bookbag and her notes, gave the old syllabus to George
with a brief explanation, and, list in hand, went to meet her
class.

"Squires?" She called the last name on her list, a late addition, out of alphabetical order, penciled in. Patrick Squires.
Everyone else had answered "Present," twenty-five of them,

all sophomores except for a couple of juniors either transfers or late entries into the major, for which this was a requirement. "Squires?" she repeated.

There was a crash at the back of the room, then a hoarse voice called "Here!" accompanied by snorts and titters and murmured "Way-to-go"s from the rest of the class. Roz craned her neck to see a dark-haired young man in the act of righting his chair. He turned around, blushing scarlet. "Sorry," he said, and sat back down, opened his notebook, hunched forward, and stared fixedly at it, in an apparent agony of embarrassment.

Roz studied him for a moment. He was tall, well-set-up, in a wrinkled cotton button-down—he must do his own laundry; she had yet to find an undergraduate male who ever ironed his shirts—mildly faded jeans, and running shoes the color and texture of moldering birchbark. His dark hair was cut short in an unsuccessful attempt to restrain the curls that tumbled every which way around a ruddy Irish-looking face made even rosier by the as-yet-unfaded blush. She couldn't see anything more of his eyes than a dark fringe of lashes across his cheeks. Then he looked up, and she saw gazing at her, still apologetic if no longer embarrassed, eyes of a self-possessed, yet clear-blue innocent sincerity. No, she decided, not the class cutup; unless, she added cynically, he was also the class actor. But that remained to be seen; meanwhile, it was time to get started.

"I'm Roz Howard," she began, standing up and coming around to the front of the desk, "I'll be replacing Professor Parsons from now on." A slight shudder rippled through the class, accompanied by sidelong glances, then all eyes were attentively fixed on her. "I'll be lecturing on *Beowulf* today just to get things started again, and then we'll try to get back on schedule with your readings. There will be a few changes in the readings, so I'm having a new syllabus typed up. You can pick it up in the English office later today." She smiled at the group of faces, took a deep breath and began.

". . . and so with the last line, 'of world-kings the mildest of men and the gentlest, kindest to his people'"—Roz paused briefly, then said with emphasis—"'*And* most eager for fame,' the Christian narrator indicates to us that in these dark times, even a man as good and virtuous as Beowulf, the great hero, the savior of his people, is mortal and imperfect. He does the best he can according to his lights, but it's just not good enough, because he is still stumbling around, unaware of the full extent of God's grace and power, in a pagan world full of treachery and vengeance and murder, an impossible world, an untenable world. He doesn't know, he's not sure, but ultimately he ignores Hrothgar's overtly Christian homily about the folly of material gain and worldly glory, and when the dragon comes, he goes for the great exploit. 'By my courage I shall get gold . . . perform a deed of fame.' And it's a bad mistake. Oh, he kills the dragon and gains the treasure for his people all right. But he also gets himself killed, leaving his people unprotected from enemies more dangerous than the dragon, because they're human. The accursed treasure is buried as useless, and in her lament the Geatish woman sings of her fear that now Beowulf is gone her people will be attacked, destroyed, wiped out." Roz paused briefly for effect, then went on.

"And so they were. Overrun by Viking hordes, the Geats vanished from the face of the earth, leaving only those who recall the legends to say their names." Roz shut the small Donaldson translation of *Beowulf* she had been reading from—the text was the same as the *Norton,* but the little book easier to handle if you liked to walk around while lecturing, as Roz did—stepped back, and perched herself on the desk. The class had been almost unnaturally attentive while she talked, not even the usual small restless noises, sniffs and throat clearings, pencil-tapping and head-turning, that every teacher is aware of even as her mind is occupied by what she's saying and is about to say. She wondered if they had taken it all in, or if they were just totally over-whelmed, confused by a new and different view of the poem, a new and different presence in the classroom. And yet from what she had read of Parsons's articles, his papers and class notes, his ideas had not been very different. So what was wrong? Why was everyone so quiet?

She looked at the clock; there were a few minutes left. "Any questions?" she asked encouragingly, hoping someone would break the barrier of silence.

Rustle, rustle. Shuffling of notebooks, creaking of chairs as students leaned down to pick up their belongings. Several throats were cleared, several stomachs gurgled. "I have a question, Professor Howard," a voice said clearly above the noise. All heads turned toward the back of the room. It was Squires.

"Yes, Mr. . . . Squires is it?" Roz replied, more tentatively than she felt. Of course it was Squires. And he might very well have a question or two; every time she had glanced at him in the course of her lecture, he had been sitting with his head leaned back against the wall, eyes shut, apparently asleep.

"What's the evidence that Beowulf is imperfect? I mean, is it just that he's eager for fame and glory, or does he have other character faults?"

It was a good question. It appeared he had been listening after all. Roz looked around the room. "Anybody want to answer that?"

They looked at each other, back at her. No go. Roz sighed inwardly. Oh, well, give them a few days, they'd loosen up. This couldn't be easy for them. She addressed Squires. "Aren't there times when you don't entirely approve of

Beowulf? When he boasts, for instance, even though it was
socially acceptable, even obligatory, in his time?" The class
nodded blankly in unison, except for Squires. Unconvinced.
Fortunately she had saved her best shot for last.

"And how about when he gets down to Grendel's mere,
kills Grendel's mother in a real no-holds-barred brawl, and
then, as if *that's* not enough, goes over to Grendel's corpse
and clobbers him with the ancient sword. Listen to this:
'For there he saw Grendel, weary of war, lying at rest,
lifeless with the wounds he had got in the fight at Heorot.
The body bounded wide when it suffered the blow after
death, the hard sword swing; and thus he cut off his head.'
Remember, he's already ripped the poor monster's arm off—
one of my favorite lines, by the way, that graphic image of
'sinews springing, bonelocks bursting'—and here's Beowulf, the mighty hero, mutilating the poor defenseless body
after death. Now I ask you, isn't he just a little out of
control?"

Silence. Not even the hint of nervous laughter, of recognition that line usually elicited. All she heard was the
faint sound of someone gagging. Roz looked over her audience. They were all staring at her, pale and wide-eyed,
apparently horrified. Oh-oh, she thought. Guess I laid it on
a little thick. And at lunchtime too. She smiled at them,
waved her hand in dismissal. "Okay, time to go. See you
on Monday. Please note the changes in the syllabus; we'll
be starting Chaucer next Wednesday. So start reading the
General Prologue. And your *Beowulf* papers are due on
Monday. Thank you."

Almost in unison the class stood up and rushed for the
door, not looking back, not even talking to one another,
engaging in none of the usual after-class chitchat and gossip.
All except Squires, who, as he passed her desk, swinging
a backpack onto a wide shoulder, gave her an odd look and
said, apparently without sarcasm: "Thanks, Professor; I think

we got the idea," then nodded politely and followed the others out, leaving Roz to ponder as she gathered her notes together just exactly what idea it was that he—not to mention his so clearly dumbstruck classmates—might have gotten from her remarks that could have elicited such a rout.

Feeling the need to unwind—she hadn't realized how tense the first encounter with her new students had made her— Roz wandered out of her classroom and over to the Art Museum next door. It was a large ultramodern structure oddly out of keeping with the rest of the campus buildings, rather like a giant petrified grand piano stuck into the side of the hill. Roz entered on the third level, where a printed placard on an easel in the lobby announced that there was a series of landscapes featuring well-known regional artists from the permanent collection on display in the Main Gallery, and, in the Lower Gallery, a show of current faculty and student work. She opted for the Lower, partly out of interest in her fellow faculty members, and partly because it was a longer walk.

Two flights of stairs and several dead ends later, she found herself in a fairly large high-ceilinged ground-floor gallery, with burlap walls and soft indirect lighting. Large French windows looking out on a cobblestone sculpture court let in additional light. Roz walked over to them, thinking she would go outside and take a closer look at the massive wood-and-metal construction that spiraled up out of the ground like a twisted roll of snow fence made of telephone poles. But the windows were fixed; there was no way of opening them.

Then why did she hear the sound of a breeze blowing gently through the room? She stood unmoving, staring out the window, while the back of her neck began to prickle. The sound, barely audible at first, seemed to be gaining in velocity and strength, until it began to come in gusts, a cold wind, a wild wind, whirling and whistling around corners, along the edges of eaves and clapboards, rattling the gutters and banging the shutters. . . .

Now just a minute here. It was probably some sort of malfunction in the air conditioning, and if so, she ought to report it. Roz examined the walls of the gallery for openings, then walked briskly across the room toward a large partition set up in the middle and peered around it.

She nearly jumped out of her skin. Someone was in here with her.

A very large man wearing a baggy gray-striped coverall and a baseball cap stood stooped over with his back toward her close to the partition, staring at some sort of sketch. Roz relaxed slightly. He must be the custodian; she could tell him about the strange noise. But why would a janitor be squinting at a drawing and scribbling in a matchbook cover he was holding? He seemed completely unaware of her presence.

"Hello," she said.

The figure lurched forward, nearly banging his baseball cap on the partition, and the eerie wind noise stopped as abruptly as though someone had slammed a door. He whirled around in her direction, his mouth fixed in an odd grimace, as though he were about to put two fingers up and execute a loud wolf whistle.

"Was that you?" Roz demanded incredulously.

The young man straightened up. Roz saw he was very tall indeed, well over six feet, and quite strong-looking, almost a giant. She took a step backward. Then the giant blinked large gray eyes and smiled at her with an expression of the most extraordinary sweetness, two deep dimples framing a tentative, rather shy smile. "Gee, you scared me," he said in a voice oddly light and soft for so large a person. "I didn't think anyone else was in here." He blinked and looked puzzled. "Is what me?"

"The wind noise. I heard...I thought..." Roz broke off, confused. Maybe he wasn't a janitor after all.

The man grinned, and, as Roz watched, the grin widened to resemble a Moebius strip or an infinity sign, and there was a soft rustling, as of leaves being blown down a street. The sound grew in strength, changing to the rush of a strong breeze blowing through the masts of tall ships, flapping the sails, rattling the halyards, then rising in intensity to the level of a gale that seemed to emanate from everywhere around her, harsh and threatening. Oddly apprehensive, Roz put her hands up over her ears, her eyes fixed on her companion. The infinity grin relaxed into a smile, and abruptly the noise stopped.

"Is that what you heard?"

Roz nodded, wide-eyed.

"Well, then it was me. I always do that when I'm working. Helps me concentrate. I can do other sounds too; bagpipes, farm animals, famous people." He set his lips again, and Roz heard the sound of a jet plane revving up for takeoff, louder and louder.... Noticing Roz's dubious stare, he broke off suddenly and laughed. He took a stride forward and extended a huge paw. "I'm Thor Grettirsdottir," he said in a normal voice. "Sound effects are just a hobby. I'm in the art department here. Sculpture, actually."

"I'm Roz Howard," she said, feeling her hand engulfed in his, shaken gently, like a very small child's, then released.

"Nice to meet you," said Thor Grettirsdottir. "You must be new around here."

"I've been here since Wednesday," Roz answered. "I'm Professor Parsons's emergency replacement in the English department."

"Oh." Her companion looked mildly distressed, ducked his head, and scuffed the carpeting with the toe of one of the largest and grubbiest running shoes Roz had ever seen, even worse than Squires's. He seemed momentarily at a loss for words. Maybe Parsons had been a friend of his. Giving him time to recover, Roz walked over to the partition to see what he had been looking at. It appeared to be some sort of preliminary drawing of a stage set. A gallows—or was it a Murphy bed?—stood center stage, around it suggestions of tenements and storefronts of an earlier time and place, low arches running across the stage like a bridge abutment or a series of drains. After a moment she turned back. Thor Grettirsdottir was watching her curiously, hands in the pockets of his striped coverall.

"Is that yours outside?" she asked.

He nodded. "Want to take a closer look?" Roz nodded back, and he took out a ring of keys, walked over to a metal door prominently marked "DO NOT ENTER/Door Electronically Alarmed," twisted a key in the lock, and motioned her through. Roz stood contemplating the massive twist of wood and wire cable. It did look like a half-buried snow fence, but Paul Bunyan–sized.

"What's its name?" she asked by way of conversation.

"I call it 'Pick Up Sticks.'"

Roz gazed at the construction, feeling rather dazed. Art was not her province. Time to change the subject. She turned to Thor.

"Grettirsdottir?" she asked speculatively.

"It's Icelandic," he replied.

"Yes, I know," Roz said mildly. "I just wondered why it wasn't Grettirsson."

Thor Grettirsdottir blinked, his mouth falling open. Then he smiled. "Ha," he said. "It's not every day you meet someone conversant with the ins and outs of Icelandic patronymics. How about a cup of coffee, or . . . have you had lunch?"

Roz and Thor Grettirsdottir sat at a small table in the corner of the college coffeehouse, their empty cups pushed to one side, along with eight cellophane-decorated toothpicks, the sole remains of a couple of club sandwiches, hers chicken, Thor's cream cheese, sprouts, and avocado; it seemed he was a vegetarian. Out of his baggy coverall Thor was not nearly so enormous-looking, still very tall but fairly slender in a long-muscled way. He had not, however, removed the baseball cap. "Montreal Expos, closest baseball team to Greenland" had been his only explanation. "Now as to Grettirsson or -dottir, what's your best guess?" he said to Roz.

"Either your mother was a feminist, or..." She paused, not wanting to embarrass him. He had challenged her, but...

"Or I'm a bastard." Thor threw back his head and laughed. "Very good. Actually, neither one, at least not legally; a hospital clerk's mistake. She saw my mother's maiden name first on the birth papers, got very dizzy, and just bunged it down for me. After my father took off on us, I decided to keep my mother's name anyway, easier than coping with deed polls and all that later on. And it sounds better with the rest of it. Can you imagine Thorkel Gralewicz?"

Suppressing a laugh, Roz asked, "Is that your real name? Thorkel?"

"Oh, no. There's more. That's my middle name. I decided to drop my first name too."

"Why?"

"Well," he said slowly, lifting a hand to the visor of his baseball cap, "my given name is Balder, and aside from the usual juvenile usages—'old Balderdash' and so forth—of late it has become entirely too appropriate." With a flourish Thor pulled the cap off and grinned. Except for a fringe of hair the color and texture of raveled, sun-bleached rope approximately level with the top of his ears, he was completely bald.

"Thor," Roz said emphatically.

"Yes, indeed," he replied. He looked down at his watch,

then rose, sighing. "Back to the salt mines, I'm afraid. Come on, I'll escort you back to your place."

As they were walking over to her office Thor inquired how her first class had gone. Roz had almost forgotten the lecture earlier and its unexpected effect on the students. "You know, that was really a little odd," she remarked, and proceeded to describe what had happened.

Thor listened carefully, pacing along slightly stooped, with his hands clasped behind his back in the manner of a very tall man habituated to conversations with much shorter persons. As soon as she described the white-faced reaction to Beowulf's tearing off of Grendel's arm, his revenge on the corpse, he stopped, nodding thoughtfully. "That's not hard to understand. Didn't anyone tell you?" he said. "Parsons was found in the woods tangled up in a wood splitter..."

"I know, but..." Roz began.

"...with his arm ripped completely out of the socket."

CHAPTER

4

*R*oz was rather shaken by Thor's enhancement of the circumstances of Parsons's decease, so she was relieved when, at the end of the day, the phone in her office rang and it was Luke Runyon with an impromptu invitation for drinks and dinner. She accepted promptly, and two hours later they were sitting at a table in a nearby restaurant somewhat oddly and perhaps too eruditely called the "Epicene." But then, this was a college town. After the usual greetings and queries of "How's it going" and so forth, Roz turned the conversation to her recent enlightenment about Parsons's death.

"Why didn't you tell me what happened to Parsons?" she demanded in a tone of mild and only partly mock annoyance. "I wish you could have seen those students' faces. . . ."

"As the students would say, hey, give me a break," Luke remarked, with that sidelong glance of his that somehow suggested intimacy. Really, the man was a born flirt. "If you will recall the conversation, you brought me to a dead halt with your no-nonsense 'never mind,' and that was that. I figured you were the squeamish type, so, like the true gentleman I am, I skipped the gory details." He paused, bouncing a thin steak knife on the padded tabletop. "Besides,

there's some doubt about exactly what *is* the 'whole story';
there are still some details the police are trying to get sorted
out downtown. Officially it's being called an 'accident.'
Just like the Nelson case."

"Nelson case?"

"Alison Nelson. She was the girl who was found dead
last November just down the hill below the campus."

This was the case that Judy had mentioned, the one Roz
had been on the point of asking Luke about in the airport
lounge when their flight was called. "What happened to
her?"

Luke sighed and leaned back in his chair, a somber look
on his face. "It was a real mess. She was a sophomore
transfer from out West, Pomona, I think, and had some
friends downtown she'd gone to visit. This far north it gets
dark early in November—this was right after the end of
daylight-savings time—and it was pitch dark when she
started back to campus. The lower part of the campus road
is owned by the town, so there are streetlights every dozen
yards, but there were no streetlights on the upper campus
road—there are now, of course—and there was about a
quarter-mile of dark street to walk up. And it was foggy,
unseasonably warm for November, but then there was a
sudden drop in temperature, typical late-fall weather around
here—one minute it's balmy, the next it's snowing like
pillow-busters."

Luke hesitated, then sat forward, his high-cheekboned
face thrown into relief by the single candle. He hunched
his shoulders and clasped his hands in front of him on the
table. Roz noticed the knuckles were white.

"To make a long story short," he went on after a moment,
"she was found by a jogger the next morning. The cause
of death wasn't clear. They found part of a note, some grains
of angel dust, a few flakes of pot. But when they did the
post-mortem, there wasn't enough stuff in her system to kill

her by itself. So the theory is that she got good and stoned from some stuff she'd gotten—or been given—downtown, wandered up the hill alone in the fog, started to feel funny, staggered off the road, and sat down before she lost consciousness. Somewhere along the way she had pulled off her down jacket, so hypothermia and exposure did the rest. At least that's the theory. We'll never know for sure though; by the time the police got there, the campus security patrol, not to mention reporters, neighbors, gawkers, what-have-you, had swarmed all over the place, moved the body, carried off evidence, messed up the scene with footprints." Luke shook his head. "Incredible incompetence, but of course this is a small town in a rural area, and, as you said, sudden deaths under mysterious circumstances are fairly rare."

Roz watched Luke. He had picked up the steak knife again and was now tapping it softly on the tabletop, apparently lost in thought. Then he began to draw a line, indenting it into the padded cloth, reminding Roz of Alan, with his artist's insistent, restless sketching of anything and everything, on paper, on tablecloths, even in the air. Suddenly she missed him with a palpable physical longing, and noticed once again the resemblance between him and Luke. She would have to watch herself. Really, they were not at all alike; still, there was something about Luke's physical presence... She gave herself a shake. "You don't think the deaths are related, do you?" she asked after a moment.

Luke looked up sharply, as though startled. "Related?" He snorted. "Are you kidding? In a place like this—rural, isolated, folks huddled together in the North Woods—*everything*'s related, right? It's a small community, everybody living cheek by jowl, in and out of each other's houses; nobody ever locks a door around here..." Abruptly he broke off, glanced around the room as though aware he had been talking too loudly, then turned back to her. "Sorry," he said curtly. "I got carried away by the niceties of small-town campus life. It just gets to me sometimes. To answer your question: No, I *don't* think they were related."

Roz stared at him, puzzled by his impatient, even condescending tone. A small-town girl herself—in fact, that had been her primary reason for taking herself off to Berkeley, with its cast of tens of thousands—and a resident faculty member of a medium-sized liberal arts college for several years, she was perfectly cognizant of the living-in-everyone-else's-pocket aspect of small-town campus life. Then she softened; of course he couldn't know that, since they'd met only a few days ago. It was probably just that he didn't like talking about these things. As a matter of fact, neither did she. She looked at him, sitting across from her, wide shoulders hunched, elbows on the table, eyes hooded, looking depressed. They didn't have to sit here retailing morbid gossip; there were plenty of other things to talk about. He knew very little about her, and she knew next to nothing about him, only that he was Dean of the college, and—if yesterday's department meeting was any indication—fairly embattled in that position. She felt a surge of sympathy for him; she'd certainly hate to go head to head against the likes of Manciple, let alone the formidable Iris LeBeau. But that all had to do with his professional life. Why, she didn't even know whether or not he was married, had children. It was time to turn the discussion in a more personal direction.

In the next several minutes she found out that Luke was in fact married, but separated from his wife, who had moved to Florida with their two teen-age boys. That probably explained his irritation with small-town campus life, Roz thought; family crisis and no doubt a busybody lurking around every corner. "She just couldn't hack being the Dean's wife, so she split. Said she felt unfulfilled as a person," he said with a trace of bitterness. "But maybe when I step down—*if* I step down..." He shrugged. "Eventually I'd like to go back to teaching, do a course like yours." He stared off into space. "Those bright young faces, those lithe young bodies," he murmured, while Roz watched him, bemused, wondering whether he was serious. Abruptly he widened his eyes and leered at her with a comically lascivious expression. Roz relaxed; he had been kidding. Then just as abruptly he turned serious. "I've been thinking about what you said about antifeminism having its roots in medieval times. Is that some sort of new wave in literary history? Something all these modern feminist critics have whipped up?" Luke leaned forward across the table, squinting at her with such an expression of suspicion on his face that Roz almost laughed out loud.

But really, she thought, patting her mouth with a napkin to cover up her rude smirk, how out of touch could you be? Modern feminists indeed; the crooked-rib theory was as old as Adam, or anyway Genesis. But she didn't want, in her turn, to seem condescending to him. So without comment she simply went through the list of the world's great classic examples of antifeminist sentiment, starting with Juvenal, moving right along to the Church Fathers, St. Paul, St. Jerome, St. Thomas, to wit, through the mixed bag of medieval lyrics and satires, full of what she was fond of calling the Rebecca-Rowena motif, Courtly Love versus Fleshly Lust, right up past Chaucer, her favorite advocate of women's rights, whose the Wife of Bath's Prologue was one of the best catalogues—and parodies—of antifeminist literature up to that time. Luke's eyes were beginning to glaze over, so she wound up with Milton, in her opinion the most egregious male chauvinist who ever lived: "'He for God, and she for God in him'—now really, I ask you, how sexist can you get?" she concluded. That line, among others in *Paradise Lost,* never failed to infuriate her. Luke just stared at her, uncomprehending. Obviously he'd lost the thread of her argument. "It's not really new," she said, trying to break it to him gently. "After all, it's been a pervasive theme in

Western culture, and one of the most important aspects of cultural history since the Bible."

"Oh, really?" His expression was neutral, but she thought she detected in his tone the same trace of bitterness—or was it disappointment?—she'd heard earlier when he was talking about his wife. Maybe she'd come on a little strong with the women's rights. Still, this was an intellectual discussion, wasn't it? His next remark caught her completely off guard. "I guess that means you must be one of *them*."

It was Roz's turn to level a glance. She didn't like being lumped in categories, and she could well imagine what "them" entailed. But she wanted to hear it from Luke in his own words. "One of what?" she asked quietly.

Luke didn't answer right away, just continued to stare at her with that inscrutable look. Roz stared right back, thinking about their earlier encounters. Had she been wrong about his apparent sexism? She had been taking it all along as a kind of joke, an extension of his flirtatiousness, a caricature of macho male chauvinism, as his airport garb had been a caricature of cowboy. Surely there weren't any self-respecting men left in the groves of academe who still believed in the art of keeping women down. It simply wasn't fashionable, not to mention that it was morally reprehensible. Probably he was only joking.

Or was he? So far she hadn't been able to tell quite where she was with Luke; most of the time he seemed perfectly natural, the two of them on equal terms, but then he'd give her one of those odd sidelong glances that suggested there was something unspoken between the two of them, going on below the surface, the two of them in cahoots . . . or was it conflict? And his voice, that soft near-drawl, so low and intimate that she found herself leaning closer and closer to hear what he said, until they were nearly sharing the same breath. Then the pause, the slow grin, the brief acknowledgment of mutual attraction. Maybe that was it, just that simple; the old sexual tension, the battle of the sexes. He liked his women to be women. On the whole, Roz thought she would take a pass. Not that she didn't find him attractive, but as for songs without words, she herself preferred the direct approach. Meanwhile, he hadn't answered her question. "One of what?" she repeated.

"A radical feminist. You know, a woman in a man's profession, having to look out for yourself, lower pay, menial courses. Right?"

"Wrong," she began, then hesitated, trying to frame a proper response to a very complex question. But at least they were back on intellectual ground, not some quagmire of thwarted sexual telepathy. Roz sighed. In fact, she did not consider herself anything more than an existential feminist, her main activity over the years having consisted of seeing to it that no one ever got away with discriminating against her or anyone else in her vicinity and her profession on the basis of sex, or anything else, for that matter. But before she could explain this to Luke, he went on.

"Alice got into consciousness raising and feminist support group and all that before she left. That may even be *why* she left," he continued, his inscrutable expression changing to one of pure bewilderment. "I couldn't understand it. She was perfectly happy at home with the boys before those women got their hooks into her."

Suddenly Luke bowed his head over his folded arms, so that Roz could not see his face at all. There was a long pause. When he looked up, his face had changed completely; it looked drawn and vulnerable. Roz felt a stab of sympathy for him; how much of his day-to-day male heartiness was sheer bravado?

He smiled a lopsided, mildly rueful smile, then broke into a broad grin, the jovial old cowhand once more. "Aw, but you don't want to hear about my broken marriage," he said. "Let's go back to what you said about the dichotomy

between the body and the spirit, women representing the
flesh and men reason. Don't you really think there's something to it? One of the things that always got me about
teaching was that there was always some lovely girl—excuse
me, 'woman'—who would invariably show up just about
final-exam time, or when a paper was due, in one of those
little gauzy embroidered shirts you can see through, braless,
of course, and then if that didn't get my attention, crossing
her legs ankle to knee, all the time talking lickety-split about
some aspect of the course as if butter wouldn't melt in her
mouth. All totally unconscious, of course, but if that isn't
one of your instinctive feminine wiles, I don't know what
is. Don't tell me you ever got that sort of thing from your
male students." He leaned back in his chair. "I rest my
case."

Roz tried not to laugh out loud. It was clear now he was
joking, for whatever reason, baiting her in a good-natured
way. Well, she wouldn't rise. There was no point in arguing
with him, no point in describing the times without number
that she had been vamped by young men in open-necked
shirts and tight jeans, no point in telling him it was a part
of college life, of life in general, and there was really no
difference between her experience and his. He was back to
his corny-gent-of-the-old-school routine, where men were
men, and women were women, and never the twain shall
meet, except in bed. It was probably easier for him, perfectly
natural given the recent breakup of his marriage. She understood, and they could still be friends. She smiled. "Why
don't we change the subject?" she said.

And so they did. Roz talked about her family, described
in vague terms what she had been doing for the last few
years, briefly mentioned her relationship with Alan Stewart,
which for the sake of privacy she painted more in terms of
friendship than she might have otherwise. After all, what
business of his was her love life anyway?

She found that out a while later when, at the outside entrance to her apartment, he suggested that she might ask him in for a nightcap. Roz fended off that line in the usual manner, said she was feeling rather tired, suggested politely that they leave it for another time. As she was turning away, he gently touched her hair, which as usual was starting to pull out of its bun in the back in unruly wisps and tendrils around her face.

"Why do you wear it pulled back like that?" he said almost wistfully. "Makes you look so severe, forbidding. You're going to end up like Iris LeBeau if you don't look out." He bent forward quickly and, before she could even think of resisting, kissed her lightly on the mouth.

Whoa! The direct approach, after all, Roz thought as she pulled back to avoid another and no doubt slightly less chaste kiss. She gave him her best Medusa glare, thinking that even Iris LeBeau couldn't do any better.

Luke straightened up, smiled, and said with perfect good humor, "Okay, I can take a hint." He raised both hands as though she were holding him at gunpoint. "I thought . . . well, never mind what I thought. But you can't blame a guy for trying."

"Of course not," Roz said, sounding more severe than she felt. "Let's just leave it at that."

Luke ran his hand through his hair, ruffling it, stared at the ground, scuffed his loafers on the step—no cowboy boots tonight—and looked contrite. "Roz, you must know how I feel about you . . . us. But I guess I was rushing things a bit. It won't happen again unless you say so. I can wait." Then he grinned so boyishly that Roz expected freckles to pop out across his nose and cheeks, a gap to appear in the large, white, evenly spaced teeth, straws in his hair. Now really. She continued to glare at him.

"Hey," he said, looking startled. "No hard feelings, okay? I'm basically harmless. If you want, we can stay just friends.

I promise." He held up a palm in what was either the Indian
gesture of peace or Scout's honor; Roz couldn't help smiling. Luke relaxed visibly, then went on: "Anyway, I hope
you'll come with me to the first Cloak and Dagger production. It's the big social event of the fall term. It's not until
next month, but I wanted to get my bid in early, before you
get too popular. You'll have a chance to see your colleagues
dressed to kill; some of them are even in it."

Roz hesitated. Maybe she should refuse and be done with
it. She didn't believe for a minute staying just friends was
what he had in mind, and a romance with Luke Runyon
was a complication she could do without.

"Aw, come on," he urged. "I appeal to your better nature."

Better nature indeed, Roz thought, her uncertainty turning
to annoyance. That old ploy of woman's irrationality versus
man's reasoned behavior, the world, the flesh, and the devil,
or the word according to Milton, as old as Adam and Eve.
It was almost as though he were challenging her. He wasn't
giving up, and she wasn't having any, but he could be just
friends, he could wait. There he stood, watching her patiently,
the picture of gentlemanly aplomb. Well, two could play
that game.

She looked him straight in the eye, said sweetly, "Of
course, Luke, I'd love to."

"Good, it's a date then." He held out his hand. Roz took
it gravely and gave it a firm shake. Luke regarded her with
amusement. "Thanks, but actually I was going to unlock
your door for you. Where's your key?"

Roz stared at him in utter disbelief, then spluttered into
helpless laughter, while Luke stood by, watching her without
expression. Gentleman of the old school indeed. Shaking
her head and giggling helplessly, she waved him away.

"Okay, okay, I get the idea," he said, starting down the
steps. He went down the path to his truck and got in. Roz
had just opened her door when he called out the car window,

"You can let your hair down now!" He grinned happily as she flushed scarlet, then drove off with a roar and a squeal of tires. Roz watched him go, fuming. He'd gotten the last word—and her goat—after all. But there would be another time.

CHAPTER

5

*T*he next week went smoothly enough for Roz as she settled into a comfortable routine at the college. That Monday she finished up *Beowulf*, collected most, but not all, of the papers due from her class, briefly went over the revised syllabus, and on Wednesday, October 14, launched into Chaucer's General Prologue, on which she planned to spend at least three classes.

If there was animosity among the various constituencies at Canterbury, as the department meeting she had attended seemed to indicate, it had not yet carried over into her relations with her students, all of whom appeared to accept her readily, if with some reserve. Her colleagues were a different matter; they were friendly enough at the office, but so far, except for Thor, who was not even in the English department, no one had made any overtures of friendship, and she found herself feeling rather left out. But then, they did have a lot on their minds, between the curriculum review on the one hand, and the fraternity issue on the other, and the members of the English department in the forefront of both controversies. So Roz kept to herself, trying to learn her way around both the people and the place.

Iris LeBeau, seeing her in the corridor one day, invited

her to go on an impromptu foliage tour of the surrounding countryside; the two women set off happily that Saturday afternoon in Iris's very spiffy and well-cared-for bright red Volkswagen pickup. (Did *everyone* in Maine own one? Roz wondered as she saw the little truck roll up to her door.) The leaves were beautiful, incandescent, flaming: "Caught them right at the peak," Iris commented as they drove down winding back-country roads so rough Roz was convinced several times that they were bumping along on four flat tires. Iris invited her in afterward for a light supper, and the two of them chatted far into the night about life and literature in general, life at the college in particular. Iris had been at Canterbury for close to twenty years, and Roz was surprised to hear that she was in fact senior to both Franklin and Manciple.

"Oh, yes," said Iris as she crocheted yet another purple-and-green daisy square for an afghan she was making. "I've been passed over any number of times. You wouldn't catch *that* bunch making a woman chairman. They're always muttering behind my back about menopause. And the Dean's no better, of course. No, the status of women here"—Iris paused and raised her fierce eyebrows over the wire-rimmed granny glasses she had informed Roz she used for close work only—"is appalling to say the least. But no one seems prepared to do anything about it. Yet," she added ominously.

Most of the statement had been made with cheerful irony, but behind it Roz thought she sensed a lingering bitterness, the depth of which she couldn't gauge. She recalled Iris's numerous abstentions on important issues in the last department meeting, and wondered if they were a kind of subversion. Nobody was going to co-opt *her*. Yet Roz got the sense that Iris had made her peace with the place, and as the conversation went on, along with the bottle of red wine Iris had opened, she seemed much less forbidding, more gossipy and casual, wanting to know all about Roz's life, her career in academia, and her course here at the college. But Roz went home still bothered by Iris's grim account of a woman's lot at Canterbury.

So she was quite relieved and even gratified when the following Friday a group of women students, one of whom she recognized from her class, a pale, rather plain girl with a modified punk hair style who seemed always to be dressed in loose, well-worn army pants and tattered camouflage shirt, came to her office to invite her to join the Women's Association Advisory Council. Roz said yes at once, happy to find that there even was such an organization at Canterbury, though at the moment they did not have a faculty sponsor.

"Or support," a girl who seemed to be spokesperson remarked wryly.

"Who needs them?" the pale girl remarked quietly, her eyes fixed on the floor. Roz turned her attention to the girl, whose name was Dori, but she had nothing more to say until the delegation was on its way down the hall. Then she turned back and called to Roz, who was standing in the doorway of her office, "Our next meeting is about the issue of sexual harassment, and it's pretty urgent."

Now there's an exit line, Roz thought as she watched them shamble down the hall in the drab, baggy clothes they must have purchased from an army-surplus depot. A real grabber. She could practically hear ears pricking up behind all the closed doors of the English department. She would certainly attend the meeting, whenever it was.

She sat down at her desk, wondering how serious the sexual harassment issue was around here. On her way to the office through Frat Row, she herself had been the recip- ient of a few catcalls, wolf whistles, mock faintings of the "Be still, my heart" variety off the fire escapes of the various houses, all of which she had studiously ignored. There had been the usual half-naked bodies sprawled all over campus—and each other—between classes in these last few weeks of Indian summer, but these, while annoying and distracting, hardly qualified as sexual harassment. Still, students were so vulnerable; she wondered if there had been any actual incidents involving them, or, worse yet, physical attacks. She hoped not, but it was always a possibility. She and Judy Laster had compared notes now and then over the years, and she remembered a story about a hulking young man holding the unwilling girl of his dreams prisoner in the elevator of the Student Union with a ripped-open beer can. But that had been several years ago. Now, the young women dressed like refugees, in clothes that hid their presumably lithe young bodies. So much for Luke and his opinions on the subject; times had changed. You'd need an x-ray machine to find any vibrant young flesh beneath those outfits.

Speaking of Luke, she had hardly seen him since their dinner together two weeks ago, and the few times she had run into him on campus he had behaved with the gravest of courtesy to her, even as he was on his way somewhere, always busy. But so was she, with part of a set of *Beowulf* papers to read, and *The Canterbury Tales* to get through as well. She had finished the General Prologue, the Miller's and the Nun's Priest's tales, and was looking forward to doing the Wife of Bath's (speaking of sexual harassment), on which she planned to spend the next two classes. She would have to find out when the Women's Association meeting was, and meanwhile there was plenty to keep her occupied. Doubtless this was true of her unforthcoming colleagues as well. With a sigh, she picked another *Beowulf* paper off the pile and commenced to read, continuing to do so until her stomach began to growl alarmingly, and she realized with a sinking heart that her cupboard back home was once again bare. So she put the papers aside, went home to pick up her canvas tote bags, and started down the road to town.

Roz had decided not to get a car while she was at Can-

terbury. For one thing, she really couldn't afford it, and for
another, she'd been told that the campus and the town were
within easy walking distance and she wouldn't need one.
This was technically true; the downtown area was not quite
two miles from the center of campus, but the way back was
all uphill, and when one was loaded down with grocery
bags, the trek was laborious and long, really out of the
question. There were taxis, of course, but using them habit-
ually ran into money. She had tried taking the college jitney
a few times, but felt conspicuous and uncomfortable riding
along as prim as a governess while the student passengers
either cavorted self-consciously or sat unnaturally quiet,
pretending she wasn't there. And she couldn't lug more than
two bags back at a time, which necessitated more numerous
trips to keep her larder stocked.

Still, since she didn't want to impose on any of her colleagues for rides—not that anyone had offered as yet—the
only alternative to walking appeared to be hitchhiking. Her
students had informed her there was a spot on the campus
road where you could catch rides with people driving to and
from the college. You had to be a little careful whom you
rode with, of course, stand there looking like you really
didn't want a ride at all, in case some sleazebag came along,
but most students did it, they assured her, and even occasionally faculty members. Never one to dismiss possibilities
out of hand, and feeling rather weary after a long day of
teaching and reading papers, she decided to give it a try.
Since it was well past the middle of October, this Friday
was bound to be one of the last of the fine Indian summer
days, and Roz was still considering walking as she stood
at the appointed spot with her canvas bags in hand. Just
then a dilapidated pickup truck swaying drunkenly on four
bald tires squealed to a stop beside her. Certain that no
element she might possibly want a ride with could be
ensconced in such a battered heap of rust and dented metal,

she resolutely looked the other way and began walking casually down the hill. With a sound of grinding gears, the truck lurched forward a foot or two so that the driver's window was once again directly adjacent to her. The horn beeped insistently.

Roz peered with great interest at the sky, the trees with their rags of leaves, the buildings nearby, and kept walking. Beep beep, again. The driver was certainly persistent, she thought with annoyance; couldn't he take a hint? The engine hiccuped, threatened to stall; the driver gunned it so that the truck exuded noxious fumes in a cloud of blue smoke. Clearly the vehicle was a menace, and so, no doubt, was the driver. Roz turned her head slowly, ready with her most witheringly haughty glance to go with the curt shake of her head . . . and saw the baseball cap silhouetted in the open window. It was Thor. She was already wrenching open the cab door when she heard his soft voice meekly offering her a ride.

"You should have called me," Thor said in a tone of mild reproach as they rattled down the hill past Faculty Row. Roz could see why Luke had described it as living cheek by jowl, for these few blocks nearest to the campus contained in close proximity the homes of Art Franklin, Iris LeBeau, Luke himself, Shipman, Huberd, Clark, and assorted other members of the faculty and administration, some of whom even shared driveways and backyards. "I go this way all the time—I live in on that road in back of the campus—so it's no trouble. In fact, I wondered how you were going to manage when you told me you weren't going to have a car."

Roz told him about the jitney and about hitchhiking, and Thor just shook his head. "Don't be dumb," he said unceremoniously. "I'll take you."

They had driven downtown to a vast parking lot surrounded by an assortment of stores, large and small. "Here we are," Thor remarked as he unfolded himself from the battered cab. He slammed the door hard and started off toward the largest store.

"You left the keys in," Roz called after him. "Aren't you going to lock it up?"

Without breaking stride, Thor shook his head. "Who steals my truck steals trash."

Laughing, Roz followed him into Southwark's one chain supermarket. They made their rounds, Thor filling his basket with assorted fresh produce, dried beans, vegetables and the like, Roz loading up on frozen entrées, cans of tuna, assorted large boxes of cereal, numerous convenience items, which, when they arrived at the check-out counter, Thor looked down upon with barely disguised horror.

"You're kidding," he said. "You're going to eat that stuff?"

Roz shrugged. "I hate to cook. I'd rather pay more and not have to think about it. That's one of the things that keeps me from even considering being a vegetarian; it takes so much time. Chopping, peeling, cracking, grinding..." She waved her hands in the air in a pantomime of frenzied preparation.

Thor grinned. "Hey, have I got a store for you."

The store, across the parking lot and down several side streets, was the Mairzy Doats Organic Health Fast Food Store. Thor proudly led her in and introduced her to the manager, a seedy-looking young man who greeted her happily with a bow almost Oriental in its stiffness. Thor pointed out several features of the place, including the dehydrated, all-natural, all-organic convenience entrées, full meals in boilable pouches, both meat and ersatz meat, whole-wheat macaroni products, eggless and cheeseless dishes, "a full selection for gourmets of all persuasions." Roz took down a package and studied the list of ingredients. How ingenious, she marveled.

"Developed for campers and mountain climbers," Thor explained. "They're good. I take them with me when I go out in the woods." He left Roz studying a package with a picture of instant spaghetti and meatballs on it—at least, Roz thought they were meatballs, but meat was not listed among the components—while he went to collect some items undoubtedly not available in the supermarket.

Roz took one instant freeze-dried entrée, Swiss steak with vegetables—more to be polite than anything else, but why not?—and had just picked up what appeared to be a large economy-size shredded wheat biscuit in a cellophane wrapper she thought she might try instead of Frosted Crispy Puffs, when Thor appeared behind her. She turned to him, holding up the shredded wheat.

"This looks good. But how do you eat it? Break pieces off it as you need them?"

Thor looked at her gravely. "That's not to eat. You rub it all over your body."

"Huh?"

"It's a loofa," Thor said. "It's a kind of all-natural, all-organic vegetarian sponge. The Scandinavians developed it. You get in the sauna, get good and hot, then run out, roll in the snow, and scrub yourself with this. Wonderful for the circulation. We used to use bundles of sticks tied together, but there were too many slivers. If you'd like to try it some time, I have my own sauna, built it myself. There's plenty of room." He grinned at her.

"Is that a proposition?" Roz said lightly, putting the loofa back where she'd found it.

"Of course," Thor answered. "Come on, let's go check out."

Thor had driven her back to her apartment, helped her carry the groceries in and put them away. "You'll have to have dinner with me sometime," he said as he stacked the various supermarket fast-food items in her freezer. The Swiss

steak in its little bag evidently just went on the shelf. He
turned to her. "I wish I could say when, but the fact is
I'm pretty out straight right now. I'm on the Committee to
Abolish Fraternities, and also the Curriculum Review; then
there's the play. . . ." He shrugged apologetically.

"Gee, thanks, Thor," Roz said with mock acerbity, "a
proposition one minute, a put-off the next."

Thor looked horrified. Hastening to reassure him—she
knew that he had not really meant either—she stood on
tiptoe and kissed him lightly on the cheek. "Anytime. And
thanks for the ride and the tour of lovely downtown Southwark."

"Pronounced . . ."

"I know, I know," she said, laughing, as she followed
Thor to the door. Bowing slightly, he tipped his baseball
cap, winked at her, and loped off down the path, wrenched
open the door of his truck, and was gone, leaving a loud
and smoky backfire in his wake. Then the phone rang,
and she ran to pick it up, thinking it might be Alan, which
it was.

CHAPTER
6

"*D*ear Alan:" she wrote the following Tuesday night. "A lot has happened around here since I talked to you last." They had agreed, after a week of almost daily transatlantic phone calls, desperately unsatisfactory despite the huge expense, to try writing letters, resorting to phone calls only on weekends and for emergencies. "So much, in fact, I don't know where to begin."

The Saturday before, she had dutifully attended the Women's Association meeting, at which the women had voted to picket the Dean's office because of his refusal to allow a rally called "Bring Back the Light" they had wanted to schedule on Halloween, which was this very weekend. It was to dramatize the sexual harassment issue, but the Dean had claimed there was already something scheduled by the Interfraternity Council, and they had taken this as more evidence of his tacit support of fraternities. As Roz excused herself, the women were already making signs reading, among other things, "I smell a f—— rat." But at this point, disturbing as all this was, as far as Roz had been able to ascertain there had been no actual instances of harassment, physical or otherwise. So the issue remained, at least in her judgment, theoretical and abstract.

The increase in volume of her campus mail, on the other hand, was not. Every day since she had agreed to be on the Council, countless envelopes stuffed with pamphlets and folders and lists of books on everything from rediscovered women's literature from the Termagant Press to long-term lactation had ended up in her mailbox, accompanied by a peremptory checkoff list "for you to look over and pass on," which she dutifully did, ever more cursorily, feeling at times as though she were a helpless participant in a particularly persistent chain letter. Still, she could not let it go; the issues were serious, and the women certainly deserved her support. Speaking of which, there had been no evidence of Iris LeBeau as a member of the Advisory Council, or even an interested party, which was odd, given her status as the most senior woman faculty member. She had been here since long before the place went coed. Now *there* was a woman who had made it in a man's world. But maybe there was a certain lack of sympathy. She would have to ask Iris about it sometime.

But this somewhat cavalier attitude had changed that following Monday. In the middle of the discussion of the Wife of Bath's Prologue, Dori, the pale young woman with the punk hair style and refugee clothes, had broken down and had to leave the room. After everyone had left and Roz was still picking up a few stray late papers, she crept back, eyes red from crying, the sleeves of her worn camouflage jacket streaked with damp.

"I'm sorry, Miss Howard," she said in a voice still shaky with emotion. "When you got to that part about the guy grabbing her and slapping her around, I just couldn't..." Tears started running down her cheeks again.

Roz had sat down on the desk and patted the girl's cold hand. "Do you want to tell me what happened?" she asked gently.

Dori gave a haunted look over her shoulder, then went

and shut the door. "Um," she stammered. Then the words came out all in a rush. "I don't know if you heard, but the last couple of weeks this guy has been, like, flashing girls in the Gym, in the Library, out walking, all over the place. He'll leap out from between the stacks, or a row of lockers, or the bushes, and . . . you know." She blinked quickly several times, not looking at Roz, and ran her hand through her short bristly hair. "He's never really touched or hurt anybody, just jumps out in this silly black karate outfit with a mask over his face, and drops trou real quick, then turns and runs away laughing like crazy. The kids sort of thought it was one of the frat guys, or a bunch of them taking turns, just a dumb joke really, but it's not that funny, you know, and so we all started going places in pairs, and there was more security and all. Then all of a sudden it stopped, and we all thought it was okay, that he'd left town or gotten tired of it or something." She took a deep, shivering breath.

"Well, last Saturday night I'd just got back to the dorm from the Women's Association meeting, and I had to go to the bathroom, you know, and I walked over to one of the stalls and yanked it open, and . . . and . . ." Dori took another deep breath, closed her eyes as if to shut out the worst of the memory, and then the words came tumbling out. "There was this guy standing there, all in black, with some sort of ski mask over his face. I screamed and shut my eyes. And then . . . and then I was just so freaked out, I don't really know what happened next, but I thought I felt this hand snake out and grab my wrist and I screamed some more but he didn't let go, and was trying to pull me in, and I was so scared I couldn't even scream any more. But I heard the other girls coming and . . ." The girl paused, took another breath, and burst into fresh tears.

Roz put an arm around the girl's shoulder and let her cry. So much for abstract and theoretical. When the sobs finally subsided, Dori seemed to feel better, and Roz suggested

they walk back across campus to her office. They took the
long way around, out of the major lanes of traffic, never
mind the spread-eagled bodies, and on the way the rest of
the story came out. When he heard the other girls calling
out and running down the hall, the figure had jumped up,
sprung across the top of the bathroom stalls from one partition to the next, and disappeared out the window into the
night.

The police had wanted to know everything, particularly
if she had in fact been flashed, but Dori couldn't tell them;
she had kept her eyes shut, and when she got the courage
to open them, the figure in black was going along the tops
of the stalls to the window. So no one quite knew what had
happened, whether they were dealing with a flasher, a bur-
glar, a voyeur of some sort, or a misguided student prank-
ster. Dori had been hysterical, couldn't sleep or eat, had gone
to see the school counselor, but no amount of pointing out
that she wasn't hurt, had not been raped or even badly
assaulted, had helped. Finally the counselor told her that
she was overreacting, and to pull herself together. Meanwhile, the incident had been filed for lack of evidence; none
of the other girls had seen the figure. This upset Dori even
more, and her friends as well—not just the idea that it was
the flasher, and that he could strike anywhere, anytime, but
that the school, and the administration, did not seem to be
taking this incident seriously enough. "Flashers don't grab,"
the counselor had said. "And voyeurs don't rape. They're
too scared themselves. If you challenge them, they cut and
run." Dori had insisted that she was grabbed, physically
assaulted, but the incident had been minimized, the whole
thing swept under the rug by the college. But of course the
members of the Women's Association were pursuing the
matter, as well they should.

They stopped at the entrance to Tabard Hall. "Don't worry
about your work for now, Dori," Roz said. "Just try to put

it behind you, and meanwhile you can take my word that we won't let the matter rest."

Dori looked relieved, her face fresher, less pale. "Thanks, Miss Howard," she said.

"Call me Roz," Roz replied, at the same time wondering exactly what it was she thought she could do, in this still unfamiliar place. Talk to Thor, talk to Luke? Or maybe Iris LeBeau?

Dori smiled wanly, and turned away down the steps. At the bottom, two of her friends joined her, and they began to talk quietly as they walked away. Roz watched them thoughtfully for a moment, then turned and went inside.

Depressed by the recollection, and the fact that she still hadn't done anything about it, Roz turned her attention back to the letter, and tried to distract herself with a detailed redaction, complete with dialogue, of the latest department meeting, which had taken place that afternoon, followed by, and—though the mind boggled—even outdone by, the first Canterbury faculty meeting Roz had attended.

"The political atmosphere is even more tense than I realized when I talked to you on the phone last Sunday," she wrote. As a matter of fact, in that last lonely middle-of-the-night phone call, they had spent very little time on superfluous issues such as campus politics and shop talk. "I've really never been in a place where there is such a distinction, even a division, among the administration, the faculty, and the students. It's like a bunch of armed camps here, and the English department, along with its allies History and Modern Languages, the two other largest departments, is in the vanguard. It comes down to a rift between the Dean of the College and the faculty over matters of educational policy and campus life, the continuation of required Freshman English, on the one hand, and the elimination of fraternities, on the other. The students are restless and a little distracted, but they haven't done anything spectacular yet, unless you count that bomb scare on the trip up and a few minor acts of vandalism. Everyone except the Women's Association seems to consider this business with the deviate just a drop in the bucket. 'The least of our worries,' Win Manciple was heard to proclaim loudly, the insensitive twerp. . . .

"Meanwhile, as far as fraternities go, things seem to have come to a complete standstill, and nobody knows what will happen. Luke Runyon is on the wrong side of that one, and has managed to alienate a large segment of the faculty, including the Women's Association Advisory Council, most of the English department, and an interdisciplinary Ad Hoc Committee on Housing Organized for Order (ACHOO) led by Thor Grettirsdottir. It's too bad, because Luke seems like a fairly nice person [here she left out any mention of Luke's trying to put the make on her outside her door, addressing herelf only to his public image; she had been perfectly capable of handling the situation herself, and besides, the unpleasantness had not been repeated], until you get him in front of a group of faculty, and then he comes on like a cross between the warden of a maximum-security prison and a government spokesman trying to convince a group of lunatics that wholesale frontal lobotomy is really in their best interests. Not the smartest move for a man who wants to be the next president of this place.

"Anyway, the Freshman English issue came to a real showdown in the faculty meeting. But first the department meeting. The Dean had sent back the recommendation of the department to keep the yearlong requirement, saying that it wasn't what he was looking for, and that set off Shipman, he of the famous 'That sucks' rebuttal, and Huberd, the one who looks like Lord Byron with a migraine from trying to hold up his eyebrows. Then Franklin stood up and orated for fully five minutes on the senior staff conspiracy to undermine the faculty, citing the secret expansion of staff positions over there in Boughton Hall. 'Why it's a veritable rabbit warren, breeding administrators, exploding out of offices like wads of cotton batting. Before you know it they'll be given faculty status, attending faculty meetings, voting us down, and we'll all be going to hell in a hand-basket!' Then Manciple sneered and made one of his jaggy remarks, and Shipman waved his arms, and everyone began to shout and argue until Knight had to stand on the table (well, almost) and yell for order so he could present the next piece of business, also from the Dean, asking us to agree to allow the literature requirement to be fulfilled by courses in other departments, and of course this was voted down out of hand—I did get my name down, along with Iris, for an abstention this time, however—and then every-body trooped over in a phalanx to the faculty meeting.

"The first thing that happened there was that Thor brought up a resolution to abolish fraternities, with Manciple of all people seconding it and leading the discussion, and Luke Runyon doing his best to let everybody know the faculty had no power to legislate in such matters, they could only advise, until finally he was shouted down completely, and the resolution passed by an overwhelming majority. Of course Runyon told them in no uncertain terms that unless the trustees agreed, the faculty could wait until hell freezes over to see the measure implemented. He seemed quite angry in a white-lipped, soft-voiced way, and Manciple in particular was very rude, and finally there was a tremendous con-frontation between the Dean and several of the senior pro-fessors that ended in a walkout. But after they'd gone—get this—the Dean made and pushed through a motion to do away with the English requirement altogether. When Knight heard this the next day he sent in his resignation, so the department is now without a chairman at all, acting or otherwise. We have a meeting tomorrow afternoon that people are talking about almost as a council of war, a lot

of whispering in the halls, phones ringing back and forth
... it's really a zoo around here. I'm trying to keep out of
it, of course, but I'm going to the meeting to observe.

"One thing all this wrangling has done is to unite the
English department, no mean trick for such a bunch of prima
donnas and territorial imperators. Even Iris LeBeau changed
her vote on the English requirement, and she also voted for
the antifraternity resolution. There's some talk of student
retaliation over the fraternity issue, but no one knows yet
what form that might take. Anyway, that's the least of Canterbury's worries, and so far the campus is still fairly quiet.
But more anon...

                                        Much love,
                                        Roz"

And more anon there was. By the end of the next afternoon's
meeting, the English department had decided to go on strike
if Dean Runyon did not give in and retract his motion by
the end of the week, and had elected Art Franklin the new
acting chairman. Art had sworn to fight the threat of lowered
standards to the bitter end, and to get rid of the fraternities
by hook or by crook, even if he had to personally strong-
arm every member of the Board of Trustees. Only Win
Manciple, whom Roz suspected of wanting the chairmanship himself, had refused to support his candidacy. Roz
herself had abstained, and, somewhat to her surprise, so
had a thin-lipped Iris LeBeau, muttering under her breath
about the male power structure, seniority, and Title Nine.

By the next morning, Luke Runyon had made it known
that he would not accept the department's election, that he
would see each member of the English faculty individually
in his office, starting in one-half hour. Anyone who did not
appear would be suspended. Shouts could be heard down
the corridors of Boughton Hall, and even through the triple-
glazed storm windows. The worst of these screams and

curses came during the meeting with Professor Manciple, who was heard to yell something about making the Dean's life an open book.

"Thought somebody was going to go right out the winder before they was done," an awed secretary told Roz as she was waiting in the outer office of the Dean's suite. "Not that there was much to choose from between the two of them, as far as that goes," the woman went on. "They both give as good as they got. They're a real noisy bunch, those English professors, always rowing and quoting racks of high-brow litra-chure at a person. I should know; I used to work there," she finished, shaking her head and making tsking sounds with her tongue.

But when Roz herself went in with some slight trepidation, Luke was the picture of calm deliberation. He greeted her warmly, told her he'd heard good things about her class, that he hadn't forgotten her, but he'd been a little busy, as she might have guessed. He waved her to a comfortable chair in one corner of his elegantly furnished office, offered to send out for coffee or tea, which she refused, then sat down at a small table covered with stacks of important-looking documents, and inquired what she'd been doing with herself. So Roz found herself describing her schedule, the people she had met, and, with Luke's prodding, practically every place she had been in the last two weeks, including the health food store.

But instead of being amused, Luke looked quite serious. He gazed at her for a moment, as if weighing what he was going to say next. Roz waited patiently, but when he finally spoke, she was completely taken aback. "I hate to say this, but I think you'd better be more careful about the company you keep."

"What do you mean?"

"Well, to be a bit more specific," Luke went on, with an odd note of reluctance in his voice, "remember that girl I told you about? The one who was found dead? And you asked me whether there was a connection between her and Parsons?"

Roz nodded. "Alison Nelson."

"Well, a connection can certainly be made; whether it's a valid one or not is another matter. As I think I mentioned, the official conclusion was that the girl had died of hypothermia brought on by a drug overdose; in other words, an accident. But the girl was found sitting up, without her jacket, with a book open in her lap. As though she'd deliberately removed it, then sat down with the book, to read until she fell asleep, knowing she'd never wake up."

"That sounds more like suicide."

"Exactly. She was not a known user, but of course that sort of thing is all-pervasive now, and she had been consorting that evening with known users of the so-called recreational substances—hash, coke, assorted gumball drugs like Quaaludes, uppers, Thorazine. Anyway, none of her friends saw, or would admit to seeing, her take any drugs, but they all agreed she seemed very depressed. Then the question is, what would make a nice, pretty, smart girl with her whole life in front of her depressed enough to take her own life? This is where your predecessor, the esteemed Professor Parsons, comes in. It seems she'd gotten behind in her papers for the survey, the same course you're teaching now, and Parsons had told her that day that he was going to fail her. It was too late for her to withdraw from the course without the failing grade going on her record, and she needed the credits to stay in school. He really had her over a barrel, saying in no uncertain terms that a deadline was a deadline, and there was no way he would accept those papers." Luke leaned back, and extended his hands, hanging on to the corners of the table to keep his chair from going over. Roz watched him, utterly fascinated. He certainly knew how to tell a story. But where was it heading?

"So her adviser got into the fray and told her to appeal the decision as cruel and unreasonable punishment; he even called it academic terrorism of the worst kind. It was brought up before the Faculty Appeals Board and..." Luke stopped, obviously for effect.

"Isn't this a rather long preamble to a tale?" Roz remarked dryly. Luke ignored, or perhaps did not recognize, her allusion to the Wife of Bath. She gave in, curiosity overcoming her annoyance. "And...?"

"Parsons's buddies in the English department, Win Manciple and Art Franklin—behind that genial exterior he has a heart of brass—shot her down. It was a real power play; they'd show the rest of the college what real standards were. Her adviser was beside himself, nearly attacked Parsons and Manciple—simultaneously and in tandem—in the Faculty Club when he found out, accused them of pillorying the girl for their own ego satisfaction. He had to be physically restrained; took two men *and* Iris LeBeau to get him out of there."

"Who was it?"

"The Viking, as some students call him. Thor Grettirsdottir."

Roz felt her jaw drop. She stared blankly at Luke. "Thor?" Luke closed his eyes briefly and nodded.

"You never know with these mild-mannered, soft-spoken types; apparently he's got a really violent temper. And just imagine somebody six seven, two-hundred-forty pounds, all muscle from slinging those giant constructions of his around, roaring mad. Anyway, there's no love lost between him and most of the members of the English department. So now do you understand why I suggested you be careful about the company you keep?" Luke paused, and his next words horrified Roz even more than what he had already told her. "Especially with these latest incidents of possible sexual assault."

Roz sat there, unable to speak. Now that was really preposterous. A violent temper she might accept, but Thor as
the Grabber, Flasher, whatever? Luke must have taken leave
of his senses. She shook her head in disbelief.

Abruptly Luke stood up. "But that's enough gossip for
the moment. I just wanted to make sure you knew what you
were getting into." He watched appreciatively as Roz rose
from her chair. "As far as this English department thing
goes, of course I won't inquire how you voted." He paused,
gave her his disarming Huck Finn grin.

Roz's head was still buzzing. "I abstained," she said
absently, turning away toward the door. Thor in a black
suit, Thor reaching out . . . ? Never.

"Acting according to your better nature again, I see,"
Luke said. "But 'Do what you list, I wol youre thral be
founde, / Though ye to me ne do no daliaunce.'"

Roz turned and stared at him open-mouthed. "I thought
you didn't know anything about Chaucer," she said accus-
ingly. "*The Scarlet Letter, Moby-Dick,* Hank and Willy . . ."

"I looked it up," he said imperturbably. "'To Rosamond,'
right there in the index. How could I resist?" He walked
across the room, leaned toward her. "Allow me," he said,
and as Roz started to pull back, reached forward and opened
the door for her, still smiling.

I should have been faster, she thought as she nodded curtly
and sidled out. I could have opened my own goddamned
door. "To Rosamond" indeed. Index to what? She was almost
through the outer office when Luke shouted after her, "Don't
forget our date for the play." The secretary looked up, startled, and gave Roz a quizzical look as she marched out the
door.

She walked somewhat aimlessly back over to her office,
not knowing what to think. She had liked Thor, and now
that she thought about it, still did. She could see how he
might have been goaded into what he did, particularly since

she had seen Win Manciple in action. If ever there was a goader ... Maybe Luke had exaggerated, with his love of tall stories, made it sound more melodramatic than it was. Thor had always been the perfect gentleman with her. Which is more than I can say for you, Mr. Luke Runyon, she thought wryly. Anyway, in the end he had dismissed it all as gossip. She could check with Iris, or ... just leave it alone. She was as good a judge of character as anyone, and Thor was her friend. Almost her only friend, as a matter of fact. Except for his invitation to the play, Luke had certainly lived up to his promise of leaving her alone, and everyone else was so distant that she was still feeling like a total outsider.

She wandered into the deserted English office to see if there were any more student papers on *Beowulf* in her mailbox. There weren't, but there was an invitation: dinner that Friday night, October 30, at the Franklins'. Well, that was a switch. She wondered briefly and somewhat cynically what this was all in aid of, the social amenities being preserved, or the new acting chairman trying to co-opt her in his campaign against the powers-that-be? Maybe she should just stay completely out of things and not go?

But it was her first invitation from anyone in the department, and she was feeling rather isolated and sorry for herself, so she called up Mrs. Franklin on the spot, and gratefully accepted.

CHAPTER

7

*R*oz read student papers all Friday afternoon; she wanted to get them back the following Monday, before the Chaucer papers started coming in on Wednesday. She had still not gotten over her sense of playing catch up and she was certainly doing less with *The Canterbury Tales* than she would like, but the response of the class had been good; the students seemed to be coming around.

She was particularly impressed by Rick Squires, as he had politely informed her he was called. He seemed bright and intelligent, a good deal more mature than the other students in the class. He also seemed to be a loner. It was not that he wasn't friendly; Roz often saw him chatting after class with some of his classmates, but he did not appear to hang around with them outside of class. Whenever she saw him on campus he was alone, sitting in the lower study area of the Library reading, walking along the road to the Arboretum, always with his backpack and his books. He was serious, attentive in class (even when he appeared to be sleeping), and more often than not came up to her at the end of the hour to ask a question or make a comment on the day's lecture. His paper on *Beowulf* was the first one she read, and it was quite a decent job of trying to pull together the so-called digressions into coherence with the more fantastic elements of the work, which he did by focusing on the persistent themes of treachery and vengeance.

Roz glanced at the clock; time to get ready to go to the Franklins'. She yawned and stretched, then climbed out of the lumpy lounge chair that, with a similarly beat-up oak student's desk stuffed into a small cubbyhole, passed for a study in the college apartment she'd been lent. It was certainly Spartan enough. She wondered what kind of quarters the Franklins lived in. When she had talked to Mrs. Franklin, the woman had offered to have someone pick her up, but the weather was still fine, the Franklins' house not very far down the hill from campus, so Roz had said she would walk. When Mrs. Franklin asked her if that was really a good idea, given recent events, Roz, not one to give in to infringements on her freedom of choice, reiterated her resolve. After all, it wouldn't be that dark yet, there was lots of traffic at that time, and the street was well lit. But this did raise the question of who her fellow guests might be; she had been too polite to ask, but she was left wondering whether this was simply a social occasion, or a council of war. Well, she would soon find out. She carefully stacked the marked papers on one side of her desk, lined up her pens and pencils, and went to take a shower.

Roz arrived at the Franklins' early; it had taken her less time than she thought to walk the half-mile or so down the hill. It was a nice walk, still in daylight, though just barely, so that the streetlights that marched up the hill at regular intervals were not yet lit. She passed a little grove filled with white birches, ghostly in the fading light, and noticed across the way the small open shelter built of rough stone in the medieval style, crenelated battlements and all, at the entrance to the Canterbury Arboretum and Bird Sanctuary, a nine-mile trail through the woods she reminded herself she should try sometime before the snow fell, which this far north was probably in about two weeks. But that was all right too: she was an eager cross-country skier, and looked forward to being able more or less to step out her door and go off on a tear down what she had heard were very well-maintained and challenging trails.

Art Franklin opened the door with a hearty "Do come in, my dear; so glad to see you," and a brief pull on his nose, a nervous habit Roz had noticed in her earlier encounters with him. His nose, now that she thought about it, did look as though it had been elongated over the years, a yank here, a persistent stretch there, and lately it had been getting quite a workout. Mrs. Franklin was right behind, a tall, pleasant-looking woman, slightly dithery, who greeted her with an equally hearty "Do call me Griselda" and took away her jacket while Roz stood in the foyer of a surprisingly modern and attractive house, all wood and glass, with a large field-stone fireplace visible at the end of the hall.

Roz followed Franklin down the hall into a room that opened high to a cathedral ceiling, with a wall of glass overlooking more white birches and a declivity that must be an extension of the ravine she had passed on her way. The room was sparsely but elegantly furnished in the modern style, but what was most striking about it were the number and variety of *objets d'art*: Etruscan vases on the mantel, twisted brass candlesticks, huge copper bowls with Coptic lettering, a head of a Greek boy with the familiar stylized curly hair, looking as if the stone itself had been oiled and combed, and the usual slightly abraded nose and lips. She found herself thinking of Rick Squires, but not for long, because Franklin was at her elbow inquiring robustly what she would like to drink. While he was getting her a dry sherry Roz studied the huge amphora hanging from the rafters; nearly every piece in the room was from Greece or

a nearby country. Franklin must be quite a Graecophile, for
this collection intimated numerous trips to the Aegean. Not
to mention independent wealth; she couldn't imagine anyone
being able to afford all this on even a full professor's salary.
Maybe Griselda was an heiress.

But who had collected the odd clump of twisted metal in
the corner there? Roz walked over to take a closer look. On
second thought, maybe it wasn't metal; certainly those were
tree branches wound around each other, knots and all, complete with tiny pores and striations of bark. But why painted
to look metallic? She flicked a branch with her fingernail;
it pinged. It *was* metal.

"Oh, do you like our steel birches?" Griselda Franklin
fluted behind her. "We thought they were so clever, and
with our view down the hill through all that heavenly birch
forest—so spiritual, don't you think?—they seemed so
appropriate. Of course they're only on loan. Thor won't sell
his little experimental whimsies, but he's very kind about
letting people display his things, such a dear and generous
friend...."

Roz blinked at Griselda, then at the metal birches, then
back at Griselda. Thor Grettirsdottir? Dear friend? Hadn't
she heard there was no love lost between Thor and the
English department? Blows with Parsons and Franklin? But
who else around here would have a name like Thor? And
it had been Manciple and Parsons he'd nearly come to blows
with, not Franklin, now that she thought of it. But hadn't
Franklin been involved somehow? Roz put her hand up to
her forehead. She couldn't keep all these people straight.
Meanwhile Griselda was looking at her strangely.

"Are you all right?" she inquired.

"Thor Grettirsdottir? I...I...didn't realize he worked
in metal," she stammered, trying to order her thoughts.

"Oh, you've met Thor then. Isn't he a lovely person? He
does both wood and metal—casts these smaller pieces in

his foundry. He built it himself in the basement of the Art
Museum; have you seen it?" Roz shook her head. "Oh, you
really must. His studio is quite remarkable. But you can
ask him tonight," Griselda added brightly. "He should be
here any minute."

The doorbell tinkled faintly, and Roz's hostess hurried
down the hall, saying enthusiastically over her shoulder,
"Perhaps that's Thor right now."

But it wasn't. It was Shipman and Huberd, with their
wives.

It was clear to Roz, as she sat next to Art Franklin at what
could only be described as a groaning board—food and
drink and glassware and candles and fine linen, five courses,
including cold watercress soup and oysters Rockefeller, lamb
à la Grecque with garden vegetables, *Crème Brulée* and
now a savory of creamed mushrooms on toast—that she
and Thor were the matched pair (metaphorically speaking,
of course, since Roz was a good foot shorter than Thor),
she on Franklin's right, Thor on Griselda's at the other end.
She wondered briefly whether Griselda, blissfully ignorant,
apparently, of all the burgeoning controversies at the college, had planned this little do in order to bring together on
spec two nice (presumably, since she hadn't met Roz before
tonight) young people. Roz and Thor were the youngest
people in the room by at least ten years; even though he
was nearly bald, Thor couldn't be more than thirty-one or
-two. And unexpectedly self-conscious about his lack of hair;
tonight, though he had forgone the baseball cap, he wore
instead a red bandana wrapped around his head, which,
together with a large tunic of some velvety material and
navy-blue sailor's pants, gave him the look of an amiable
pirate.

He sat there now, beaming beatifically at Griselda Franklin and Emily Huberd as they chattered on about the latest

plot to raise money for the Art Museum; Griselda was president and Emily treasurer of the Faculty Wives Art Guild, Tea and Poetry Society. He had certainly done justice to the meal, being personally responsible for putting away several helpings of everything except the meat, eagerly passing his plate along for more at the urging of Griselda, who had concocted some sort of special dish of brown rice, tofu, ground-up mushrooms, tomato paste, and other unidentifiable ingredients molded into the semblance of medium-rare lamb chops especially for him.

It was just as well he was distracted by the food and artsy conversation, because Roz had been aware, before Thor loomed in the door some minutes late, of some tension in both Huberd and Shipman, possibly even in Art Franklin, though he must have known Thor was coming. But greetings had appeared friendly, if somewhat formal, everyone behaving cordially, so that Roz wondered for a moment about the alleged bad blood between Thor and members of the English department. But here he was, seeming the mildest of men, and the gentlest, kindest to his people, downright meek by comparison with the increasingly bellicose Professors Franklin, Huberd, and Shipman. Anyway, bygones appeared to be bygones, at least socially. Whatever the professors might be thinking in their heart of hearts, the social amenities were certainly being preserved.

They had sat down not too long after his arrival, Thor with a large flagon of beer—apparently he eschewed hard liquor of any kind, and a good thing too; imagine someone his size, never mind the alleged violent temper, roaring drunk and you had *Götterdämmerung* in a nutshell—the rest with their wineglasses, filled so promptly and generously that Roz finally rested her fingers more or less permanently over hers to indicate she wanted no more.

Now, her head buzzing slightly, she listened to the conversation of Franklin, Shipman, and Huberd. In the relative privacy of a mere social occasion, none of them talked or gestured so extravagantly as they had in the recent meetings, but there was no doubt that they were now engaged in the ongoing council of war Roz had predicted. They were determined to stop Luke Runyon at any cost, force him to resign, embarrass him, do whatever necessary to obviate what they saw as a treacherous betrayal of college standards in general, and the English department in particular.

"And to think the s.o.b. was one of us. We got him elected; you know that. And now he's angling to succeed President Bailey," Huberd announced, his disgruntled satyr's face made momentarily sinister by the guttering candle directly in front of him.

"If you ask me, Manciple's the real problem," Shipman interrupted, his narrow, pale face piqued with cynical amusement. "He's rocketed right out of control. Why, he had the nerve to accuse me of stabbing him in the back after the meeting the other day. The idea of either of them, Manciple *or* Runyon, in charge of anything frankly beggars the imagination. They're both so hostile and alienated." Shipman tossed back his wine and smacked his lips complacently.

"But Manciple's still one of us," Franklin remarked. "And Runyon's not."

Listening, Roz wondered what they all would think if they knew she had a date with the alienated and hostile Luke to go to the play next weekend, or what they would think when they found out. Things were beginning to get a little awkward; she really ought to do something besides sit here and listen to all this. Hadn't she promised herself she was going to stay out of campus politics, not get involved?

She could get up and move, go talk to Thor and Griselda, offer her services to the Art and Tea Society or whatever. Maybe that was too obvious, maybe...

Her dilemma was solved by a strident interruption on the

part of Mrs. Shipman—Madelayne, her name was, Maddie
for short, and she was Viennese—who was sitting next to
Thor, near the center of the table, and had obviously had
her fill of fund-raising brainstorms, as well as wine.

"Ha!" she shrieked. "Did you zay Luke Runyon? Dat
monster!" She leaned conspiratorially toward Roz, and said
in a loud whisper, "Vun time I vuz talkink to his vife—
dear lovely pearson and those two byootifool boyce, und I
asked her what it vuz like, beink married to zuch a—how
you say?—a male chauvinist pik, and she sayd, 'Not good
enuff,' dat's all, and the next veek, poof! she vuz gone.
Viz da boyce, lock, stock and bananas!"

Roz simply blinked at her, but Emily Huberd had heard,
and immediately chimed in with more tales of horror, never-
home nights, or else trustees brought home unexpectedly
for dinner, important alumni wined and dined on short notice,
and Alice such a perfectionist about these things, not to
mention the bottom-pinching, off-color jokes. But, Emily
Huberd added seriously, her feeling was that it was really
his ambition that caused the breakup. No time for his family,
nothing to stand in his way. "You mark my words," she
said. "If not here, he'll be president of someplace before
long."

Roz shut her eyes; obviously none of them realized how
well she knew and, yes, even liked Luke. And this certainly
didn't sound like the Luke she knew. It was more like
character assassination. The women had taken sides; but
that was inevitable. So she was relieved when Griselda
leaped to Luke's defense—how good he was to his two
children, how much time he had spent with them, how
conscientious a teacher and so forth—which only served to
set Maddie Shipman off again.

The women ranted on, and she opened her eyes to find
Thor gazing at her with a mildly amused but sympathetic
expression. She was wondering how she could politely excuse

herself and go sit next to him without seeming hoity-toity
when Art Franklin, things apparently getting a bit rowdy
even for the junta, stood up and announced he would furnish
after-dinner drinks in the living room. Everyone else moved
back into the high-ceilinged space, where a fire was crackling merrily, and Roz managed to sidle up to Thor.

"I like your piece over there in the corner," she said
awkwardly, not quite knowing how to strike up a noncon-
troversial conversation with him. She hadn't seen him since
that day he had taken her shopping, had even wondered
once or twice if he might call her. When he didn't, and after
she'd heard about his feud with members of the English
department, which now appeared exaggerated to say the
least, she had figured with mild regret but complete understanding that when things really got going, he had had to
choose sides and dissociate himself entirely from the rest
of the department, including her. But that did not appear to
be the case after all, for here he was.

"My twigs?" he murmured happily. "That's nice. If you
come over to the foundry sometime, I'll show you how I
make them." He beamed at her, two large dimples deeply
furrowing his cheeks. She was taken on the spot with the
conviction that he was every bit as nice and dear and gentle
as she had first thought him. She was beginning to think
this place—so small, so isolated—did odd things to people's perceptions of reality, or at least their perceptions of
other people. The atmosphere at times seemed almost poi-
sonous. But she was an outsider, thus more objective because
less involved, and she certainly planned to remain that way,
for the time being, or for the nonce, as Chaucer—and
Alan—were wont to say. She sternly reminded herself to
form her own opinions from the evidence of her own eyes
and ears, and keep her own counsel, taking everything she
learned with a grain of salt. So much for Luke Runyon and
his gossip.

Just then Franklin came in, looking puzzled. He held up an oddly shaped bottle, brown and heavy-shouldered, like a squatting troll, with a small card attached to its long neck. "Where did this come from, Gris?" he inquired, waving the evil-looking bottle at his wife.

Equally perplexed, Griselda answered, "I have no idea, dear. What is it?"

"Grappa, no less, the very best imported Livorno," Franklin intoned with a delighted grin. "Which of my wonderful guests is responsible for this unexpected extravagance?" he asked, directing a slightly addled glance around the room. The guests all looked at one another; no one spoke up.

"Perhaps the card says, dear," Griselda remarked.

Franklin opened the folded card and read it aloud: "'This treasure hath Fortune to you given/In mirth and jollity your life to liven.' Aha! Pop quiz! Who said that?"

"Sir William Davenant," said Huberd with authority.

"No, never!" shouted Shipman. "It's John Skelton."

"Sounds like Chaucer," ventured Thor.

"Too obvious," Franklin said dismissively. "Spenser perhaps?"

The rest of the company looked blank as Franklin swept the room with a pedagogue's expectant glance. Roz racked her brains. No, it wasn't Spenser.... On the whole, she agreed with Thor; it sounded like Chaucer.

"Who cares?" said Madelayne Shipman, and everyone laughed.

"So! The unknown benefactor chooses to remain nameless. Well, Fortune, I salute you, whoever you are!" Franklin chortled, and hastily set to prying the cap off the bottle. That accomplished, he smiled expansively at the company, lifted the mold-encrusted bottle with a flourish, and waved it around with a proprietary expression. "Who's first?"

The wives shook their heads, Madelayne with a little hissing noise in the back of her throat.

"Ugh! Nasty stuff, like rotten leaves and river slime mixed oop. No sanks!"

Roz tended to agree with Madelayne's description; the last time she had tasted the Italian liqueur had been five years earlier, in Naples with Tony. She hadn't liked the taste then, and she didn't welcome the memory now, of either the drink or the companion. Nevertheless, she was about to accept a glass, more out of politeness than anything else, when Thor whispered *sotto voce* next to her, "I wouldn't if I were you."

She looked up at him, startled. "Why not?" she whispered back.

"It's the real dregs," he answered. "Not only that; you don't know where it's been."

Bemused, Roz put her glass down like an obedient child, the phrase he had used reminding her sharply of what her mother had always called her reasons of last resort, along with the exasperated "Because I said so." She hadn't wanted the stuff anyway. Thor didn't even have to refuse; Franklin passed him right by, obviously aware he took no strong spirits. Not only that, he was still holding a half-empty stein of beer. But how many beers? Roz looked up at him and was reassured; he beamed at her with his usual beatific but completely lucid expression. Of course he wasn't even the least bit drunk; it would be totally out of character.

On the other hand, Huberd and Shipman, already a little tipsy, eagerly held their glasses out, and the three English professors happily toasted each other in the center of the room on a raucous note. They were antitoasts, really. "Death to tyranny!" Shipman shouted, and Huberd and Franklin laughed uproariously. "All for one and one for all!" shouted Huberd. Everyone else tittered nervously, except Thor, who sat there apparently lost in thought, contemplating the huge stone amphora suspended overhead.

"To us! The last bastion of Western culture and standards!"

bawled Franklin as he hurled his glass into the fireplace.

"Hear! Hear!" said Shipman, similarly smashing his, followed by Huberd. Griselda winced and then smiled weakly, putting her hands over her ears.

"Heh, heh," laughed Franklin heartily, and yanked his nose.

"Hee, hee," snickered Shipman, holding another glass out for more grappa.

"Ho, ho," boomed Huberd, his awesome eyebrows waggling as he too grabbed another glass.

"Thank you very much," Roz said to her distracted hostess, "but I really must go. I had a lovely time."

"Oh, must you?" Griselda said shrilly, her attention fixed on her husband and his two comrades in arms, the growing pile of glass shards in the fireplace, the diminishing tray of glassware. She looked very uneasy, and rather frazzled around the edges. And dishes yet to do, if there are any left, Roz thought guiltily. But she had to get out of here before she had hysterics. She'd never heard anyone actually say "heh, heh" in real life before, let alone "ho, ho" and "hee, hee." Not to mention the Three Musketeers routine with the glasses. Things were getting more than a bit too riotous in here. It was time to make like a crumbling battlement and fall away, she thought, remembering Alan with a pang, suddenly missing his dependable nature, not to mention his . . .

There was a gentle tap on her shoulder. She looked around, and there was Thor, holding her jacket.

"I'll see you home," he said. "It's about time I left too."

"Well," said Thor as he and Roz walked slowly up the hill toward campus. "That was quite a show."

"Do you see the Franklins often?" Roz asked. She was still trying to sort out the various bits of conflicting information she seemed to be collecting faster than she could verify. Was Thor really on the outs with the whole English faculty? Apparently not any more: in fact, she had a hard time imagining him on the outs with anybody.

Thor thrust his hands deep in the pockets of his tunic—his only outerwear was a large wool scarf wrapped around his neck, but then, it was warm for the last weekend in October—cocked his head, and grinned at her.

"Not really. Why do you ask?"

Roz hesitated, not wanting to be a purveyor of gossip, or whatever it was she had heard from Luke. "I heard you had a . . . a slight misunderstanding with some members of the English department. . . ."

Thor had turned to face her and was walking backward up the steep sidewalk, looking about nine feet tall. He regarded her quizzically. "Who told you that?"

Staring up at his mild-featured face, with its expression of benign, disinterested curiosity, Roz was even more convinced that the story of Thor's violent tendencies had been exaggerated, to say the least. If there was ever anyone she felt safe with, it was Thor. "Oh, never mind," she said. "It wasn't important."

"Griselda's the one, as a matter of fact. She's a great admirer of mine, and she invites me over once in a while. She thinks I don't eat well. Tells me I need to keep up my strength to do my stuff." Thor chortled softly. "Art and I aren't real pals, though we speak. He's not my type. Matter of fact, neither is Griselda. She just wants to be friends with everybody. And she's a great cook. Maybe she'll invite you over sometime for her medieval banquet." His large hands scalloped the air. "You know, a turkey stuffed with capon stuffed with pheasant stuffed with game hen stuffed with pigeon stuffed with lark, stuffed with an olive stuffed with a pimento, or roast boar's head with apple, syllabub, and sawdust on the floor . . ."

"I thought you were a vegetarian," Roz interrupted.

"I go just to watch. I eat the olive and the pimento."

Roz laughed. They walked on together comfortably for a while, until Roz, her curiosity overcoming her *politesse*, remarked, "Then there's nothing to the story that you came to blows with Win Manciple and Professor Parsons?"

Thor jerked to a halt, nearly toppling over her. "You heard *that*?"

Roz nodded. "The Alison Nelson case..." She stopped, sorry she'd brought it up at all, for Thor had turned visibly pale, even in the blanching moonlight. When was she going to learn to leave well enough alone?

"Oh, God," he moaned, passing a huge hand over his face.

They had just gone by the small stone shelter in the woods near the Arboretum; through the large openings that were obviously meant to afford a relaxing view down the hill and out over the valley, Roz caught a glimpse of rough stone benches.

"Why don't we go over there and sit down?" she murmured, taking Thor's arm.

He looked in the direction she was pointing, then back down at her with an expression of absolute horror, turned on his heel and loped off down the hill without a word. Without even a backward glance. Roz stared after him for a moment. What, she wondered, did I say?

After one more brief look around, only to discover that Thor had completely disappeared from view, those long legs of his as effective as seven-league boots, she shrugged and continued walking slowly up the hill.

She was just getting into her nightgown when she heard a knock on her door. But at this hour? It was past midnight. She pulled on her bathrobe, scuffled into her slippers, and went to the outside door.

"Who is it?" she called.

"It's Thor," a voice said from the other side. Roz put on the chain and opened the door a crack. It was indeed Thor, standing on the steps, his pirate's kerchief pulled down over one ear, his scarf dangling unevenly, nearly ready to fall off. And fall off it did, with a soft plop onto the doormat. He did not stoop to pick it up. "I wanted to make sure you got home all right," he said, ducking his head. He looked rather abashed.

Roz unhooked the chain and opened the door. She bent forward and retrieved his scarf from the doormat, handed it to him.

"Thanks." He made no move to come in. Or to go away. He raised his eyes and looked at her. "I'm sorry I took off like that," he said somewhat sheepishly. "It's just..."

"Would you like to come in?" Roz interrupted. "I can make some coffee, or herb tea, if you prefer," she added formally.

Thor nodded gratefully and moved inside.

"Alison Nelson was found in that little stone hut, and when you mentioned her name, and then I turned around and saw where we were, I...I...." Thor put down his teacup, sat back against the lumpy couch.

Roz nodded sympathetically, but said nothing. It was clear that Thor wanted to talk. She could ask questions later, if she wanted to.

"The case has never really been resolved, you know." Thor paused. "I really can't talk about it very well even now. She was a student of mine. Did you know that?"

"Yes, I did hear that," Roz replied. She waited for Thor to ask her from whom, but he did not seem to care. It was as if it were common knowledge.

"She was really quite a good artist. She was a combined English-art major, but the art major was sort of taking over; she was beginning to do the kind of mature work that one seldom sees in an undergraduate." Thor sighed. "But she had some personal problems—I was her faculty adviser; you must have heard that..."

Roz nodded again.

"...But she was very reluctant to say anything to anyone, even me. I tried to smooth some things out for her. Parsons had threatened to flunk her and wouldn't listen to mere vague references to extenuating circumstances, even from me; he wanted the straight dope—no pun intended—or else. He gave us an ultimatum, and...well...I did get a little hot under the collar, pushed and shoved a little. But it was only momentary. We'd gotten things worked out; she was going to withdraw from his course—the one you're teaching now—pick up the credits some other time, and drop the English major entirely. Then one day I woke up and she was dead." Thor shook his head, his eyes closed. "What a goddamned waste."

"So arbitrary," Roz murmured. "If only someone had happened along, seen her in time..."

Thor went pale again, stared hard at her for a moment, while Roz watched him curiously. Was there something else wrong? Or was he just wondering how much more to tell her? After all, they hardly knew each other. Still, there were advantages to being an outsider; she was objective, could be trusted. But she was disappointed.

"I have my own ideas about that," Thor said darkly, and that was all. Abruptly he stood up, towering over Roz in the low armchair. "I've got to go. Thanks for the tea and conversation, and I'm sorry I left you in the lurch there. It was inexcusable of me."

"That's all right..." Roz began as she stood up, holding out a hand for Thor's cup. She found it grasped in a huge warm paw instead.

"No, it isn't. Listen, it's not safe to walk alone around here, particularly if you're a woman. Promise me you won't.

After Alison's death, when they asked if anyone knew anything that might shed some light, the women students came forward with seventeen reports of attempted assaults. They were afraid to say anything before, and didn't think they should because nothing really happened. Then there were the cases of what is now fashionably called 'acquaintance rape,' that and a gang bang involving one or two of the more disreputable fraternities. The frats have been heavily implicated in charges of sexual harassment. That's one of the reasons we're so anxious to get rid of them. Not that this had anything to do with Alison's death, as far as anyone knows." He paused, gazing at Roz's expression. "You've heard about the latest incidents with the Grabber, haven't you?"

Roz nodded. Not only that, she'd also heard the girl Dori, who had been assaulted in the bathroom, had withdrawn from school.

"Well, I don't mean to frighten you, but I just want you to be careful. No more hitchhiking, okay? Call me."

Roz, who was accustomed to taking care of herself, withdrew her hand. "Thanks, Thor. I'll keep it in mind." Then she added, with the gentlest of irony, hoping to lighten things a bit, that obscure old English tag phrase Alan was so fond of, "For the nonce."

Unexpectedly, Thor answered, "You mean 'For the Norns.'"

"What?" Oh, but of course, Roz thought. He must be using a peculiar Maine pronunciation of the word, the *r*'s missing from one word turning up unexpectedly in another. Maybe it was the one from Southwark, pronounced Suthwahk. She gave him a skeptical look.

Thor grinned at her. "You should say, 'I'll keep it in mind, for the Norns.' Oh, I know the theories about transposed consonants and metrical fill-ins, but the truth is, nobody knows exactly where 'for the nonce'—or the earlier form, 'for the nones'—came from." Assuming an exaggerated attitude of scholarly concern, he cleared his throat and, much to Roz's amazement, went on. "For my part, I've always thought that that phrase was the Norse equivalent of 'God willing' or 'by God,' stuck in there so the Norns, those dear old gray ladies with but one eye they pass around among them, won't think you're goosing the gods about your fate. They *are* the Fates. You knew that, didn't you?" he asked, peering at her cautiously. "Hence, 'For the Norns.'"

Roz gaped at him, startled by this unexpected and—if she was not mistaken—possibly even original contribution to the etymology of an obscure Middle English phrase. In fact, she'd just run across it last week in the Miller's Tale, in Chaucer's description of the manservant as "a strong carl for the nones." She had always thought it meant "for the occasion," which in that case had been summarily ripping a door off its hinges. She contemplated Thor's massive figure for a moment, concluding that, unlike many of the artists she knew (Alan being the one notable exception), he must have a literary as well as a plastic imagination. He must not spend all his time blissfully slinging around telephone poles, bending chicken wire, and pouring molten metal after all. Not that she was an intellectual snob, but the truth was, she found Thor's literary expertise quite refreshing: someone else to talk to about words. She beamed at him.

Thor beamed back. "And another thing. I wanted to tell you that I would have called you after we went shopping that day—I thought about you several times—but I've been out straight with classes and the stage set for the play next weekend. I designed it, and I've been building most of it myself. That's what I get for being so damned ingenious." He shrugged, some of his old charm and easygoing manner reemerging. "I can't take you to the play because I have to be backstage, but I wondered if you'd like to go to the cast party afterward with me."

"Oh, Thor, I'd love to. But I've already..." She hesitated briefly. "...made plans," she finished, having decided on the spot that she'd rather not tell him she was going with Luke Runyon. Maybe Thor did not share the same opinion of him as the members of the English department, but she'd had enough *Sturm und Drang* for one night, and it wasn't worth the risk.

Meanwhile, Thor was looking disappointed, but then he brightened. "Never mind; it was a bad idea. I'll probably be a nervous wreck anyway, thinking about all the things that went wrong, didn't work, fell apart, and so forth. Not to mention totally exhausted. But what about coming over to my studio sometime? I'll show you my foundry, how I make those branch castings you liked."

"Oh, Thor, I'd really like that."

"Good. Tomorrow okay? It's Saturday, so neither of us has classes, and it'll be quieter."

Roz smiled and nodded. Thor happily wrapped his scarf several times around his neck, threw the end over his shoulder with a flourish. "Good. About ten o'clock?" He peered at her. "Or is that too early?"

Roz laughed. "No. I don't sleep in on weekends. Too many papers to grade."

"All right then. I'll see you tomorrow. And thanks again. I guess I needed to talk. I feel much better now." With that, Thor Grettirsdottir bent forward in a slight bow, gave Roz a mock salute, and marched out the door.

Seeing his broad back disappear down the path, she wished briefly that he had told her more about his connection with Alison Nelson, but on second thought, she'd had enough of that too for tonight. Yawning, she took off her robe and went to bed with the phrase from Chaucer's Miller's Tale

running through her mind: "a strong carl for the nones."
She tried Thor's version. "A strong carl, by God." And so
he was, she thought as she drifted off, imagining Thor's
huge figure heaving doors off hinges, striding over the white
permafrost northern landscape in his giant's boots, cuffing
villains aside with one mighty stroke....

And then she was asleep.

CHAPTER

8

At a little before ten the next morning, Roz made her way across campus to the Art Museum. The building, in contrast to the older ones that surrounded it in the so-called New Quad, was starkly modern, dug into the hillside at one side like a bunker, and stretching up as though on stilts three glass-fronted stories high on the other. Architects of the college's most recent building boom had declared that the Wren-style colonial architecture that had made Canterbury resemble an academic Williamsburg was out, and the powers-that-be had decided that sufficient structural unity would be preserved if every building were faced with the same iron-impregnated limestone the college quarries had been supplying for nearly two hundred years. So there it was, all rust-streaked stone and glass and copper roof. The only problem was that Roz had no idea how to get to Thor's studio. She knew it was in the basement, but where was that?

She had no choice about which door to enter; only the main entrance was open, a navy-blue-clad security guard posted nearby. As she pushed through the heavy glass door she was surprised to see Rick Squires sprawled in an armchair in the lobby. He looked up from his book, obviously surprised to see her as well.

"Hello, Rick. How are you doing?" she said, coming to a halt beside him.

"Oh, hi, ah, Professor Howard," he replied, sitting up awkwardly, and flopping the book he had been reading face down in his lap, obviously not sure whether he should stand politely or not. Resisting the urge to say "Call me Roz," Roz glanced down at the cover; Queen Elizabeth in a ruff and jewels. It was Volume One of *The Norton Anthology*, the book for her course.

"Hard at work, I see," she commented, wondering why this nice, attractive boy was sitting here all alone. There was not another student in sight. Come to think of it, what was he doing in the Art Museum in the first place? It seemed an odd place to study. Not wanting to seem too inquisitive, she said casually, "That was a very good paper you turned in on *Beowulf*, Rick. I think you really hit the mark on the issue of violence and evil stemming from the need for revenge."

The young man ducked his head, and Roz saw the familiar flush spread across his prominent and lightly freckled cheekbones. But when he looked up at her, his face was deathly pale.

Concerned, Roz said quickly, "Is there something wrong?"

"No, no, gee thanks, Miss Howard. I'm glad you liked my paper. I worked pretty hard on it. I liked *Beowulf* a lot."

Not the most articulate of conversationalists, Roz thought, but then, it was still fairly early in the morning. "What are you reading now?"

Rick looked down at the book in his lap as though it had just flown there from outer space. "Um, oh, I was . . ." He grinned disarmingly. "Actually, I was asleep. I was out kind of late last night." And he blushed again.

Okay, thought Roz, I'll leave you to it. "Well," she said
brightly, "I'll be seeing you. I've got to find the basement
studio somehow. You wouldn't know how to get there by
any chance, would you?"

He looked at her blankly. "Basement studio?"

"Yes. The sculpture studio. I'm supposed to meet Thor
Grettirsdottir there"—she glanced at her watch—"five minutes ago."

To her surprise, Rick leaped up, no mean feat, since the
Muppet-style chair immediately slid squishily out from under
him and fetched up against one of the French windows
overlooking the front entrance. Ignoring this, he quickly
stuffed the anthology into his rucksack, slung it over his
shoulder, and said, "Come on, I'll show you."

Because the museum was partially built into the hill, the
entrance and main museum gallery were on the top floor of
the building. Leaving the watchful eye of the guard, Rick
and Roz descended a flight of winding tunnel-like poured-
concrete stairs and then a corkscrew metal flight that clanged
more sepulchrally the farther down they got. There were
doors leading out, but they were barred and alarmed, with
red lights and buzzer horns, and minicameras of the type
used to film bank robberies, all ready to go into noisy
operation the minute anyone tried to violate them. Rick went
ahead of her down a damp-smelling corridor toward a set
of heavy double doors, and pushed them open.

The room roared.

Roz's hands flew immediately to her ears and she shrank
back against the wall, certain that they had just opened the
door on some sort of explosion, some terrible accident. But
the noise went on, loud and continuous, surrounding her,
assaulting her, a conflagration of sound. She'd never heard
anything so loud in all her life.

"Oh, hi! Come on in!" a cheerful voice shouted above

the pandemonium. "I just fired up the blast furnace; it'll be ready in a minute."

Roz crept toward the door and peered inside, hands still held protectively over her ears. In the middle of a room that seemed to be the size of an airplane hangar, filled with piles of railroad ties, stacked-up trash barrels, bits of broken furniture, and what appeared to be the remains of several demolished buildings, Thor Grettirsdottir was standing in his striped janitor's coveralls, peering with a smoke-blackened face into a hole in the floor about a yard in diameter. The rim of the hole flickered and glowed, and apparently it was from there that the roaring emanated. Unless, Roz thought crossly, this was more of Thor's sound effects. But she didn't think even he could make that unearthly racket.

She moved inside. "Hi, Thor," she yelled. "Is it all right if..." She was going to ask if Rick Squires could come in too, but when she turned to motion him inside, the boy was gone.

"Well, that's it," Thor said breathlessly as he pushed the huge overhead dolly back against the wall. "Your very own set of steel birch twigs." Roz looked down at the beds of wet sand set in frames along the floor. The sand had stopped burning; she could see the little melted and fused bits where the white-hot metal had ignited the grains and made them flame. The metal Thor had poured into the molds was still red hot, but beginning to solidify after running like liquid mercury into every whorl and fissure.

"What a fascinating process," Roz said, a little too loudly now that the furnace had been shut off. She had been surprised to learn that the incredible noise could be turned off with the twist of a valve; the furnace, Thor had explained, was fired with high-pressure natural gas to a temperature of twenty-three hundred degrees Fahrenheit. The furnace itself was the size of a large steel-drum barrel, buried in the concrete floor. When it was heated, Thor ran a dolly that was suspended from the ceiling on two large tracks over to the hole, attached a crucible that looked as though it were made of gray alabaster but was in fact graphite, containing a chunk of scrap steel, to the metal basketlike affair at the end of the dolly, and maneuvered it with large tongs into the opening. In a matter of minutes the metal chunk was molten, and Thor, in welder's helmet and insulated gloves, manhandled the whole contraption along the tracks overhead until it was suspended over the frames where earlier he'd pressed several birch branches into the sand, tilted the graphite beaker over ever so carefully, until the hissing white metal had streamed like lava into the molds. Then he'd shoved back the helmet, mopped his brow with the self-same red bandana he had been wearing on his head last night at the Franklins', and beamed at her. "They'll be cool in a couple of hours," he said. "How about a grand tour, and then maybe you'd have lunch with me somewhere?"

Roz had agreed, so Thor had first showed her some of his works in progress, including the piled-up railroad ties that looked like a corral for Babe the Blue Ox but were actually entitled "Don't Fence Me In" (I'm getting closer, she thought), and the bolted-together trash barrels hung on chains from the ceiling, which Thor proudly pointed out as "Oranges and Lemons" (No, I'm not, she concluded).

She and Thor had spent the rest of the morning in the museum, of which Thor, with his keys, appeared to have free run, alarms and buzzers notwithstanding. Then they had gone directly to Ludwig Van's, a fine German restaurant in an adjoining town, where they had spent the better part of the afternoon, Thor instructing her in the finer points of various forms of vegetarianism, and introducing her to one of his favorite dishes, beanburger à la Lindstrom, a thick mixture of coarsely ground garbanzo beans, macerated beets, tofu, capers, and other mystery ingredients, mixed up and then baked into a square pattie that looked to Roz like a slice of raw meatloaf with raisins. Thor had eaten his, and finished Roz's as well. Then he had spent some considerable time trying to convince her to join him in his favorite seasonal pastime, cross-country skiing and winter camping. "You're in the Frozen North, you know," he had admonished her cheerfully. "Any day now you'll wake up and, pow! snow all over the place. It'll be here; winter six months of the year!" He grinned happily. "That's one of the reasons I came here; it goes with my race memory. Or, as your old friend Chaucer says, 'Thanne is it wysdom, as it thyn keth me, / To maken vertu of necessitee.' In other words, if you can't fight it, you might as well join it. Right?"

"Right!" Roz answered, and they both laughed and laughed.

At Roz's request, after lunch Thor dropped her off at the office, where she found several more papers to grade, which she did right on the spot. And so it was that she did not hear until late that afternoon about the terrible accident involving their erstwhile dinner companions Professors Shipman and Huberd, who had been found smashed up against a lamppost in Shipman's car, or about the considerably more serious and certainly more bizarre circumstance of their host, Professor Franklin, who had been found in his own living room underneath a pile of shards, all that was left of the huge Greek amphora that had once depended from the rafters, clutching in one hand the bloody bunch of metal birch-tree branches forged by Thor Grettirsdottir, who was even now being questioned as a suspect by the police.

As soon as she got inside her apartment, Roz dialed Luke Runyon's number. The phone buzzed insistently in her ear— busy. She began to pace around the room, stopping to redial his number every minute or so. She was downright startled when the fifth time she dialed he answered right away; she must have caught him between calls.

"You heard?" he said without preamble.

"Yes. I can't believe it. They were all fine, if a little raucous, when we left." Roz shifted the receiver to the other hand; she had been gripping it so tightly her fingers ached. "Luke, shouldn't I go down to the police station, tell them . . ."

"What *you* are going to do, my dear, is stay out of it. There's absolutely no reason for you to get involved."

Roz held the receiver away from her ear and stared at it. What did he mean, stay out of it? Wasn't she already involved? Thor was her friend, Franklin et al. her colleagues. And she didn't care much for that condescending tone of Luke's, either. My dear, indeed. She wasn't going to stand for being dismissed out of hand like this. "Listen, Luke," she began, "I was there last night—"

She was interrupted by a couple of loud beeps that seemingly emanated from inside her phone. Was the damned thing bugged? She held it away from her ear, while Luke's voice jabbered like a chipmunk.

"What did you say?" she asked, gingerly holding the receiver back against her ear.

There was a groan of frustration. "Sorry, Roz, but would you hang up now? That beep signal means there's an important call on my line. Something big—an emergency situation—has come up, and I have to take care of it."

"Emergency!" Roz snorted. "What's more of an emergency than having three of your faculty members grievously injured, and another one questioned as a possible suspect?"

Luke sighed impatiently. "Last month the Interfraternity Council scheduled a monster rally for tonight—'Screech Out and Clutch Somebody' it's called—ostensibly for Halloween. It's supposed to start at midnight, and they got several of the younger professors to agree to dress up and read scary stories, Poe, LeFanu, Jacobs, you know. But in view of the accidents last night, it seems to be in really rotten taste, not to mention the fact that it will probably turn into a pro-fraternity demonstration, so I'm trying to get it canceled. I hate to be rude, but will you please hang up? I'll call you later." Luke sounded breathless, even desperate. Roz felt a sudden stab of sympathy for him. What a mess for a dean to be in. What a mess for anybody to be in. She wished she could help, but she knew when she wasn't wanted.

"Bye," she said abruptly, and hung up. She sat there, staring at the telephone, wondering what to do next.

Wait a minute. Accident, he said. No, *accidents*. That wasn't so bad, then. The students had been wrong; surely the police were only questioning Thor as a witness. But she had to know more. She picked up the phone again, dialed Luke's number. Busy. Then there was no answer. Iris LeBeau was not home, either. No answer at Thor's; that probably meant he was still at the police station. Completely frustrated, as last she gave up, fixed herself a light supper and sat herself down in the living room with her papers and her books. It was nearly ten o'clock when the phone rang, making her jump. She grabbed it up like a squalling baby.

"Hi, Roz." It was Luke's voice, sounding apologetic. "Sorry to cut you off like that, but everything's okay now." For a split second, Roz thought he was talking about Thor. But Luke went on, "More or less, anyway. We couldn't get them to cancel entirely—there would have been a riot tonight for sure—but they've agreed to put it off until the weekend after next. They settled for Friday the thirteenth. But this'll give things a chance to settle down." There was a huge sigh at the other end of the wire. "I'm ready for a drink. Want to join me?"

Curiosity overcoming caution about Luke's real motives, she agreed; he could certainly fill her in on what had happened, and she could take care of herself. She need not have worried. Luke was, as he had promised all those weeks

ago, the perfect gentleman. But he had learned no more
about the accidents and Thor's questioning than she had, so
Roz came home an hour later none the wiser and no less
concerned than she had been before.

"It seems that Shipman and Huberd between them," Roz
wrote to Alan on Monday night, "finished the whole bottle
of grappa in very short order and then started singing and
yelling and generally carrying on, and before anyone knew
what was happening, the three of them got into some kind
of argument over what Griselda swears she heard them call
'the treasure,' probably a reference to the quotation on the
card which, by the way, is from the Pardoner's Tale. Shipman and Huberd started struggling with Art Franklin and
the women tried to stop them, but they were incredibly
strong and totally out of control, practically raving, so that
finally the three women were so frightened they ran over
to Emily Huberd's house and called the police. Before they
could get there, Huberd and Shipman, apparently drunk out
of their minds, hollering 'Death to tyranny! Death to Mr.
Death!' roared off down the hill in Shipman's car, straight
into one of those tall arc lights. Meanwhile, Franklin apparently grabbed up the steel birches, clobbered the amphora
as though it were a piñata—maybe under some sort of
delusion that was where the mysterious treasure was hid-
den—and knocked it right down smash on top of himself.
He's in the intensive care unit at the hospital with a concussion and lacerations; Huberd and Shipman are both in
pretty bad shape, head injuries, respiratory problems, and
possible kidney failure; none of them is lucid enough to
remember a thing about what happened. The whole place
is in an uproar. My class was absolutely bug-eyed this morning; I don't know whether they understood a word I said
about Chaucer's 'Retraction.' A few people have suggested
that the opening of the play scheduled for this weekend be

postponed, but Win Manciple, who, it seems, is the star, has declared 'the show must go on,' that Franklin and Shipman and Huberd would want it that way. . . ."

Roz's account of these unfortunate events at Canterbury was interrupted by the telephone. She put her letter aside and picked up the phone to find Luke Runyon on the line, wanting to know if she wanted some company. Roz looked at her watch; it was half past ten. Company for what?

"I'm fine, Luke, thanks anyway," she told him, hoping he wouldn't insist. He did, briefly, but Roz remained firm; she did not want company. There was a puzzled silence on the other end of the phone, during which Luke apparently decided once again not to press her. "Aw, shoot" was his clearly understated and mockingly hayseed response. Laughing, Roz found herself perversely flattered; he *was* persistent, in his gentlemanly way. And attractive; she couldn't deny that. But . . . She looked down at her unfinished letter to Alan.

"Just remember our date for the play Saturday night, okay?" Luke said finally. "If I don't see you before then, as seems entirely likely given the latest horror show, I'll pick you up for dinner at five-thirty. Wear something sexy. Bye now, and take care."

Roz hung up the phone, suddenly weary. I'll finish the letter tomorrow, she thought, yawning hugely. She tucked it back into her letter case and went to bed.

Roz paused in her lecture on *Dr. Faustus* and looked over the class. Heads bent over notebooks, hands moved busily, scribbling notes. One or two faces looked up expectantly, waiting for her to go on. She wasn't sure she could go on; she had spent two restless nights thinking about recent events. Tuesday a police detective had come to talk to her, and she had told him everything she could remember about the eve-

ning of the dinner party. He had seemed particularly interested in Thor's actions, his whereabouts at all times,
particularly during the half hour or so during which he had
gone back down the hill, before he showed up at her door.
Of course Roz could not account for that time, but she could
tell from the detective's manner it was important. Chasse
was his name, a burly, red-faced man about thirty-five, with
a cadence to his speech that Roz found unfamiliar enough
to inquire where he was from.

"Madawaseedumkweag, ma'am," he had answered
politely. "It's a four-hour drive north from here, about as
far north as you can get in these United States." Roz had
been surprised to find how much more of Maine there was
up north, not to say Down East; she had been under the
impression from Thor's account of the winters here that she
was situated just below the Arctic Circle. They had chatted
a little about life in the farthest reaches of northern Maine,
which people assumed, Chasse ruefully explained, was pop-
ulated entirely by potato farmers, lumberjacks, Maine guides,
the Furbish lousewort, and moose, none of these with more
than a third-grade education, except perhaps the moose. He
himself was very proud of his degree from the University
of Maine at Fort Kent, where he had been captain of the
football team.

They actually got on quite well talking about their respec-
tive small hometowns, and Chasse had seemed open and
friendly, but when, as he was leaving, Roz had asked him
in passing the reason for all these questions, he had smiled
a tight, professional smile, and answered, "Just routine,
ma'am, just routine."

But she did not believe it was routine, not one bit. That
night she hardly slept, and it did not make her feel any
better to learn from Chasse, who had called again earlier
this morning with more questions, that, for the moment at

least, the whole thing was being treated as a dreadful accident.

Then why was he asking her so many questions about Thor?

Behind the lectern she shuddered briefly, trying to regain her train of thought. It was Wednesday morning, November fourth, and she had begun lecturing on *Dr. Faustus*. "The sin that damns Faustus to eternity," she concluded, "is not greed for money or power, as the Pardoner would have us poor simpletons believe, but pride—hubris, the belief that we are smarter and more powerful than everybody, including God. And this is expressed finally in Faustus's cynical belief that he has damned himself irrevocably, in his terrible despair thus denying God's will and power to save." She paused briefly, indicating the end of the lecture, sighed inwardly with relief. Was it her imagination, or was there a similar faint exhalation from the class? "We'll be coming across this theme again, the awful pride of evildoers, whose ultimate act of pride is to cut themselves off from God's power, so keep it in mind as you read along. We'll be talking about the last act of *Faustus* on Friday, and on Monday we'll be starting *Othello*. I expect to have your Chaucer papers read and back to you by Friday the 13th" (muted groans) "at the latest." She nodded her head in dismissal, and twenty-six notebooks clapped shut, twenty-six bodies stood up, yawned, stretched, and made for the door. She scooped up her books and went to her office to finish the few remaining papers, grateful for the prospect of some work to distract her from her depressing thoughts.

There was a department meeting that afternoon, so she had packed herself a lunch to save time. She ate her sandwich and picked up Rick Squires's paper on "The Pardoner's Ultimate Sin," and began to read.

"The consummate arrogance of the Pardoner finds its ultimate expression in his brazen attempt to cozen the pilgrims, after he has already let them in on his fraudulent tactics. One must remember that the Pardoner, unlike the Miller and the Reeve and some of the other less savory pilgrims, is not just your average run-of-the-mill lowlife. He is in fact a walking emblem of the Seven Deadly Sins— lust, sloth, gluttony, avarice, envy, anger, and pride—the epitome of evil. He may argue that love of money or *cupiditas*—avarice—is the root of all evil, but it's clear from Chaucer's characterization of the Pardoner that he wants us to realize that it is pride—horrendous, deformed, and over-weening pride, what we would now call 'egomania'—that lies at the heart of his, and possibly all, evil. The Pardoner is so convinced of his own intellectual superiority that he believes he has the absolute power to make anyone act however he wishes, including God." Hmm, Roz thought with some amusement, sounds like Manciple. She read on with interest. "And the only recourse the pilgrims have, as we see, is the threat of violence, both in word and deed." Zowie, Roz thought, the boy is brilliant. She read on, and was just finishing the paper when an odd thought struck her. She picked up her variorum Chaucer and read through the text of the Pardoner's Tale. She turned to the Miller's Tale and read that as well. She put the book down and thought for a moment. "No, that's ridiculous," she said aloud. Shaking her head, she picked up the next paper, a feminist reading of the Wife of Bath's Prologue and Tale, yawned, and read on.

In a brief meeting that afternoon a subdued English faculty elected Win Manciple acting chairman. "I want you all to know right now," he said somberly, "that in spite of the recent tragedy of our colleagues, I will not give any ground, either to these terrorist tactics or to the pressure being applied to us by certain members of other factions in the college; I will not lower our standards or give one *inch* of ground. The Freshman English requirement must stay, and fraternities must go."

"Hear, hear," the rest of the department had murmured wearily. Several of them were working double shifts, having taken on some of their stricken colleagues' courses, including Roz, who was scheduled for several classes on Milton in Franklin's course. Roz got the feeling that most of them were fed up with the whole business; she certainly was. It had certainly sounded like a call to arms. But what did he mean by terrorist tactics? Pressure applied? Or was this just more of Manciple's theatrics? As soon as the meeting broke up she took Iris LeBeau aside in the corridor and asked her what was going on.

"Haven't you heard the latest?" Iris asked, her heavy eyebrows lifting practically into her scalp. She motioned Roz into the unisex bathroom—Roz had been right the first day; there was no women's room per se—and shot the bolt, "So no one else will come barging in here," she explained. Then with evident relish, in a hushed voice, she started in on the latest, which was that the police had confirmed from laboratory evidence that the grappa had been heavily drugged, with enough LSD and PCP—"That's angel dust," she explained unnecessarily—to send the whole front line of the New England Patriots as high as the Goodyear blimp, let alone three puny professors. But unfortunately the bottle was nowhere to be found; the police were still searching. From fingerprints on the amphora and the birch twigs, they also knew that Franklin had not accidentally knocked the stone jug down on himself, after all; it had been deliberately cut down and smashed over him, after which, the new theory went, Huberd and Shipman, crazed with drugs, had worked him over with the steel birches, then jumped into the car and driven themselves full speed into the nearest lamppost.

As to who was ultimately responsible for this havoc, that was anybody's guess, since nobody had ever locked doors around here—though they surely would now—but Iris had it on good authority that a campus investigation was in full swing, room-to-room checks for drugs, questioning of students the three professors had in their classes, questioning of witnesses before and after the unfortunate events. After the bomb scare on the airplane, it still seemed logical to suspect some sort of student underground in operation, and the possibility of a student prank that had gone too far.

"Some prank, huh?" was Iris's wry comment. "The only trouble with that theory," she went on, "is that no one can figure out what the students would have against those three in particular, or how they would have gotten hold of the grappa bottle, or known that Franklin and Shipman and Huberd were so nuts about the stuff. After all, it is an acquired taste," she added with a slight shudder. "So..." Iris paused; Roz stood tensely, waiting for her to go on. "That's why the police suspect Thor Grettirsdottir."

Roz slumped back against the hard tile wall, feeling dazed. So Thor was a suspect after all. And he had stopped her from drinking the stuff. She shook her head blindly as a wave of nausea swept over her.

"You look kind of green," Iris commented. "Is something wrong?"

Roz shook her head numbly. It couldn't be; she mustn't say anything. Surely there was some other explanation.

Iris waited until she had recovered, then filled her in on the rest of the gossip. According to Iris's information, which seemed to Roz exhaustive, one theory was that sometime after he had left with Roz, Thor had gone back to the house, found the three professors unconscious, beaten up Franklin with the steel twigs to which he had applied Shipman's and Huberd's fingerprints, cut down the amphora for effect, then lugged the other two out to the car and run it into the lamppost to make it look like an accident, and gotten rid of the grappa bottle he had drugged earlier and brought with him to dinner. "Seems like rather a lot, doesn't it?" Iris added unnecessarily. "But then, Thor can move fast when he wants to."

It had made Roz sick to think of it. It still did. Of course the possibility of Thor's involvement was mere speculation, she told herself, standing in the now-empty third-floor corridor of Tabard Hall, and really, now that she thought of it, quite preposterous. Could he have done it in that short time after he had left her on the hill? No, clearly it was impossible. Why, he hadn't even been out of breath when he showed up at her door half an hour later. There must be another explanation. Unfortunately, all three victims were presently still out of it, unable to give any information. When they did recover their wits, *if* they did, she was sure they would explain everything. She wouldn't be surprised to hear that they had given the drugs to themselves. Stranger things had happened, as witness many of the faculty parties Roz had attended over the years. Not all professors, in fact damned few of them, were what you might call staid and conservative straight arrows. She'd probably been offered more hits off joints and lids of coke by her colleagues than by any other segment of the population.

Not that any of this would help Thor. But still. She for one did not believe a word of it. What could they possibly think was the motive? As she slowly descended the dinosaur metal stairs, she made up her mind what to do next, and once outside in the brisk fall air, walked quickly over to the Art Museum to see if she could find Thor.

They found a quiet corner of the Main Gallery in which to sit and talk. Thor seemed very depressed, sitting on a low hassock with his elbows on his knees, long legs folded up like a grasshopper's. He was dressed in street clothes instead of his usual working garment of coveralls and baseball hat. With his head bare, he looked years older, his face lined and strained and grim.

"What I don't understand is why anyone would think that I doped the grappa in the first place, let alone leave it around for just anybody to drink, and then go back when they were all stoned out of their minds and . . . do all they think I did. I mean, what kind of degenerate do they think I am?" He shook his head, staring fixedly at the floor.

Then why did you stop me from drinking it? she wanted to ask. But she couldn't bring herself to do it. Instead, she said, "That's a good question, Thor. Why would they think you'd do something like that in the first place? I mean, really . . ." She stopped short as Thor lifted his head, regarding her with the look of a large and gentle hurt beast, and was suddenly aware that her tone of loyal disbelief had fallen flat, and anything else she said might end up sounding like an accusation. "I'm sure it will turn out to be an accident, or . . . or a student prank that misfired," she finished lamely.

Thor sighed. "There's a lot you don't know, Roz, and I guess I'd rather you didn't at this point. There's more to this business than meets the eye." Abruptly he stood up, looked down at her mournfully from his great height for a moment, then said, "I've got to get back to work; I'm finishing the set for the play this weekend. There's a crew downstairs waiting for me. One of them's in your class, by the way, says he likes it a lot," Thor went on with a pathetically labored attempt at normal conversation. "Name's Rick Squires. Nice kid. A transfer."

Roz stood up, uncertain what to do, to say. But Thor took that decision out of her hands.

"I think we'd better not see each other for a while, until this is all cleared up," he said in a serious tone. When Roz started to protest, he merely held up his large, callused, strong-looking hand and shook his head. "No, really. I appreciate your trust in me, but I'd rather you didn't get involved any more than you are already." He regarded her for a long moment. "Things may get even messier before this is over. Please, Roz, stay out of it." With that cryptic remark he turned and stalked off, while Roz stood gaping after him, completely at a loss.

And things did indeed get messier, although not in a way Roz or anyone else had foreseen. The next morning the Class of Ought Seven's Commemorative Fountain, which had so unobtrusively and cheerfully burbled its recirculated water over artfully deployed boulders into a rounded declivity in the center of the West Quad yea these many years, was discovered to have been entirely filled during the night with great quantities of concrete, which had then hardened to a petrified mass, into which was stuck a crudely lettered sign, "Death to the Tyrents."

The faculty, alumni, and, to their credit, most of the students were completely outraged, not to mention mystified, by this act of vandalism, which had involved at the very least commandeering a cement mixer from a local contractor, driving it into the quad, and discharging its contents, under cover of darkness, into the hapless fountain. Certainly some collusion, at least in their silence, by the inhabitants of the quad, who happened to be mainly fraternity men, was suspected, but by the end of the week none of the miscreants had been apprehended. Classes on Friday were conducted to the raucous jittering of jackhammers, and even after days of excavation, the fountain was not yet restored to its former glory, nor ever would be. There were rumors that a group of students dressed in black hoods had hired themselves out and were wandering the campus at will, terrorizing antifraternity partisans with cream pies, threatening to and even succeeding in applying them to the faces of many professors and administrators as well as students whose views they disagreed with, including one esteemed professor known for his agility who, distracted by the sight of a gorilla traipsing down one aisle of his lecture hall, turned around in wonderment only to be pied in the face by Batman. This was regarded as serious, although President Bailey was heard to remark that it was better than switchblades or tire chains.

Officials sighed and met and met again, declared that this lawlessness and vandalism must stop, and announced the addition of several more security guards to the campus force, who could be seen at any hour, pacing conspicuously, bouncing night sticks in their extremely competent-looking hands. The number of pies in the face fell off considerably, and no more black-clad figures were seen roaming the campus, for whatever purposes, at least for the time being.

CHAPTER

9

"*B*ut why would they consider Thor a suspect in the first place?" Roz asked Luke Runyon over dinner at Ludwig Van's that Saturday night. They were going to the play, which was, Roz had discovered earlier in the week from posters liberally tacked all over campus, *The Rover,* by Aphra Behn. This seemed rather an odd choice for a largely undergraduate college production; in fact, Roz was not even sure the play had been produced *anywhere* since the eighteenth century, but then, hers not to reason why, at least about that. She had had enough other problems to reason why about, the most pressing of which was what had become of Thor. So she had been relieved to hear from Luke that he was no longer the only one under suspicion in the drugging and assault of the professors three; after the fountain incident the police had given renewed attention to several student suspects, and were now tending to treat both incidents as deporable examples of criminal mischief.

"Well, for one reason, he was there," Luke said as he picked up his coffee cup and drained the last few mouthfuls. A waitress in a dirndl and lace-trimmed cap appeared from nowhere and filled his cup again, looked inquiringly at Roz, who shook her head. She was keyed up enough as it was.

"So was I," Roz said after the waitress had moved out of earshot.

"Ah, but they questioned you too, didn't they? And Manciple, who wasn't there, and Knight, and Pierce, and any number of students. Not to mention me and Iris LeBeau." He gazed at her with crinkled-up blue eyes, briefly waggled his mustache, then composed his handsomely chiseled face into the picture of disinterested sincerity.

"It isn't the same," she persisted. "They just wanted to know what I had seen. No one thought I might have done it. Why should I? I hardly know any of them. I just got here."

"Well, now, that's the point, isn't it? Why not stop worrying about it and let the people who have been around a while, who know everyone involved, solve the problem? I was a fraternity member myself when I went here; I don't believe they meant any real harm," he said, and smiled at her. Then, leaving her to wonder what in fact they *did* mean, he turned in his chair, signaled the waitress for the check, scrawled his name across it, and handed it back. He stood up, held Roz's jacket for her. "We'd better hurry now, or we'll be late for the opening curtain."

With these words he led a puzzled Roz through the dining room, out the door, and to the car.

Really, Roz thought as she settled back in her seat in the third row of the Major Theatre, a former stable converted into an elegant if somewhat improbably tall, narrow stage and precipitously stacked risers, even though Luke didn't see fit to discuss it, the idea of Thor as a suspect to begin with in the Franklin incident was patently ridiculous. Fortunately the original—the simplest—hypothesis about Franklin and the other two appeared to be the right one, that it was all a tragic accident stemming from a misfired practical joke. Anyway, people didn't go around killing each other in real life. Especially sweet gentle people like Thor. Why, he was even a vegetarian, for Pete's sake.

She sighed and shook her head. Here I go again, she thought. It was her nature—carefully nurtured by her anti-Calvinist parents, who had both actively disagreed in their relatively short lifetimes with the previous generation's sin-guilt-and-depravity theory of human motivation—to assume that people acted from the best of motives, or, she had learned more realistically lately, from the least worst. Why should the guilt settle on Thor? Just because he was there?

Roz sighed again. She would have to see some evidence beyond mere hearsay before she'd believe Thor Grettirs-dottir was guilty of assault and battery. And apparently the police now thought so too.

Luke must have heard her sigh; he dropped his arm, which had been lying casually along the back of her chair, down around her shoulders and gave her a brief, friendly squeeze obviously meant to be reassuring. Since that night several weeks ago, he had been warm and affectionate in an offhand sort of way, not the least bit overbearing. This had had the perverse effect of making her more attracted to him. And he *was* rather charming, if often difficult, and, she was beginning to think, certainly the least eccentric person around here.

The way he was with her, informal, amusing, respectful, was occasionally at odds with his professional attitudes and behavior, but this seemed reasonable, given the demands of the position, his apparent total commitment to his job, and the recent troubling events on all sides. So it was understandable that his reaction to criticism was sometimes anger. She remembered his remark as they were driving to the theater, in answer to her question about the latest academic stalemate: "If those prima donnas in the English department don't start to toe the line, believe me, heads will roll." But a moment later he had chuckled; fortunately his anger did not seem to last. And she was sure he had the good of the college at heart; that much was clear. So did Manciple and the others, even if it was from a more traditional and insular, less practical, but no less arguable standpoint. But if forced, she would probably side with the horses of her own color. She hoped it would not come up, that somehow this would all be settled, and also the business with the three professors who still lay unconscious in guarded but now stable condition in the hospital down the road.

"Should be starting up any time now," Luke murmured, removing his arm and crossing one leg at the knee; she saw he was wearing his cowboy boots, part of what she had come to think of as his mountain man outfit, leather jacket, tight pants, string tie, wide-brimmed hat, and embossed boots, all reserved for social occasions. In the office he was the picture of Brooks Brothers conservatism.

Roz turned her attention to the stage set; she had been staring at it for some minutes now, but not really seeing it. The curtain was pulled back into the wings so that the whole stage was exposed. What the audience saw was a three-story set connected by a series of catwalks, stairs, and balconies, surrounding a cobbled street that extended by some miraculous feat of perspective arguing considerable professional expertise to the vanishing point around some convincingly squalid and distant corner. On either side the old-fashioned timbered houses bent in, brooding over the street with some inscrutable intention, perhaps of falling down. It made Roz tense to look at it, a tribute to the artist's care. It also looked familiar; and Roz recognized it presently as a large version of the sketch she had first seen in the Art Museum, being studied by a large young man who made strange noises—Thor. That thing that had resembled a Murphy bed was in fact a curtained alcove in one of the houses high on the third level, and the low arches running partway across the stage were obviously meant to be, among other things, the sewer the villain, arch-antifeminist Blunt, would be cast into in the third act. Roz couldn't remember much more of the plot, not having read the play since graduate school, but she did remember that. It was a farce, with many exits and entrances, people in disguise, mistaken identities and intentions, Mrs. Behn following the fashion of the day, which was somewhere around the late 1670's. Which raised again the question of why now, and why here?

She opened the program. "A Joint Production of Cloak and Dagger and The Women's Association, in celebration of Women's Awareness Week." Aha. That explained it. Aphra Behn, the rediscovered Restoration playwright, first Englishwoman to earn her living entirely by the pen, thought for many years to be a kind of literary transvestite, slavishly copying the male dramatists of her time in a desperate attempt to survive and support herself, now being reevaluated as a feminist heroine and radical. *The Rover,* although certainly a prime example of the fashion of the day in bawdy comedy, could also be seen as subversive; the male characters were all such lecherous, opportunistic, and irresponsible miscreants, not an attractive male among them; Willmore, the Rover, a handsome but fickle twit, and Blunt, his counterpart in the subplot, a lascivious blowhard with vicious proclivities. She glanced out of the corner of her eye at Luke, wondering what he would make of all this. He was sitting patiently, hands folded over his program, waiting for the play to begin. He probably had no idea what the play was about; he was certainly in for a surprise.

She turned back to her program to see who was playing whom, and was surprised to see Win Manciple as Blunt, Rick Squires as Willmore. Several of the members of the Women's Association had parts. Now that was interesting. She settled back in her seat, crossed her legs, and tried to remember more of the plot as a small orchestra in white

periwigs struck up a baroque overture and the lights in the
auditorium dimmed. Instead she found herself thinking about
Rick Squires.

She had not realized he was appearing in the play as well
as helping build the set. How did he ever get all his school-
work done? A bright boy, and also very attractive. She
recalled her class the day before. Things had loosened up,
as she had predicted, so much so that instead of lecturing
she had found herself in the middle of a freewheeling discussion sparked by one of Squires's questions. "How did
they stage Faustus's descent to hell?" he'd asked. "Drop
him through a trap door?" This had led to class speculation
about the staging of the last scene in *Faustus,* where the
only stage directions are "The throne descends" and "Hell
is discovered," and about what kind of stage set might be
used to show Faustus being dragged down into hell. The
discussion had concluded with Roz drawing a composite
stage set on the board, incorporating everyone's suggestions, and pointing out, "But really, the idea is that hell is
all around us, as Mephistophilis says, so heaven descends,
and hell is discovered in the curtained alcove, where it's
been all the time." (In fact, Roz decided, looking at the set
in front of her, this one would do very nicely. Times had
come round again; the modern penchant for an open stage,
no curtains, one set for all the acts and scenes, duplicated
the stagecraft of Marlowe's and Shakespeare's time.)

The class had ended on a raucous note, Roz recalled with
amusement, as a hulking student named David Oblonsky,
who usually spent the whole hour looking either mystified
or hostile, remarked that Faustus should have known better
if he was so smart, but then had shrugged philosophically
and added: "Oh, well, you win some, you lose some, but
you gotta get dressed for 'em all." Everybody had broken
up, including Roz.

It had been the best class yet, Roz thought; though she

was perfectly willing to listen to the sound of her own voice, she preferred to listen to the students, see them taking in the reading, relating it directly to their own lives, understanding it in their own contemporary terms. That way, she knew, it would always be a part of their lives. And there was always something to be learned from their fresh encounters with the material. She chuckled to herself. You gotta get dressed for 'em all.

There was a rustle through the audience, a ripple of attention. Lights struck across the stage, illuminating behind a scrim a scene in an upstairs room of one of the beetling houses. A murmur of admiration, sporadic clapping. Really, the set *was* brilliant. Roz thought of Thor once again, and found herself hoping vehemently, as if her hope could conjure it, that the Franklin affair would turn out to be no more than an unfortunate accident, and Parsons's death too; no one's fault, no one's guilt. Meanwhile, she hoped the directors and producers of the play had used their ingenuity, as Thor had his, to edit some of the farce; most of Behn's plays suffered from an excess of complication, not to mention language, as if poor Aphra felt she had to go her male counterparts one better just to stay even. As probably she had. But surely the play had been cut, simplified, or else they would all be either confused or bored to death.

In fact, neither was the case. Oh, some scenes had been cut or transposed—for which, Roz recalled, there had been ample precedent in these modern times, Olivier's *Hamlet* being the most prominent example—that plus a combination of skilled acting (relatively speaking; they were, after all, rank amateurs) and marvelous stagecraft involving the use of the set made the play move along rapidly, and the outrageousness of the plot soon engaged the audience thoroughly. It was clear that the director had seen the play as a send-up of antifeminism, and had instructed his male players to exaggerate their roles to the limit. So by the time Helena made her plaintive remark in Act I, "Why must we be either guilty of fornication or murder if we converse with you men? And is there no difference between leave to love me, and leave to lie with me?," it was greeted with cheers, Willmore's self-serving machinations and Blunt's cock-of-the-walk lustful antics with boos and hisses. Everyone in the audience, as well as on stage, seemed to be having a wonderful time, including Luke, who, Roz surmised, might even be learning something. And she had to admit that the casting was brilliant—Rick Squires played the feckless Willmore with deadpan wide-eyed sincerity that managed to give the effect of total amorality, and Manciple's snarling arrogance as Blunt gave that silly character a whole dimension of nastiness and brutality that bordered on true corruption. All the actors were marching around in masks and dominoes, the scene being Naples in carnival time, and there had been several sword fights interspersed with abortive love scenes—something for everyone.

The real star of the show was of course the set, stunning in its versatility, brilliant in the sense of space, ingenious in the use of all its parts: the backlighting of a scrim here, pulling of a curtain there, moving of a partition, props casually brought on by actors at their entrances, and the stage altered from lodgings to square to street to lodgings and back again to street or square. The audience had actually applauded the set at several points in the production as the actors casually made a few motions, shoved a few bits and pieces around as they moved past, and totally transformed the space into what was needed for the next scene. And it certainly made the play move right along.

It was near the end of Act III and the despicable Blunt was holding forth alone at center stage, whipping himself up to confront the fair Lucetta in her chamber above. "Cruel?

Cruel?" He snarled and raged and gesticulated, overacting in the most shameless fashion, yet it worked:

> Yes, [he went on] I will kiss and beat thee all over,
> kiss and see thee all over; thou shalt lie with me too,
> not that I care for the enjoyment, but to let thee see I
> have taken deliberated malice to thee. I will smile and
> deceive thee, flatter thee and beat thee; embrace thee and
> rob thee, fawn on thee and strip thee stark naked, then
> hang thee out my window by the heels, with a paper of
> scurvy verses fastened to thy breast in praise of damnable
> women!

The audience went wild, hooting and booing, catcalling, standing and throwing wadded-up programs in lieu of tomatoes and rotten oranges, and Manciple obviously loved every second of it, swirling his cloak around himself in the manner of an arch-villain, sneering at one and all (the man had a show-stopping sneer, no doubt from years of practice) and storming up the stairs toward the topmost story in search of the unfortunate Lucetta. He disappeared behind a screen ... and the house lights came up. A collective sigh rippled over the audience. Intermission.

Luke rose and stretched, smiled appreciatively at Roz. "Quite a play," he remarked. "Manciple's just perfect for the pervert. Real type-casting," he added as he ushered Roz out into the aisle and, lightly touching her arm, guided her out into the lobby. Roz nodded agreement as they milled through the large crowd, all talking enthusiastically about the play.

She had just emerged from the ladies' room, where there had been a considerable wait for the two stalls, and was talking to Julia Knight when there was a commotion near the front of the lobby. People swept back against her, and there were gasps of alarm, the sound of running feet, shouts and yells. Alarmed, she stood on tiptoe, and saw several black-suited figures wielding signs and chanting, "Down with tyranny! Up with fraternities! Aphra Behn unfair to men!" as they jostled their way through the crowd. Only a demonstration, Roz thought as she relaxed back against the lobby wall. Then she was galvanized by a shrill scream.

"He flashed me! Did you see that!" followed by another scream and shouts of "She's fainted. Stand back!" Carefully Roz edged around the crowd toward the door into the theater itself and reached it just as four black-clad and masked figures pushed by her, ran down the aisle, and disappeared out a door marked "Exit" next to the stage. She stood gaping after them, only to be flung aside in turn by three security guards, who thundered down the aisle with Luke Runyon hard on their heels.

There was pandemonium in the theater now, people rushing into the auditorium, people shouting, screaming, people in the aisles looking wildly around at each other, at the stage, at the exit doors. Roz turned dizzily, looking around for someone, anyone, she knew. Someone should do something about this panic, restore order; after all, it was just a prank, a joke, no one had been hurt, and the security police were in control. Surely the best thing was for the play to go on. She started to giggle, then clapped a hand over her mouth. Wasn't anyone going to take charge?

"May I have your attention please!" an authoritative voice boomed from the stage.

Immediately the entire place was silent, unmoving. All heads turned toward the figure. It was Luke, standing center stage. Strangely enough, the chamois leather jacket, the tight Western-style jeans, even the cowboy boots, did not look one bit out of place. Luke looked completely at ease, totally serious, and very much in charge. The audience breathed a collective sigh. Luke went on, his voice carrying right to the back of the auditorium. "Would you all please return to your seats. This disruption has been unfortunate, but everything is now under control. The authorities are in pursuit of the demonstrators..." Here a loud guffaw was heard somewhere in the audience; not in the best of taste, as Luke's frown and momentary silence indicated. "... So if you would all return to your seats, the play can continue."

The audience, murmuring quietly, milled aimlessly for a while, then small groups began to sit down in their seats, whispering quietly, with occasional glances at the stage. Order was restored, the house lights dimmed, and the orchestra struck up its tune.

Roz settled back into her seat, quietly joined a few moments later by Luke. "How was I?" he whispered.

"Just great," she answered, then shushed him as the lights came up behind the third-story scrim—Lucetta's chamber—and the actors began speaking.

This was the part she had been looking forward to, the despicable Blunt getting his comeuppance from the clever prostitute Lucetta and her sidekick Sancho. Roz sat forward, not wanting to miss a line or a nuance, watching Blunt slavering over the prospect of hopping into bed with Lucetta, eagerly shedding his clothes across the floor, blowing out the candle so the chamber was lit by a single dim light, then ostentatiously groping his way toward the bed where, presumably, Lucetta waited. But meanwhile, obvious to the audience but not to him, the bed moved back out of the way, and Blunt, groping after it, muttering "Sure I am enchanted! I have been around the chamber, and can find neither woman nor bed... enough, enough, my pretty wanton!" as he stood with his arms on his hips in shirt and drawers, and, bang! the trap door opened, and Blunt dropped straight down, flailing and yelling "Ha, pimps! Rogues! Help!," his cries abruptly terminated by a splintering crash and, somewhat tardily, a loud and clearly recorded but nevertheless effective splash.

The audience went wild, clapping and cheering, some coming to their feet, the incident at Intermission all but forgotten. It was some moments before the applause quieted down, but finally everyone settled back, and watched the stage attentively for the next scene, Blunt's appearance, much besmirched, from the city sewer where he had been so summarily dropped.

Roz watched the lower arches, relishing the thought of Blunt's emergence, wiping smut from his eyes, realizing his own folly, but the moment stretched on, the stage was silent, bare, and so it remained. The audience began to move restlessly, murmuring to itself, as time seemed to drag interminably. Damn, Roz thought, they were doing so well, such a great scene; too bad it's ruined by a missed cue....

Then a shaken-looking Willmore walked out on stage, holding his eyes up to shield them from the glare of the footlights, and said quite clearly, in a quavering, nonacting voice: "Is there a doctor in the house?"

CHAPTER 10

Roz swam up out of a deep but certainly not dreamless sleep. There was something she had to remember, something important about her course, the books, something she had forgotten; in her dream she was standing in front of the class when she suddenly realized, looking at all those expectant, fresh young faces that she had not read the books, not any of them, that she was responsible and she was not prepared, and the students, sensing this, had begun to stomp on the floor, in unison, then pound their desks, demanding a replacement, demanding justice, demanding revenge, and she had looked down and realized that she was standing there in nothing but her filmy nightgown, with the light streaming through, exposing her body, and the students were dressed in costumes from the play last night, knaves and whores, battered broken corpses lying at the bottom of a narrow shaft, their necks at odd angles, while others in black hooded robes were pounding, pounding, screaming "Down with tyranny! Aphra Behn unkind to men..."

She struggled to the surface of consciousness. The loud knocking continued, someone banging on the door of her apartment.

"Just a minute!" she shouted, and threw back the covers. There was the filmy nightgown, but at least the rest wasn't real. She looked at the bedside clock—seven o'clock. She had slept exactly five hours, from shortly after she'd gotten home at 2:00 A.M. She could have slept longer too; she felt exhausted as she threw on a robe and scuffed her feet into slippers. But with such dreams . . . She hurried to the door and flung it open without thinking.

"Hi," said a disheveled Rick Squires, leaning against her door frame in what appeared to be the remains of his *Rover* outfit. "Can I come in?"

And of course she had let him in, had sat him down on the sofa while she went and put the coffee on and herself into some real clothes. When she came back into the living room, he was bending forward, grinding the heels of his hands into both eyes. He looked up at her bleary-eyed, apologetic. "I guess I woke you, huh? Sorry, but I didn't know where else to go."

"Never mind that." She sat down next to him, handed him a steaming mug of coffee. "What's up?" The last she had seen of him was just before she and Luke had left, after the police had finished questioning witnesses in the audience.

He inhaled the steam of the coffee, sipped it, then put it down, still too hot to drink. "They kept us there, the cast and crew, I mean, until a little while ago, asking questions. It was really bad." He stopped abruptly, gulped a few times, and reached for the coffee, drank off at least half the cup, hot as it was. For one awful instant, Roz thought he might break down and cry.

"I didn't know what to do, so I came straight here. I know that you guys are friends, and I thought maybe—"

"Wait a minute, Rick," Roz interrupted. "Who're friends? What's happened?"

"You and Thor—I mean, Mr. Grettirsdottir. They've taken him to jail. They think he did it. Rigged the trap door. Killed Professor Manciple."

After sending Rick out to the kitchen to fix himself something to eat, Roz dialed the police station. They didn't give information on prisoners, sorry, but that was confidential, and did she know it was only 7:15 A.M.? "Why don't you just go back to bed, lady?" the clerk said in a patronizing voice.

Roz hung up, furious, thought a moment, then looked up the number of the local daily newspaper, the *Morning Courier*. If it was a morning newspaper, there would probably still be somebody there, even if they hadn't had time to run the story in this morning's edition. Then she remembered it was Sunday; there was no edition.

She dialed the number anyway. Sure enough, a sleepy-sounding reporter covering the graveyard shift—not the best choice of words, Roz thought—at the news desk had the full report; police called to the Major Theatre, tragic accident, one person dead, one person taken into custody. The reporter, whose name was Gagnon, pronounced Gag-none, obviously another case of names being fate, told her, off the record, that the suspect was that tall art professor with the funny name, and that he was really only being questioned. But he'd built the contraption, and apparently had some grudge against the victim. If it *was* a homicide, why he thought he'd ever get away with it was beyond him, Gagnon opined chattily; the guy must be nuts or something. Roz let him rattle on, but got no more useful information than that Thor had been taken to the police station. If he was going to be bound over, then he would doubtless be removed to the County Jail before too long.

Roz thanked him and hung up just as he was asking her what her interest was in the case.

"Bad, huh?" Rick said between mouthfuls of toasted bagel
and cream cheese. "Is he in the big slammer?"

Assuming by that he meant the County Jail, Roz answered
simply, "Not yet."

"Shit," Rick commented. "What are we going to do now?"

What they did was to get in Rick's battered 1976 Honda
and drive downtown to his apartment—where he lived by
himself, Roz was not surprised to learn—so he could change
his clothes. Roz waited in the car while Rick ran inside and
emerged almost instantly in jeans and a rumpled shirt, pulling some sort of hooded ski jacket over his head. Then they
drove over to the police station.

"Are you his wife?" the officer in charge asked, looking
dubiously at Roz, and even more dubiously at Rick.

Roz shook her head, her heart sinking.

"His lawyers?" the officer inquired. "Close relatives?"
Roz debated telling the small lie, just to get in to see Thor
for a minute, let him know . . . Know what? The air palpi-
tated with doubt. She decided not to risk it.

"Can we leave a message?"

"Sure," the officer replied, handing over a large yellow
legal pad. "Write anything you like. I'll see he gets it."

Roz took the pad over to a counter suspended from the
wall. Pen poised over the pad, she hesitated. What could
she say? "Hi, we came to visit you in the slammer. Hope
everything's okay. Best wishes, Roz"? "Sorry to hear about
your misfortune, good luck, Roz and Rick"? She might as
well send a get-well card. Finally she scribbled down: "Rick
Squires and I came by but they wouldn't let us see you.
We'll try to do whatever we can. Do you have a lawyer?
Sincerely, Roz Howard." She folded the note in half, handed
it to the officer, who promptly opened it and read it over.
He nodded, refolded it, and came out from behind the desk.

"Okay, I'll see the prisoner gets it. Want to wait?"

Roz nodded stiffly, annoyed that he had read the note. What did he expect, instructions for a jailbreak? The officer must have noticed her cross expression, for he shrugged at her and smiled. "Can't be too careful, ma'am." He disappeared through a heavy wooden door that had a single small window reinforced with chicken wire. Beyond that Roz could see bars. Lots of them. But, "the prisoner"? Weren't people innocent until proved guilty or something? Oh, forget it. So what else were they going to call him? A client? She turned around. Rick was standing over by a bulletin board, studying Wanted posters.

"Holy smoke," he said in a wondering tone as she came to stand beside him. "There are some really bad dudes out there. Ugly too. No wonder they're criminals," he added with the casual heartlessness so often unconsciously displayed by very good-looking people toward their less handsome fellows.

"Mnnn," Roz said noncommittally. She was busy wondering what she—they, actually, since Rick seemed to be in this with her, at least for the time being—were going to do in the somewhat impulsively promised realm of "whatever." She didn't even know who the good lawyers were in town.

The door banged open behind them, and the officer in charge walked directly to his desk and sat down, picked up a pen, and scribbled briefly. Roz looked at him expectantly. Finally he glanced up and saw her.

"Oh, sorry. No answer, ma'am." He returned Roz's stare. "Was there anything else?"

"Ah, no," Roz answered, somewhat at a loss. "Thanks." She took one last look around the dreary jail lobby. "You ready, Rick?"

"Yeah, right," Rick said, tearing himself away from the Wanted posters. He followed her out the door. "No dice, huh?"

Roz shook her head.

"That's weird," Rick commented, casually taking her arm as they crossed the street to the car. Roz looked up at him, mildly startled by the gesture. Oh, well, maybe he was used to helping little old ladies across the street. She helped herself into the car—evidently his chivalry didn't extend to wrestling open car doors—and sat there, feeling both depressed and perplexed, while Rick went through the series of operations necessary to start his car.

"What I don't understand," he said to Roz on the way back up the hill, "is why they think Thor did it?" Rick looked confused. "Why would he take out Professor Manciple? If you ask me, something just went wrong with the machinery and wham! Three stories straight down. But deliberate murder... hey, come on."

"You helped build the set, the props, presumably including the trap door," Roz asked in turn. "You were there, right? You tell me. Could it have been an accident? How could it have happened?" What had happened was that Blunt, instead of jumping down through the trap door onto a stairway landing that would allow him to run down, dirtying himself sufficiently on the way, and emerge from underneath the arches for his next scene, had fallen through the trap door into thin air, and crashed three stories to the concrete floor of the theater. He had died instantly of a broken neck.

Rick was silent, staring straight ahead, his hands clenched on the wheel. "I don't know. Thor did that part himself. All the scaffolds came apart, or folded up on hinges so they could be changed for various scenes. I suppose someone could have folded up that part of the stairs by mistake." He thought for a while, then shook his head. "I...I just don't know."

"Did you see anything strange while you were standing there?"

The boy thought for a moment. "No. I was waiting backstage for my entrance with Florinda, and I had the scene right after that in the garden on the second level. We heard the trap door go, and Manciple hollering his lines, and then this crash. We ran over and looked..." He stopped, swallowed hard, looked at Roz. "He was lying there, kind of broken-looking, and both of us just sort of froze. I don't remember much after that, except... being out on stage and blinded by the lights, calling for a doctor."

There was a moment of horrified silence; Roz looked at Rick, again afraid he might break down and cry. He looked so young and vulnerable. Trying to distract him, she asked, "What about the guys in the black suits who disrupted the place during Intermission? Did you notice any of them behind the scenes?"

Rick turned and looked blankly at her. "Oh, you mean the Fraternity Ninja Brigade." He shook his head. "There were a lot of people running all over in those hooded cloaks and masks most of the time, but none of them were Ninjas. Besides, bad as they are, I don't think they'd do a thing like that."

Roz took a deep breath. "And Thor?"

He shook his head again. "I'm sorry... I just can't remember."

After some discussion, sitting in the car outside Roz's apartment with the engine running—"It's easier to let it run than try to start the bugger up a dozen times a day," Rick told her—the two of them ascertained that Rick had been concentrating so hard on his stage business and the one or two lines he had to say at just the right moment for his entrance that he hadn't seen anybody he recognized, let alone someone dismantling the set. But there must be other witnesses, not so preoccupied with an imminent entrance; someone would come forward and, they hoped, put Thor in the clear.

Or not. Anyway, it wasn't her responsibility. She reached for the door handle.

"Bye, Rick. Thanks for coming by," she said as she started to get out of the car.

"Hey, wait a minute, Miss Howard..."

"Call me Roz," she said without thinking.

"Thanks, ah...Roz. Back there, when we were talking about Thor and it being murder, you never told me what the motive was supposed to be."

Roz bent down and peered at Rick through the open door. "It's a long story, one that I don't even understand myself. But I can give you the gist of it. Last year a girl died under suspicious circumstances, and it's just possible that Manciple's death—and maybe the other assaults on professors as well—are a case of...of..." Roz hesitated. She could not even say Thor's name in this connection. It seemed so absurd. And yet, the evidence, the coincidences... "Of someone wanting revenge."

Rick gazed at her in patent disbelief. "You're kidding. That sounds really nuts." He paused, then asked, "Who was the girl?"

"Her name was Alison Nelson." She thought she saw a flicker of recognition in Rick's eyes. "Did you know her?"

He turned to look out the windshield. "Alison Nelson?" he said, his eyes fixed on some distant point. "Never heard of her." Then he looked back at Roz. She was surprised to see that he was blushing. He smiled that disarming, slightly embarrassed smile of his and added, "But I'm a transfer, remember? I wasn't even here last year."

Roz paced restlessly around the apartment for several minutes. She had to do something, but she wasn't quite sure what. Call Luke? Call Iris? No, she had it. She could call her friend Chasse, the one who'd come to question her after the Franklin incident. Maybe he wouldn't give her the time of day, but there was a chance she could hear everything from the horse's mouth. She dialed the number of the police station.

Detective Chasse was very polite, very sympathetic when she explained her concerns. No, he didn't think anyone had been seen tampering with the scenery. Yes, the scaffolding was complicated, and something could have gone wrong accidentally; the department was investigating. When she had finished asking questions, he thanked her for her interest, told her blandly that she should keep in touch, and that was the end of that.

CHAPTER

11

Classes at the college were canceled on Monday, so that everyone could attend a memorial service for the late Professor Manciple, held in the College Chapel, with readings from *Moby-Dick* ("Call me Ishmael"...), the Book of Isaiah, and a choral recitation by the college choir. The decimated English department met that afternoon, looked around the table, and in a move characterized more by desperation than practicality, elected Feeney and Kelley as joint acting chairmen. George was heard to remark, "Good idea. That way if one of 'em gets it they won't have to call another meeting." Feeney's first act as co-chairman was to call Roz into his office and ask her if she would take over Manciple's section of the survey course.

"It meets right before yours," he said. "The syllabus is the same as Parsons's, so it shouldn't be too much trouble," he added hopefully, handing her a copy of Manciple's syllabus.

Sure enough, their syllabuses were practically identical, his a carbon copy of Parsons's and hers an edited version, minus Bacon's *Essays* and *The Duchess of Malfi*. The Shakespeare was different, and she resigned herself to doing

King Lear after all, since Manciple had already started it, but that was really not so bad. Since Manciple's class was ahead of hers, she might even be able to fit in the Bacon essays. It would give her something else to think about besides Manciple's death and Thor's arrest. Roz agreed readily, happy to help out in whatever way she could. Feeney moved off wearily down the hall, muttering over several scraps of paper in his hand, knocking on doors.

Meanwhile, nothing more was heard of Thor, who presumably was still in custody; the college apparently had seen to it that as little news as possible of his arrest was released to the daily paper. Roz called Chasse's office several times on Tuesday, but when she was greeted with an obvious stone wall and less than no information, she finally gave up. Luke, her only other reliable source of information, had left right after the memorial service to attend a Deans' Conference in Milwaukee and was not due back until Thursday. Even the students seemed to know very little beyond the rumor that a homicidal maniac was trying to knock off all the English professors, and there was no gossip in the halls of Tabard, even from the redoubtable Iris. So she remained in the dark about what was going on with Thor.

Roz jumped into the middle of *King Lear* in Manciple's class on Wednesday, and found herself giving a number of extensions for the paper on Marlowe's stagecraft due the previous Monday; not surprisingly, the students were in the same state of bewilderment she was. Then she turned around and started *Othello* in her own class, hurrying through the first two acts to make up for lost time. Back in her office, she gazed in despair at the two syllabuses, wondering how she was ever going to get through everything. She came home to a letter from Alan, mailed nearly a week ago, informing her that he was off on a botanical detective expedition for an Arabian sultan who was certain he had found the remains of the Hanging Gardens of Babylon, and would be riding camels in the desert for the next two weeks, completely out of touch. So she was quite pleased when Iris LeBeau invited her for a pickup supper that night. Roz brought a bottle of wine and some carrot cake; the dinner, a savory mixture of pork chops and scalloped potatoes termed "plain fare" by Iris, was delicious, and Roz found herself feeling much more relaxed and less troubled than she had all week. She ended the evening by giving Iris a blow-by-blow description in as much detail as she could stomach of the events of the previous Saturday night, which Iris much appreciated, since she had not been present at the play herself. Iris drove Roz home, even though her house was not very far down the hill from campus, and Roz slept that night without bad dreams for the first time in a week.

Luke called her as soon as he returned from his conference on Thursday to invite her for what he described as a night on the town. Roz, who had found somewhat to her surprise that she missed his company as well as his fund of inside information, accepted eagerly, and so that night they went out for dinner and a movie.

Of course, as he pointed out wryly, it wasn't much of a town. In fact, Southwark had only one movie theater, the Depot Cinema, so called because it was housed in a disused railroad station. After an early dinner at the Epicene, they arrived in front of a quaint building made of brick, with large wooden eaves overhanging either side, set up on a crumbling concrete platform. A large, faded wooden sign read: SOUTHWARK.

"It's an alternative movie theater," Luke told her as they parked the car across what Roz assumed were two disused railroad tracks. "You know, crunchy granola flicks, all organic and natural, no additives..."

"Oh, stop," she said, looking around the rather elegant if shabby interior of the movie house. The inside was turn-of-the-century municipal Gothic, with a ceramic-tile floor in a geometrical pattern of black and white. The railroad ticket office, left as is, had been turned into a box office, and the schedule board now announced the arrival and departure of movies rather than trains. Roz thought it was quite charming. Even the railroad restaurant had been preserved and put to use as a café, serving cider, imported beer, and a variety of— Luke was right—granola and health food snacks of the semi-vegetarian variety. With a pang she remembered Thor, reminded herself to ask Luke if there was any news. But meanwhile the movie was about to start, something called *Revolt of the Ninja,* which sounded vaguely familiar, even though Roz didn't know what a Ninja was, much less why it would revolt, and wondered if Luke had brought her to some sort of alternative underground horror flick.

"My oldest boy—he's sixteen now—is really into these martial-arts movies. We used to go together all the time," he told her. There was a barely detectable note of sadness in his voice; Roz wondered how often he saw his children now. "They're Japanese, a kind of..." Just then the lights went out, and someone behind them shushed loudly. "Oh, well," Luke whispered, settling down in his seat. "You'll see."

And see she did. The movie was so revolting—packs of Ninjas, who were, she quickly observed, some kind of killing society, assassins, in fact, running around in footed black pajamas scaling walls like ants and killing each other with various exotic weapons—that Roz found herself feeling both bored and disgusted midway through. Maybe Luke and his teen-aged son were accustomed to this kind of movie, but she was not. Seeing the black-clad figures swarming all over with their uncouth grunts and strange clucking noises that made them sound like berserk chickens gave her a dizzy sense of *déjà vu,* so Roz quickly excused herself and went out into the lobby. She was in the café sipping chamomile tea, feeling a little pale and obviously looking it, when Luke came out and found her some minutes later.

"Something wrong? Aren't you feeling well?" he inquired as he sat down across from her.

"I'm fine, Luke," she answered. "There was just something about the movie that made me think of poor Win Manciple...." Which was odd, now that she thought of it, since one of the few ways the victims of the Ninja were *not* dispatched was by falling through the floor. But of course, now that she had had time to think it over, it was not the play itself she was reminded of, but the disruption at Intermission by similarly black-clad, threatening figures. Rick had called them the Fraternity Ninja Brigade. And that in turn made her think of the girl in her class who had been attacked in the bathroom of her dorm, also by a masked figure in black. She told Luke as much.

"God, Roz, I'm sorry. I never thought... Larry and I used to come to these all the time...." He gazed at her with a look of abject apology on his face. "Was it just the violence, or... ?"

Suddenly Roz did not want to answer any more questions; she wanted to go home. "Everything," she said curtly. "Too much. And now I just want to forget it, if you don't mind."

Luke reached across and patted her hand. "I understand. If you don't want to talk about it, that's okay. Come on, I'll take you home." And so he did, leaving her at her door with such a sympathetic, courtly bow and a brotherly, chaste peck on the cheek that, perversely, she found herself quite disappointed. Not only that, she had forgotten to ask him about Thor.

But that was soon remedied, for Roz had just settled down the next afternoon to read the set of Manciple's student papers she had finally gotten in when the telephone rang. It was Luke, calling to tell her that some new evidence had come up, and the police were now treating Manciple's death as an accident, caused by some sort of technical weakness in the scenery. "You'll be glad to know," he told her, "that Thor is no longer under suspicion."

Roz replaced the telephone receiver, and stood there for a moment feeling completely disoriented. So much had changed so quickly; Manciple dead, Thor arrested, Thor released and the murder now written off as an accident. It was over; she should feel relieved, but she didn't. What she felt was suspicious. Hadn't there been an awful lot of these so-called accidents lately: Manciple, Parsons, Franklin et al., and, going back further, even Alison Nelson?

Oh, come on, she told herself sternly. Obviously this had not escaped the local police, who no doubt had considered all the angles. They must know something, or else they wouldn't have turned Thor loose. Writs of habeas corpus aside, police forces didn't just turn suspected killers out on the street unless they were in the clear, did they? So Thor must be innocent, mustn't he? And Manciple's death truly an accident? So why shouldn't it be? She pondered her own suspicion. Based on what? The fact was, all she had were ideas and opinions gleaned from hearsay, gossip, personal bias, and speculation. The police were experts, supposedly, and if they thought the evidence said accident, then accident it must be, no matter what it had looked like at first.

Anyway, Thor was presumably in the clear. And two people, Luke and Thor, had told her in no uncertain terms to keep her nose out of it, three if you counted the politely unforthcoming Detective Chasse. All right then, she would. After all, it wasn't as if she didn't have anything else to do. Stacks and piles of student papers reproached her from most of the level surfaces in the living room—several of her own papers on Chaucer she had meant to hand back by Monday and still hadn't read, not to mention nearly a whole set from Manciple's class on *Dr. Faustus*. The most she had done was to sort them by subject.

She walked over to the coffee table and stared down at

the top paper of the largest pile. "Halloween Images in The Pardoner's Prologue and Tale." Right. How appropriate. Someone making a virtue of necessity, taking her suggestion literally and relating the old stuff to modern life, in spades. You win some, you lose some, but you gotta get dressed for 'em all. Win Manciple had gotten dressed. . . .

Settle down, she told herself. You're really much too rattled about this. But Thor hadn't even sent an answer to her message at the jail. She remembered the last time she talked to him, over a week ago. Don't get involved, Roz, he'd told her. No, *warned* her.

Oh, hell. Why don't I just sit down and do the job I was hired to do, starting with those blasted papers? And where have I heard that before? With a pang of loneliness she thought of Alan, reached for the phone, automatically adding hours in her head. It was 9:30—no, 8:30—in the evening over there. And anyway, he wasn't there; he was bumping along on a camel somewhere in the Arabian Desert. Nuts. Oh, well, reading papers was always a distraction. Sighing, she sat down on the couch, shuffled through the closest pile of papers for a catchy title—she wasn't quite up to Halloween images at the moment. Here was one— "Down the Pipe: Symbols of Corruption in . . ." She put that one aside with a slight shudder, shuffled through a few more. Here was Oblonsky's paper on—she might have guessed— clothes imagery in *The Canterbury Tales*. Sighing, she put aside her own stack of papers, and turned to the ones from Manciple's class.

Some time later she sat back against the couch, feeling more than distracted. All the papers in one form or another concentrated with excruciating detail on the final scene, Faustus's struggle, his ranting and raving, his final awful entry, kicking and screaming, into hell. What was distracting to Roz was not the acuity of insight or beauty of the prose as each student struggled to come up with a plausible—and playable—scenario as per Manciple's assignment, or even the various ingenious arrangements of trap doors, elevators, stairs, and other gadgetry the students had devised in their desperate attempts via the few stage directions ("Hell is discovered," "Exeunt devils with Faustus") to construct a concrete representation of Faustus's "hellish fall," as the Chorus describes it at play's end.

No, what distracted her was the odd but persistent similarity between the demise of the late lamented Dr. Faustus, discovered by his friends in the alley with his limbs broken asunder, and the descent through the floor, also kicking and screaming, to be discovered later with all his limbs asunder as well, of the late lamented Dr. Winston Manciple.

Roz shut her eyes. Images, scenes, titles, characters, names, and dates swam in her head, collided with one another. It can't be, she thought. It just can't be.

She walked into the tiny closetlike study. Her minuscule desk was useless for anything that required more space than writing thank-you notes and storing paper clips, but there was a rather nice bulletin board over it, on which she had tacked various reminders and schedules, including the syllabus for her course and, right next to it, Manciple's. She stood there in front of the desk, staring at the dates and titles. Manciple's (like Parsons's) read:

September 11 Introduction

14 *Beowulf*
16 *Beowulf*
18 *Beowulf*

21 *Beowulf*
23 *Beowulf*
25 *Canterbury Tales*—General Prologue. Paper due.

	28	The General Prologue
	30	The Miller's Tale
October	2	The Nun's Priest's Tale

Everything was spelled out. She thought, irrelevantly, that, like her, Manciple had abhorred a ditto mark, then shuddered slightly; Week 3, September 21, was where poor Professor Parsons had gone out. And where had she come in? October 7, the middle of Week 5.

October	5	The Wife of Bath's Prologue and Tale
	7	The Pardoner's Prologue and Tale
	9	Examination—Chaucer's World View

This is where she'd changed things. During that first week and the Monday after she had had to finish up *Beowulf*, then the week of the twelfth, she had started Chaucer, so her syllabus looked like this:

October	9	*Beowulf*
	12	*Beowulf*. Paper due.
	14	*The Canterbury Tales*; General Prologue.
	16	General Prologue
	19	General Prologue
	21	The Miller's Tale
	23	The Nun's Priest's Tale
	26	The Wife of Bath's Prologue
	28	The Wife of Bath's Tale
	30	The Pardoner's Prologue and Tale

Roz passed a cold hand over her face. The Pardoner's Prologue and Tale, a story of consummate wickedness and greed, the three egregiously drunken revelers finding Mr. Death where they least expected. Distracted by their discovery of the treasure, in an irony of cross-purposes they had done each other in because of their cupidity, unwilling to share three ways. The one had brought back poisoned drink, and the other two had fallen upon him, beaten and stabbed him to death, then celebrated with deadly swigs of the poisoned wine. And now she recognized again what she had briefly noted before, the similarity between this collective literary debacle and the incident involving Franklin, Huberd, and Shipman. The complexity of that series of events had always troubled her, but now suddenly she understood. Incredible as it seemed, the whole thing had been orchestrated to follow the Pardoner's Tale. Life imitating art.

It was not too big a leap from there back to Parsons, the so-called accident in the woods, the twisted arm, the rumors—Grendel, whom the mightly Beowulf had dispatched with his epic hand-grip, the grip of thirty thanes, by wrenching his arm out of his socket, the sinews springing, bonelocks bursting. . . .

Roz stood there staring in horrified fascination at the two syllabuses, then at her syllabus alone. Lines from another poem of less prodigious antiquity but similar subject matter popped into her head: "He left him dead and with his head, he went galumphing back." Roz started to giggle, then to laugh, fully aware she was hysterical. She couldn't help herself. She flopped down in the desk chair, tears rolling down her cheeks, blurring the syllabus. She didn't need to see it; she knew it by heart. There it was in purple and white:

November   6   *Dr. Faustus*: Act V

Marlowe's mighty lines boomed in her ears: "O, I'll leap up to my god! Who pulls me down? . . . Then will I headlong run into the earth . . . Ugly hell, gape not! come not, Lucifer! I'll burn my books!—Ah Mephistophilis!" Who pulls me down? Humpty Dumpty had a great fall. A hellish fall indeed.

She sat up and wiped her eyes. How could she be so naive? How could anybody? Accidents, hell. Accidents don't generally follow a pattern, do they, one after another, little deaths all in a row?

Well, these did.

Someone was using her syllabus as a program for murder.

CHAPTER
12

Suddenly Roz felt very cold, shivering in her sweater and jeans. She went into the living room, put the syllabus on the table in front of the couch and sat down. She reached for the afghan folded across the end of the couch and wrapped it around her shoulders. She had to think.

She stared at the syllabus in front of her. Now, really, talk about preposterous. Maybe she had overreacted, jumped to conclusions over what was just a spooky coincidence? After all, this was a small place, everyone in everyone else's pocket, everything connected. The students were up in arms, the faculty divided, the administration beleaguered; accidents could happen, pranks and demonstrations and practical jokes could go awry, backfire. But this was too much. There must be some other explanation.

She looked at the names, the dates. No. There was little doubt in her mind that the murders, accidents, pranks, whatever the officials were now calling them, had started with Parsons's death—and then followed the syllabus in almost exact detail, week by week, and work by work.

So what we have here, she thought, with all due respect to Agatha Christie, is a series.

So what was she going to do about it? She put her hand on the phone, on the point of calling the police. She could tell them about her discovery, about the connection with the syllabus. Surely this was evidence that the so-called pranks, the three professors' accidents, even Manciple's grisly demise, were in fact a chain of related homicides or attempted homicides. Wasn't it?

Roz took her hand off the phone. She could just hear herself trying to explain to Detective Chasse—or anyone, for that matter—what she thought was going on. Maybe she should go back over the evidence, or what she thought was the evidence, to make sure it was what she thought it was. Maybe she should just butt out, teach her classes, read her papers, and think about what she was going to do when this year was over. Let the rest of them worry about what was going on.

She put her head back, stared up at the ceiling. It was made of what appeared to be gray stucco, with the rust-colored rim of an old water stain fanning out from where the ceiling joined the wall. It reminded her of blood. Pools of blood that left a stain you could scrub and scrub, and never get rid of that telltale perimeter. No, that was *Macbeth*. She shut her eyes.

There was no question, really, of getting involved, no matter what anybody said, or who was involved. She had learned that lesson already. If she hadn't been so passive and accepting, spent so much time staying out of things, maybe...

She sat forward and opened her eyes, rubbed them vigorously. No sense in going over all *that* again. But she knew from past experience that she could not simply mind her own business and expect things to work out for the best, count on people to do what's right. That was a hopelessly naive vision; she understood that now, even though old habits of thought died hard. Most people acted for the best according to their lights, which were not always the best lights. And then there were those who just plain acted for the worst, were wound up that way from the beginning, like Grendel, like the Pardoner, some quirk or deformity of character, some feud with God, or whoever they thought was in charge of their universe. She recalled one of her favorite lines from *Beowulf*: "Grendel came, wearing God's anger." Poor monster, what an awful garment. Still, for all the tragedy of his background—the old "but look what a rotten childhood the poor thing had, from a broken home, his mother a real monster"—that was still hardly an excuse for gobbling down thirty thanes in a single gulp. Grendel had been maddened by the harps, but that was hardly a sufficient motive, either. No, it was the magnitude of his crime as much as the crime itself; like so many evildoers, he had overreached himself out of some terrible hurt and envy, that awful damaged pride that demanded revenge, in the guise of just redress, for some imagined wrong.

But maybe not entirely imagined, Roz reflected. Did Grendel, like the Pardoner, like so many others—like the grandfather of them all in fact, Lucifer, Son of the Morning, later known as Satan, that glorious name and angel beauty all besmirched—blame God for his actions, driven by some sense of helplessness before that awful power? And of course Lucifer couldn't fall back on the excuse that the devil made him do it. No, Lucifer "felt himself impaired," Milton had explained quite simply. Roz chuckled. He had suffered from what in modern parlance is known as a bad attitude.

Somebody around here had a bad attitude, that was clear. And this, she suddenly realized, was the basis for her unwillingness to believe that Thor had anything to do with it; she couldn't imagine his feeling himself impaired about anything. It didn't jibe. With his sublime lack of self-absorption, his gentleness, even his meekness, she just couldn't imagine Thor as a Grendel, or a Pardoner, or a Mephistophilis.

But never mind that for the moment; back to her syllabus. Clearly there was something to this, even if it sounded crazy. But good detectives—like good scholars—always checked themselves, going back over and over the evidence, looking for flaws in reasoning, looking for other possible interpretations, to make sure what they finally argued was the truth.

Roz brought both fists down on her knees, stood up with a sense of determination. However it fell out, there was still the matter of truth, and truth mattered. Whoever it turned out to be, even if it was Thor, she couldn't sit by and let a murderer keep on killing; she had to do something.

Abruptly her stomach agreed with her, growling noisily to remind her it was now well past lunchtime. She quickly fixed herself a sandwich and poured a glass of cider, then locked the door of her apartment, pulled the shades, and took the phone off the hook. Surrounded by all the books for her course, and all her student papers, read and unread, she settled down on the sofa, with the smoothed-out syllabus and a lined pad for taking notes attached to a clipboard in her lap.

She was definitely on her own. But it was her syllabus. And that in itself was pretty damned odd. Why hers? It was almost as if it were a personal challenge. Such ingenuity, look how clever I am. Will you figure it out? And can you prove it? Just like the Pardoner challenging the pilgrims. But who? And why challenge me? she asked herself. And found no answers.

Well, all right then, she thought grimly. Whoever you are, here I come.

She started with *Beowulf* and the first death, Parsons in the woods, his arm wrenched off. The method fit, Beowulf twisting the arm off Grendel with the greater strength of his handgrip, so that the monster, caught, expired. Grendel's mother he had killed with a magic sword, in a fiercely pitched battle that nearly cost the hero his own life. And of course in the battle with the dragon, he had finally fallen, much mourned, before the onslaught of poison breath and claws and teeth. There were no further parallels here as far as she could see, and anyway, if she was right, the moving finger, once having writ, moved on to the next victim, the next week, and the next work. And the victims in the works were villains all. That seemed to indicate that the perpetrator had some rough justice in mind, however deluded. Perhaps, like Hamlet, he—or she; let's not be sexist—felt himself or herself sent as scourge and minister to a corrupt world.

Was there something else to be learned here? Roz wondered. We know the method and the victim, but what about motive? Grendel had killed out of envy and spite, because he hated the sounds of joy, the power that was in Heorot. Beowulf had killed to rid the world of a murderous presence, out of a sense of justified revenge. . . . And he was the hero. Did the murderer of Parsons consider himself the avenging hero? There was a thought, perverse as it seemed. Roz wrote it down. Murderer deludes himself into hero role. Vengeance is mine. Beowulf does away with the monsters finally because nobody else can or will, and somebody has to rid the world of these vermin, for the sake of justice as well as safety. And of course the pride: nobody does it better. Roz shut her eyes on the image of Thor in a horned helmet, swinging a huge and terrible swift sword, a twin-handed engine. Terrific. On to the next.

And next had been Franklin, Shipman, and Huberd, the professors three, or as she persistently visualized them— three men in a tub, thanks, no doubt, to that hanging amphora that had reminded her so much of the Miller's Tale. But it was the Pardoner's Tale that was being copied here. She

didn't even have to look at the text; she already knew that
the quotation attached to the bottle had come right out of
the story of the three corrupt roisterers in those plague-ridden
times drunkenly seeking out Death, whom they take to be
a person, a murderer, in fact, and being sidetracked by the
idea of treasure. And of course, in the best fabulistic
Appointment in Samarra style, Death is what they find,
becoming the ironic perpetrators of their own just retribution. The murderer had been extremely ingenious here,
though it was unlikely now he would get away with the
semblance of self-inflicted injury. The police had been one
step behind, carefully collecting the evidence this time, the
cut rope, the meager traces of drugged grappa. Still, they
had settled on the simple explanation, the collective villainy:
a student prank. But the parallel to her syllabus, if she could
convince them, ought to clinch the case for singular foul
play.

But back to the old questions, who and why? Did anyone
still take seriously the public conclusion that it was a student
prank gone wrong? When Franklin got his memory back,
if he ever did, wouldn't he be able to tell who had attacked
him? Or would they all have been so befuddled by drugs
and drink that no one would ever know, the villain stealing
in like a thief in the night through all those notoriously
unlocked doors on Faculty Row?

If you discounted Thor, as Roz was determined to, at
least for now, partly because it seemed so out of character,
and partly because it was so obvious, then the only other
reasonable possibility was a disgruntled student. After all,
it had been those three, along with Manciple, who had
spearheaded most vocally the antifraternity resolution passed
by such a slim margin two weeks ago in faculty meeting.

Still, she found it difficult to credit this as a motive for
assault with grievous bodily harm; it certainly would seem
to be a gross overreaction to a basically frivolous issue. The

days of real student terrorism had gone out with the 70's and the end of the Vietnam War. Hadn't they? Roz certainly hoped so. This would be violence with no adequate justification, and therefore incomprehensible. But then, gratuitous violence was always difficult to comprehend. Not only that, it had been Thor who had actually drafted the resolution, and no one had tried to kill him. Yet.

Manciple was another matter. The man had been a walking insult, creating enemies with a glance. Next to Thor, he had been the most vociferous of the faculty against fraternities, most defensive to the point of paranoia against the imagined "them" of the administration, who were out to cut the heart out of the liberal arts curriculum, but that hardly seemed incitement enough to murder. Perhaps his death *was* an accident?

Not likely, given the similarity between Manciple's death and the end of *Dr. Faustus*. Both overreachers, arrogant in their superiority of intellect, for both a hellish fall. Technical malfunction, my eye. But once again, the motive fled before her, as the deed far outdistanced any wrongdoing on Manciple's part that she knew of. Nasty as he was, this was not his just deserts. Maybe whoever it was hadn't meant to kill, but only to scare? That had been the case with Franklin and the others, surely. But why? Or did it all come back to some perverted sense of justice? Faustus got his just due, no matter how he twisted and turned to evade it. A deal is a deal, and Satan, jealous of the beauty of the human soul, reaches out to spoil the best and brightest, to revenge himself on God.

Roz sighed. It always came back to these: jealousy and revenge. And power, of course, always power, power over others, even if only to spoil. But, getting back to a less metaphysical level, for what? And what did it all have to do with Manciple?

Roz rubbed her eyes, looked up from her books. She had

been at this for some time now, and seemed to be getting precisely nowhere. The hows were obvious enough, as were the whos—the victims—but the why continued to elude her, not to mention the by whom. And that was the most important, if the supposed murderer was to be stopped. She sat back against the couch and stretched her stiff arms out wide along the upholstery. She had to have some proof beyond the observation that life was imitating art, and there was none. So far it was all speculation.

Well then, let speculation reign. Maybe she hadn't answered the questions why and by whom, but there was another question equally, if not more, important.

Who's next?

If she couldn't solve the murders that had already taken place—if they were murders—could she figure out how and where—never mind if—the murderer was going to strike again?

She stared at her syllabus. Now where were we? She picked up the dittoed sheet.

November 13   *Othello*: Act V

Desdemona, the wife unjustly accused of faithlessness, smothered in her bed. Othello, in a paroxysm of recognition and remorse, dead by his own hand: ". . . with this little arm . . . I smote him, thus." Murder, but this time of an innocent victim. Then suicide. Innocent victim, but the motive was still jealousy and revenge. Wait a minute. She racked her brains for the bit of information she knew was relevant. It came to her; Luke had mentioned it after the Franklin incident, when he had warned her to watch out for Thor. Alison Nelson's death a possible suicide. That was it, of course. All the victims so far had been connected with Alison Nelson somehow, Parsons, Franklin, Manciple, even Shipman and Huberd. And Thor.

Roz stared unseeing at the paper in her hand. Desdemona dead, but Othello a victim too. Was that where this all was headed, the end of it played out in a grisly simulation of this tragedy of innocence turned against itself into gullibility, of a good man driven to murder the thing he loved by that motiveless malignity, or, rather, a malignity with motive so far overreached by the evil deeds done in its name that it becomes its own motive and reward? She remembered Iago's line near the end of the play, describing Cassio: "He hath a daily beauty in his life/That makes me ugly," this single cryptic line uttered after all plausible justifications are exhausted, and Iago himself is unable to account for the ferocity of his own evil, beyond justice, beyond revenge, beyond even his own comprehension and control. "Demand me nothing; what you know, you know./From this time forth I never will speak word."

She sat back, chewing on her pencil. That was it then, no doubt about it. The motive, clearly stated in all this, was revenge for Alison Nelson's death. She pondered the possibilities of the *Othello* parallel. Would the killer, finally having avenged the death of Alison Nelson, do himself in? Did he see her as Desdemona and himself as the tragic hero, Othello? Or was he in fact the villainous psychopath, Iago?

But there was something wrong here. Alison Nelson hadn't been murdered; her death was officially an accident. Nobody had smothered her with a pillow; she had frozen to death under the influence of drugs. It just didn't jibe.

Unless the killer knew something no one else did. Or thought he did.

Roz shivered in the darkening room. This line of inquiry was getting her nowhere fast; she couldn't put herself in the place of a demented killer. So, back to Grendel, the Pardoner, Faustus, Iago. Overreachers, spoilers, adversaries all. But who? Who could it be? Who would be next? Villain or victim? Desdemona, Othello, Iago? And by what means?

If there was to be another death, she had to stop it.

All right then. Back to the first question. Who? Maybe she could get at that another way. Who had had access to her syllabus? As far as she knew, Thor had never laid eyes on it, had shown no interest whatsoever. Maybe he'd seen Parsons's or Manciple's? She banished that thought; it wasn't their syllabus the killer was following. It had to be someone who had seen hers. Not just seen it, memorized it, or swiped a copy.

Go back to when she changed the syllabus around. The departmental secretary, George of the flowing auburn locks, remarkable red gaucho pants, see-through blouses, and non-stop conversation, had typed it in nothing flat. She'd had fifty copies run off on the ditto machine; that was more than enough for her class of twenty-six. And where were they now, besides in the hands of her students? On her bulletin board. In the English department files. Probably in the fraternity files as well, along with sample papers, in case one of the brothers in later years needed a quick fix for English 21. In other words, practically all over campus.

It could be anybody.

She sighed, rubbed her eyes. Granted she could convince the authorities there was a murderer at work, but showing that the deaths followed her syllabus would only tell them who got done, and how. And they already knew that. All she could provide was a connection between the incidents, and a probable motive. Thor was already connected; the police could see that, otherwise they wouldn't keep arresting him. With a sinking feeling she recalled that odd bit of literary talk they'd had, "for the nones," not to mention the line about "maken vertu of necessitee." He had read Chaucer. *Beowulf* was part of his literary heritage. All her information so far served only to implicate him further.

With a slight shiver she acknowledged the unwelcome thought: Maybe Thor had warned her off, told her not to get involved, because he *was*. No more Mr. Nice Guy. Oh, hell, she thought, I really liked him. I liked him a lot. How could I be so wrong? But, she reminded herself, I've been wrong before.

With her syllabus in front of her, she picked up the phone and dialed the police.

Ten minutes later she put down the phone, muttering imprecations, her cheeks flaming, teeth clenched in anger. Her friend Detective Chasse, the officer in charge of the case, had been polite and patient, so polite and patient and long-suffering finally that it was clear he considered her a complete crackpot. When she had described the syllabus and her theory about the murders to him, there had been a long, suspiciously muffled silence on the other end of the phone. Then Chasse had inquired politely if this Chaucer fella she was talking about was a Frenchman; when he was going to school up in Fort Kent he'd known a guy called Chaussier, a French kid from Nova Scotia. Smart too. She could tell her information was going to be dismissed out of hand, even though Chasse had suggested she send him a copy of the document in question. "But thanks for calling, Professor Howard," he said indulgently. "We'll be sure to take this under advisement. Call us again if you think of anything else. Bye now." And he had hung up.

She pounded her knees in frustration, crumpling the paper in her hands. Never mind, she had other copies, lots of them. So did somebody else. And that somebody had already involved her. It was her syllabus, for heaven's sake. She picked up the phone again and dialed Luke's number. It was busy. Furious, she dialed and redialed quickly several more times in succession. Finally the call went through, was snatched up in mid-ring. Luke's voice snapped, "Now what!"

"Luke?"

"Roz! You just caught me. I can't talk right now...."

"You've got to," Rox interrupted. "I've come up with something. It really sounds crazy, but listen. . . ." She had barely outlined her theory about the syllabus when Luke interrupted her.

"You're right. It does sound crazy. . . ." The phone squawked; with a sinking heart, Roz recognized the signal for an urgent call on Luke's line. "Listen, Roz, I can't talk now," Luke said desperately. "I'm in trouble again with these goddamned rallies. But I'll get back to you as soon as I can." And he hung up.

Roz sat there staring at the silent phone in disbelief. Rallies? What rallies? It was still afternoon. What was going on around here? Quickly she slapped the cradle down to get a dial tone, and dialed Iris's office in the English department. Surely Iris would know what was going on, and while Roz was at it, she could try her theory out on her too.

Iris did know, and conveyed with considerable amusement Luke Runyon's latest predicament. He had unwittingly rescheduled the Interfraternity Council's Halloween "Screech Out and Clutch Somebody" party for tonight, Friday the 13th, the very same night as the Women's Association's antiharassment (read antifraternity) rally, "Bring Back the Light." "There's going to be hell to pay, believe you me," Iris chortled.

"Iris, listen," Roz broke in. "I've got to talk to you. Will you be in your office much longer?"

"Of course. Nine to five every day except weekends and holidays. But can't you tell me on the phone?"

"I'd rather not," Roz answered. She really wanted to see Iris's face when she explained her theories about the multiple murders; that would give her an indication of what she was up against as far as convincing people went. Iris was certainly no pushover.

"Okay, come on over. I'll be here."

* * *

Seen in the cold (but already fading) light of day as she trudged across the campus to Tabard Hall, the evidence seemed a little flimsy. So what was she going to do about it? Call the police back and insist they take her seriously? That seemed unwise, considering the response she had gotten already. After all, she didn't want to acquire a reputation as a crackpot female hysteric. What if it all turned out to be coincidence? Shouldn't she at least consider that possibility before she jumped to conclusions and accused anyone of murder? Multiple murder at that! Weren't there laws about that sort of thing, libel, slander, defamation of character, false arrest? And there was her own reputation as a scholar and a teacher to consider.

She squinted up at the pewter-colored sky, blinked her eyes. It looked like snow, but wasn't it much too early? Friday, November 13th. That sounded rather ominous, but Roz was not superstitious, so she put the thought aside. Anyway, the question remained: What to do?

Maybe Iris could suggest a course of action; together they could figure out what to do. Iris was clearly not one to go off the deep end. Roz grinned. We women have to stick together.

She hurried up the steps of Tabard Hall. Anyway, she thought as she clanged her way upstairs to the English office, if worst came to worst, and the motive was revenge, with Thor the perpetrator, her syllabus conveniently providing the means and statement of theme—if there was such a thing in systematic mass murders, but how else could you describe it? And certainly great pains had been taken to make life imitate this craft and sullen art of literature, thus punishing the works as well as the men—then Manciple's death must be the end of it, for there wasn't anybody else to be revenged, was there? It was a clean sweep, Parsons, Franklin, Manciple, with a swipe at Huberd and Shipman on the side, and surely that meant that it was over. The syllabus had served its purpose, and, crazy and wrong as it was, the innocent victim, Alison, was avenged. So she could forget *Othello* and whatever means that might be, stabbing, swordplay, smothering. . . .

But speaking of Desdemona, she thought as she marched down the hall toward Iris's office, what she still didn't understand was, if Thor's motive in all this was to avenge Alison, why he had to use her syllabus to do it. The gauntlet thrown, so unlike Thor in his relations with her so far. But then, he had said there was more to this than met the eye. And more to him as well. Thor the hero, the protector of the weak. Thor the avenger.

She shook her head. Much as she hated to admit it, it made a lot of sense, awful as the sense was.

My, but the English office was quiet. But it was past five, she realized; probably everyone but Iris had gone home. George certainly had; the office was dark, the typewriter in its gray plastic cover crouching like a hooded beast next to the desk.

She walked down the hall to Iris's office. The door was slightly ajar; Iris must be waiting for her. Roz pushed the door open and peered inside. Iris was not at her desk, though she obviously just had been; a bluebook was open to a page with red marks scribbled on it, the correcting pen laid down across the page. Then, as her eyes roved farther, Roz noticed a rumpled bed pillow lying on the floor. How odd, she thought. But there was something even odder.

Just barely visible, sticking out stiffly from behind the desk, were two stocking feet, lying motionless on the floor, with what were clearly the sensible shoes of Iris LeBeau tumbled off any which way next to them.

CHAPTER

13

*I*t's not over, Roz thought as she gazed in horror at the motionless stocking feet sticking out from behind the desk. Someone has done in Iris with Desdemona's pillow. The syllabus murderer strikes again. She clapped a hand over her mouth to suppress the hysterical giggle that threatened to emerge. It wasn't over; the killer was making it a clean sweep, every English professor in the place.

"Who is it?" said a voice from behind the desk. Roz lurched backward into the door, slamming it shut. "Who's there?" the voice said more severely. The top of a head bobbed up, wearing the iron braid of Iris LeBeau.

"You're not dead," Roz murmured in amazement, staring at the stern features of her colleague.

"Why should I be?" Iris replied. She bent forward slowly, touched her toes, reached for the pillow, and shoved it under her desk. Then very gingerly she rose to standing position, toed her shoes into an upright position and slipped them on.

"I...I saw your feet behind the desk...the pillow..."

Iris gave Roz a curious look. "It's my back," she said, moving over to her desk and slowly lowering herself into the chair. "Years ago I slipped on the ice—dastardly climate, this—and fell ass over teakettle, racked up several vertebrae. Most of the time it doesn't bother me, but when I'm grading a lot of papers it acts up. So I lie on the floor with a pillow under my knees, but the pillow doesn't always help, so, as today, I push it to one side." She regarded Roz quizzically. "You're looking awfully pale. Are you sure you're all right?"

Roz was in fact *feeling* quite pale; her heart still pounded in her chest. But that didn't matter; what mattered was that Iris was all right. "Um...well, it gave me quite a turn, seeing you on the floor..."

"And you thought I was dead?" Iris gave her a dubious look, as if to say, "Now really." Roz nodded ruefully. She had to admit, now that she had had time to catch her breath, that it seemed highly unlikely. No one would dare kill Iris. The idea was patently absurd. One basilisk look from that stern visage and any malefactor in his right mind would turn tail and run. Or turn to stone.

"Well, now you're here, sit," Iris said briskly. Roz moved to a chair on the far side of the desk and sat. Iris folded her hands neatly over her papers and leaned forward, waiting for Roz to speak.

When she had finished telling Iris her discoveries about the syllabus and all the so-called accidents, including her concern that Thor might be the murderer, Iris looked serious for a moment. "Hmm," she said neutrally. Then she shook her head.

"It *is* pretty hard to believe," Roz agreed.

"All that mild-mannered charm, such a polite, serious person, with a fine intellect; one of nature's gentlemen." Iris paused. "I'm afraid I have some bad news for you. This isn't public knowledge, but for a while, until they decided the death was self-induced, one way or another, Thor was implicated in the Alison Nelson case as well."

"What?" Roz gasped.

Iris nodded. "It seems she was supposed to meet him that evening; they had an appointment to discuss her 'future.' Not only that, but he was seen walking up and down the hill repeatedly that night. Of course he claimed he was looking for her after she didn't show up at his office, but for a while the theory was that he ran into her on the way up the hill, walked her up to campus, then, when she passed out, just left her there in a fit of rage because she had decided to switch her major."

"To what?"

"English, of course. I know it sounds crazy—"

"It certainly does," Roz interrupted, forgetting for the moment her own rather shaky claim to rational explanations of behavior.

"But murder is always crazy, the sign of a warped mind, isn't it," Iris said quietly. It was not a question, and she did not wait for an answer. "Alison was Thor's protégée. He was very proud and fond of her. She was extremely talented as a sculptor, and he couldn't stand to see her throw it all away, or so the story would go. He could have been secretly jealous; perhaps he felt she'd been seduced by those fiends in the English department. I've always thought that's why she was found with a copy of *The Norton Anthology* propped open in her lap. As a symbol. So as far as your hypothesis goes, you see there is no lack of connection. In fact, the contrary."

Roz gaped at Iris in stunned disbelief. *The Norton Anthology?* Luke had said something about a book, but she had never thought to ask what it was. That clinched it; everything fell into place. Murder by the book, murder by the syllabus. Just deserts. "Do you actually think Thor killed her *and* the others?"

Iris shrugged. "If he did meet Alison that night, certainly he shouldn't have left her in her condition. I suppose you could call it negligent homicide, involuntary manslaughter.

Personally, I think *someone* left the book in her lap as a sign; she didn't put it there. But it doesn't really matter. There was never any evidence whatsoever that would lead to an indictment, then or now. As for the others..." Iris folded her hands neatly in her lap, the thumbs rubbing over one another with a soft, dry sound.

Roz shook her head. "I just can't believe it of Thor."

"Neither can I," Iris replied.

"But what other explanation is there? It's all getting so complicated!"

"What about the police theory?" Iris asked mildly. "That these are all ill-advised and ill-fated pranks on the part of a small gang of hoodlums. In which case, I would think that they might now see the danger, and desist. It has the virtue of being the simplest." Iris smiled. "Old Occam, and all that."

Roz stared at Iris, bemused. For all her severity, her martinet postures, Iris seemed, like her, to want to believe the best of people. She mulled over what Iris had just said. Occam's razor, the tool of logicians; in a series of increasingly complex solutions, go back to the simplest one. It had all seemed so complicated; now, after talking to Iris, it was less so. Maybe she'd been too immersed in her syllabus herself, all the devious evildoers, Iago and the Pardoner, liars and villains all. There was nothing devious about Thor. Then she thought of something. "Why did Thor tell me to stay out of it?" That had certainly been evasive on his part.

"Why don't you ask him?"

Roz blinked. Just walk right up and ask him?

"Why not? It will put your mind at rest," Iris answered, as if Roz had spoken her doubts aloud. "Tell him your theory, not mentioning any names, of course, and see how he reacts. You'll be able to tell if he has guilty knowledge, won't you? If you're not satisfied, run, don't walk, to the nearest telephone and turn him in. I'd do it in a public place, with plenty of people around. No sense being an idiot."

Roz nodded, although she was not at all sure about the idea. But if Iris thought it was worth a try . . .

Roz stood up. "Maybe this will settle it once and for all."

"I agree. Of course I'll keep this all under my hat until you let me know how things turn out. Just keep me posted." Iris sat forward, extended a hand to Roz, who clasped it gratefully. It was nice to have a friend.

She was on her way out the door when she thought of something else. She turned. Iris was packing up her briefcase to leave.

"I almost forgot," she said. "What was the book open to?"

Iris paused in her rummaging. "Which book?"

"The one in Alison Nelson's lap."

Iris went back to shuffling papers; Roz could not see her face. "Somewhere in the middle, I think."

"But you don't know exactly where?"

Straightening, Iris turned to look at Roz. "No. Does it matter?"

"Probably not," Roz answered. "But you never know. See you later," she said with a wave, and went off down the hall, feeling much more settled in her mind.

CHAPTER
14

*I*t was dark and chilly. Students were streaming out of the Library all around her like lemmings. Roz glanced at the clock on the Library tower, nearly six. They were probably afraid they'd miss dinner. She too should think about getting something to eat. But eating was the last thing she felt like doing. What she felt like doing was taking a brisk walk, to stretch her cramped limbs and brain. That's it, she thought, a good fast walk to get my mind off this, and then I'll have something to eat, finish my papers, and figure out how to tackle Thor.

She started off down the well-lit path from the Library at a fast pace, admiring the faint outline of trees like smoke against the skyline, the bright orange glow of the setting sun beyond the hill of the main campus. She walked toward it. But wait a minute, she thought; that's not the sun; this is Maine, my dear, and the sun set over an hour ago.

Well then, it must be a fire. Then she remembered the two rallies scheduled for tonight; evidently Luke had not been successful in his attempts to cancel them. She hoped he had succeeded in rescheduling one or the other, or else, as Iris had pointed out, there was going to be hell to pay.

She hadn't gone far before she heard the faint sound of

many voices raised in unison, then, more loudly, a cheer, a heave of raucous laughter. Against the trees, beyond the College Chapel in the Main Quad, she saw the orange glow flickering much closer. It sounded like too many voices for the Women's Association demonstration, and also the wrong tone. It must be the Halloween Screech Out and Clutch Somebody blast, postponed from two weeks ago. She paused to listen, heard a spatter of applause, a cheer, more laughter. It certainly sounded amiable enough; if Luke hadn't been able to reschedule, at least everything seemed to be under control, no doubt due to the burly security personnel, both male and female, with night sticks and holstered firearms, posted prominently at intervals along the campus paths, or patrolling in prominently marked cars down all the blockaded byways. No one could accuse President Bailey of not running a tight ship.

Curious now, she resumed her brisk progress down the hill.

The Main Quadrangle of Canterbury College had been built in the early years of the nineteenth century, and largely reflected that elegantly plain style of architecture known as Federal. The focal point of this rectangular greensward was the College Chapel, designed by Charles Bulfinch in the style of Wren, a colonial building of three austerely colonnaded stories topped by a noble recessed tower rising to a gilded cupola surrounded by what from the distance below appeared to be a white picket fence, topped in turn by a mighty wrought-iron quill pen weathercock the size of a small canoe. The whole thing, exclusive of the pillars, colonnades, picket fences, and weathercock, was built of the distinctive iron-stained limestone from the college quarries. Standing in front of the Chapel was a bronze statue of Percy Baxter, an early patron and trustee, presented here orating, holding in one outstretched hand what generations

of Canterbury College students cheerfully assumed to be a
hickory stick. At the moment he was also adorned with a
large jack-o'-lantern placed over his head, completely
obscuring the august and somewhat overbearing visage. Roz
smiled as she strolled up to the statue on its plinth, thinking
of Ichabod Crane and other Puritans terrorized by the devil
in various guises, pumpkin-headed and otherwise, on those
*Walpurgisnacht*s of yesteryear, now declined into the sere
and yellow simplicity of children's trick-or-treat.

Roz stopped by the statue and looked as far as she could
into the Quad, which wasn't very far. The whole space was
packed with pulsating bodies in varying degrees of costume,
mainly sheets, dark cloaks, or arrangements of rags and
tatters, surrounded by an outer ring of similarly attired upright
figures laced arm in arm, swaying and chanting around the
central crowd. The faces on the far side were gilded by the
orange glow of a huge bonfire that Roz could only just make
out by standing on tiptoe and craning her neck. Even then
she couldn't see very much of what was going on. To give
herself more height, she stuck the tip of one sneaker into a
small crevice in the lower part of the granite pedestal and
stepped up, reaching for Baxter's ankle.

She recoiled sharply as a hand curled around her upper
arm, and began to pull and drag her upward against the
rough granite. She looked up into the raised eyebrows and
mild eyes of Thor Grettirsdottir.

"Here, put your toes flat on the lower part and swing
around facing it," he directed, reaching down for her other
arm, "and I'll just walk you up. Then you can see everything
without having to hop up and down like a mouse in a
cornfield." Roz did as she was told, and shortly she and
Thor were sitting side by side under Percy Baxter's bronze
knickers.

"Thor, I—"

"Never mind, Roz," he interrupted, giving her a plaintive

look. "I'd rather not go into it now." He hesitated, then said all in a rush, "But I did appreciate your coming by the jail, you know, even if . . ." He was interrupted by a loud booing and hissing from the motley gathering in front of them, which seemed to be turning in a body toward the floodlit Chapel. Roz's heart lurched as she saw a line of women dressed in white robes, marching toward the Chapel steps, carrying torches and signs whose legends she could not make out. Both rallies were taking place after all, for better or worse.

"Look at that," Thor said, pointing. "Someone's climbing up onto the Chapel balcony!"

Roz looked. "What for?" she shouted over the rising din of chants and counter-chants.

What for was instantly clear. The figure, whose sex could not be determined, since its entire head was enclosed in a rubber Yoda mask, was manhandling what seemed at first to be a duffel bag full of dirty laundry. But as the figure lowered the bag down from the second-story colonnade, it was revealed as an effigy, a scarecrow figure with legs of rags and straw, a head of some heavier material, so that it lolled realistically. But from this distance, she could not make out who the effigy was supposed to represent, let alone which side was perpetrating it. A generic-brand faculty member? She craned her neck to see. Down below, the white-clad women students were carrying makeshift placards on which were lettered: "Hey, Pard! Hands Up or We'll Shoot," "Runyon Runs Scared," "A Dean in the Hand Is Worth Two in the Boot," and "Frat Is a Four-Letter Word!"

Roz watched with interest as the figure on the balcony lowered the effigy down on its noose of bright yellow rope. The entire crowd went wild, booing and hissing, surging forward in a great mass so swiftly and unanimously, even as they were shouting at each other "Down with the Faculty," "Down with the Dean!," "Down with Frats," that even though they were going to the opposite direction, Roz instinctively shrank back against Baxter's cold knees, trying to make herself as inconspicuous as possible. This was really something; she had never seen a student demonstration of this magnitude before. Then she saw several of the silhouetted dancing figures grab up burning brands from the bonfire, and run toward the Chapel steps. They were going to set fire to the Chapel!

No, it was the effigy, lowered down farther by the masked figure, so that the flaming torches could set it alight. The straw began to blaze, and she gasped as she realized that the flames were licking against and beginning to scorch the wooden cornice over which the blazing figure swung. The mob leaped, cavorted, surged, completely demoniacal. Sheets and capes fluttered, ragged figures capered in the flickering light; the chanting rose to a deafening roar. Roz gazed at the seething mass, appalled. It was a vision from hell, *Walpurgisnacht* in spades. Pandemonium, she thought, picturing her syllabus. But that was jumping ahead. Besides, this had nothing to do with her, or her theory.

Then, blazing torches held high, murmuring hellish imprecations, the crowd turned and began to run toward her.

Everything seemed to explode at once: the sound of sirens whooping and shrieking, the flash of red lights, blue lights, lemon-lime fire trucks and white police cars, screeching to a halt along the edge of the trampled grass of the greensward, streams of water suddenly gushing forth, striped by the floodlights and orange flames, directed toward the blazing effigy, the bonfire, the surging mass of students. Screams and shouts, squeals, yells of protest and delight as the crowd started to break up and run in all directions. To her amazement Roz caught a glimpse of Kelley, the man who cried at department meetings, followed closely by Feeney, both wearing yellow slickers and huge bucket-shaped fire hats, hauling happily on a large white fire hose. The Volunteer Fire Department had arrived. Relieved, Roz stuck her head out from under Percy Baxter's crotch, where she had been huddled on hands and knees, and began to climb down the granite plinth.

She heard a scuffling noise behind her, the sound of heavy breathing. "Thor!" she cried, reaching out a hand toward him. But Thor had leaped down from the plinth, his tall figure shouldering deep into the crowd, so that finally, even though she craned her neck, teetering precariously on the edge of the plinth, she could not make out even his bald head above the crowd.

She again heard a noise behind her, and looked around curiously—to find an eerie jack-o'-lantern grin with what appeared to be no face, mouthing some sort of incantation.

The next moment, unable even to articulate a scream, she felt herself pushed down, clutching, falling, her palms abraded by the granite, landing on the ground, her head pushed hard against the ground, so she could barely turn it, hands pressing down, her nose pressed into a muffling, soft heavy object so she couldn't breathe and began to choke, her chest heaving as she ran out of air, thinking, No, stop, you're smothering me, I can't breathe, managing to turn her head slightly, sucking in air, just in time to see a huge foot coming swiftly toward her, something hard crashing into her temple, thinking at the same time quite objectively, as though from far away in a consciousness buzzing with the clarity of revelation, Why, here's *Othello* after all, and here's who the next victim is: me.

Then everything went black.

"And my poor fool is hanged, is hanged, is hanged..." The words whined far away, growing fainter. Roz couldn't place them. What fool? Who was hanging whom? Why, of course! *King Lear*. Hanging was next. But who?

"Miss Howard! Professor! Hey! Are you all right?"

She took a deep breath. The air felt so fresh and cool on her face. She opened her eyes. Rick Squires was bending over her, a worried expression on his face. She smiled amiably, admiring his dark curls, the blueness of his eyes, the freshness of his cheeks. "Are you all right, Miss Howard?" he repeated anxiously, helping her to sit up.

"Call me Roz," she whispered, and began to sneeze.

After several loud explosions, Roz caught her breath and blew her nose on the large red bandana handkerchief Rick offered her. Her whole head seemed to be full of lint. It also ached furiously. Feeling as though she might throw up, she carefully lay back against the cool grass. It would be nice to go to sleep.

"Miss Howard—I mean Roz—I think maybe you ought to sit up and stay awake. That's a really nasty bump on your head." Rick's voice sounded hollow, as though he were speaking inside a metal wastebasket. Or was it her head that was inside it? That could account for the clanging noise now insistently sounding in her ears. She shut her eyes for a moment, and the world faded.

"Oh, shit," she heard Rick remark. "What am I going to do now?" She opened her eyes.

He was on his knees, palms flat against his very muscular, tight-dungaree-clad thighs, broad shoulders encased in a beat-up leather bomber jacket, staring down at her with a look of intense concern. Then he stood up, looked all around, his expression of concern turning to exasperation. "Where did everybody go?" he muttered. He certainly looked very tall and imposing from this angle, Roz thought admiringly, flat on her back next to the pedestal supporting the even more remote and imposing bronze Baxter. As she watched curiously, Rick put one hand behind her neck, the other around her shoulders, bent forward so close they were practically embracing, and carefully levered her into a sitting position. He released her and sat back on his heels. Her head throbbed.

"Ouch," she said. "That hurts."

"Come on, I've got to get you to some help. Can you walk?" He was squatting on the ground next to her, hands loosely clasped between his knees, bouncing up and down impatiently.

"Uh . . . what happened? Did the Chapel catch fire?" she said by way of conversation. Maybe if she kept him talking, he wouldn't make her stand up.

"I don't know about that," Rick said, looking at her somewhat dubiously, "but you sure clobbered yourself a good one on that statue."

Roz winced as he dabbed gently at an excruciatingly painful place just above her left eyebrow. "I don't think there's a fracture, but it sure is swelling up . . ." he was saying as he prodded gently. Wait a minute. She pushed his hand away. What did he mean, clobbered herself? Someone had kicked her! Yanked her right down off the goddamned plinth, kicked her in the head, and . . . and that was the last thing she remembered.

She struggled to her feet, grabbing at the granite, then at Rick's more conveniently snatchable form as he stood up with her. Overcome by a wave of nausea, she leaned against him. She opened her eyes wide, stared around her, trying to make the world stop whirling.

The Quad was empty. Empty of people, that is, but not of their assorted debris, most of it soggy, all of it squalid-looking in the pale light of the arc lamps, unaided by the bonfire, now no more than a pile of blackened logs from which still issued a hissing noise, an occasional sharp pop, a mere feather of smoke in the center of an acre of mashed grass. Streams of unrolled toilet paper festooned the land-scape, hanging from the leafless trees, the Chapel balcony, stuck to the window sills of classroom buildings. Rags and tatters, the more easily separable bits and pieces of former costumes, littered the grass, the Chapel steps, the gravel paths crisscrossing the greensward. "What's that over there?" she said, trying to focus her eyes on a particularly large scorched-looking heap near the Chapel steps. She took a tentative step forward. Maybe walking over there would distract her from the ever-more-compelling sense that she might throw up.

Leaning heavily against Rick, clutching his right forearm, comfortably aware of his other arm firmly wrapped around her shoulders, Roz staggered over to the pile. It was the effigy, now only a head and torso, its legs having been burned off before the arrival of the cavalry in the form of the Volunteer Fire Department. Next to it was a sign, the words still barely visible, soaked and runny. "Cry WOLF!" it read. Wolf? The big bad one? Whose side was *he* on? Confused, Roz stared at what was left of the figure. The torso was no more than a stuffed duffel bag with "U.S. Coast Guard" stenciled in pale letters, but the head had obviously been more carefully fashioned, of some sort of plaster-impregnated wrapping material for making casts— or theatrical masks. Roz squinted at the face as the light from the street lamps, the Chapel floodlights, seemed to flicker, grow dim. But not before she saw that the scorched and partly melted features, the cruel caricature of a hayseed grin, topped by a huge cowboy hat, were unmistakably those of Luke Runyon.

And then the lights went out.

CHAPTER

15

She was in the Quad, on Percy Baxter's plinth, trying to figure out how to get down, because she had to warn Luke; he was next. It wasn't her syllabus after all; it was Manciple's, and Luke was going to be hanged and burned, *King Lear* and *Paradise Lost* rolled into one; she knew it now. Fried like a piece of Bacon. He was next; she had to get down. She heard a noise behind her, and looked around curiously—to find a face looming over her with an eerie jack-o'-lantern grin, mouthing some sort of incantation. But the grin was really eyes, glittering at her intently, the rest of the face completely covered by a black hood. She tried to scream, but no sound came out. She couldn't move, but felt herself being enveloped in a heavy fabric, choking, gasping, unable to breathe. Luke! she cried out, Luke! But she made no sound. She was in a silent movie, and the Ninjas were all over her like ants.

"Pass me that cuff over there," a voice answered.

She lay still. Someone was clattering pans loudly in the background. There was an uncomfortable tightness around her upper arm, a tingling in the fingers, but she couldn't seem to open her eyes to see what was wrong. She knew if she just opened her eyes the nightmare would stop, but they would not respond to her orders. She concentrated all her energy on lifting her eyelids, to no avail, while someone stuck pins in her fingers and palm. There was a whoosh, and her hand flooded with warmth.

"Ninety over sixty-five. Not bad. A little on the low side, but she's not in shock or anything, just one of those skinny athletic broads with low blood pressure who live forever. She'll be fine. I bet she wakes up with one hell of a headache, though."

Annoyed, Roz opened her eyes and glared at the speaker. "I already have," she said.

"Well, hi there," a young man in a white lab coat with a plastic hospital I.D. card clipped to the pocket said cheerfully. "Welcome back. You took quite a knock."

Roz put her hand up to the sore spot on her skull and found it covered with a large wad of gauze and adhesive. She winced.

"Next time you go mountain climbing, be sure to take a rope," said a second voice. She looked up to see another young man in a white coat, with EMT emblazoned in large blue-and-red letters on the pocket, packing bits of medical-looking gear into a large metal suitcase resting on the end of her bed.

Her bed in her room. Her ceiling. She was in her apartment, with a doctor and a paramedic. But who was out in the kitchen rattling her pans? She sat up, started to swing her legs over the side of the bed. "What's going on around here?" she demanded. "Who's that in the kitchen?"

The young doctor gently pressed her down against the pillow. "Hey, cool it. You've got a concussion, young lady. That's a friend of yours, so just stay quiet."

Roz lay back, trying to remember what had happened. How had she gotten here? The last thing she remembered was deciding to go for a walk. The smell of the bonfire. The roar of the crowd. But who was the last person she had seen, and where? Of course. Rick Squires. The Chapel steps. She vaguely remembered walking—no, not walking, being carried—swung along like a baby in a cradle . . . no, that had been another time . . .

Dammit. She couldn't remember. But Rick must have brought her back here. She had to thank him. "Rick!" she called out, and was surprised at how weak and thin her voice sounded. "Rick?" She heard footsteps crossing the floor, looked up expectantly toward the doorway, the words "thank you" forming on her lips.

But it was not the rosy cheeks, blue eyes, and curly locks of Rick Squires that appeared there, smiling sympathetically, holding a steaming teacup.

It was the iron-gray braid so welded together it resembled the girder of a suspension bridge, the recalcitrantly bushy eyebrows, the pursed lips and austere visage of Iris LeBeau.

"We women have to stick together, particularly in *this* world," Iris LeBeau remarked, with a nod of the steel-girder braid obviously meant to encompass the entire academic community, as represented locally by the faculty, trustees, administration, student body, and possibly even the buildings of Canterbury College. "After young Mr. Squires had lugged you back here and found out from the ambulance attendants that you had a concussion, he didn't think it would be appropriate to stay the night and wake you up every two hours, so naturally he called me. Very sensitive young man, that Squires boy. Sensible too. I should know; I'm his adviser."

Roz was sitting up in bed, the remains of a hearty breakfast prepared by Iris congealing on the tray in front of her. Her memories of the previous night were fragmentary, even hallucinatory; twin Iris LeBeau faces swimming in and out above her own, grotesque rubber Halloween masks of goblins and monsters wobbling and jiggling, distorted versions of Rick's face, Thor's face, Luke's face, and, worst of all, a face with no face, only burning coals for eyes. Try as she would, she could not remember anything else beyond the sensation of being yanked down off Percy's plinth, the crack on the head coming out of nowhere, bursting into a thousand stars.

Iris had faithfully shaken her awake periodically to make sure she had not gone into a coma, had fetched a bucket when Roz thought she might vomit. Now, in the light of morning, the headache and double vision, the strange Halloween mask faces, the nausea were a thing of the past, as vague and hallucinatory as those moments in the Quad before she had passed out. Surely Iris could help her sort out what had actually happened. But first . . . what day was it? It must be Monday. She had to get ready for class. She hastily put the tray aside, started to throw off the covers.

"Hold it right there," Iris said firmly. "You're not going anywhere. Doctor's orders."

"But my class . . ."

"It's only Saturday. You'll probably make your Wednesday class, maybe Monday's too. But you're to be absolutely quiet for two days." She grinned at Roz's horrified expression. "Oh, you'll live. But you'd better take the doctor's advice. Imagine what the students would think if you turned pale and fell on your face right in the middle of a lecture on . . . ?" Iris looked at her inquiringly.

At least *she* doesn't know my syllabus by heart, Roz thought—and then realized with a shock that she didn't, either. And anyway, now there were two of them. Hers and Manciple's. Or was it Parsons's? Something about *King Lear, Paradise Lost*. "I . . . I can't remember," she said, passing a shaking hand over her face, only to encounter the large wad of bandage over her left temple. Much to her dismay, she started to cry.

"Now, now, my dear. It's all to be expected. Just a little

retrograde amnesia. You'll be fine," Iris murmured in a surprisingly gentle voice. "After all that's happened..."

"That's just it," Roz moaned. "I can't even remember what did happen!"

"You fell down the backside of Percy Baxter's plinth, hit your head, and got your clock rewound, that's what." Iris stood up and reached across Roz for the breakfast tray. "What with the riot being quelled, no one saw you there until almost everyone had been herded off. Squires was coming along to take the pumpkin off Baxter's head—police orders; don't ask me why they couldn't do it themselves, but he had just turned up and looked trustworthy so they sent him back for it—and stumbled over you huddled up against the granite with that great bloody lump on your noggin, out cold. You seemed all right at first, he said, but pretty groggy. And then of course you passed out. He carried you all the way back here."

"We walked over to the Chapel, and the effigy, and it was Luke...." Once again the irrational panic assailed her. She had to warn him. She'd been wrong. It wasn't her syllabus after all; it was Manciple's. *King Lear* was next, and my poor fool is hanged. A clean sweep, every English professor in the place. But no, no, that had been her dream.

"Oh, that. That's true enough," Iris said matter-of-factly. "It was the Women's Association. They're now calling themselves the Women's Organized Liberation Front. WOLF. Makes me glad I decided not to get involved. I can't stand fanatics. Really, so soon after Manciple and his..." There was the briefest of hesitations, then Iris finished grimly, "...unfortunate accident. Really rotten taste," she added acerbically. "Speaking of which, the police want to talk to you. I told them to come by later this afternoon."

There was an odd tone to Iris's voice. Roz wished she could see her face, but Iris had turned toward the door. She paused briefly, shook her head, and went out with the tray.

Roz stared after her. The police were coming. Something
nagged at her consciousness, something she had to remember. There was a plot, but no one would pay any attention
to her. But why? Didn't anybody care, didn't anybody want
to stop what was going on . . . ?

But what was going on? Roz felt as though she were
facing a blank wall. She couldn't even *remember* what was
going on, let alone stop it.

Suddenly she was overcome by a feeling of loneliness,
even panic; she wanted badly to call Iris back. If not Iris,
then who? And about what? There was the blank again. Her
head throbbing, she shut her eyes and lay back against the
pillows. Think, Roz, think. Remember last night. You banged
your head falling off the plinth, and Rick found you . . .

Somehow that didn't seem quite right. There was something else, someone else before Rick . . . Eyes shut tight,
she groped in the ragged shards of her memory of last night.

Something about *Othello*. Of course, *that* was next on
her syllabus, and poor Desdemona . . . smothering . . .

That was it. Her syllabus. The whole thing flashed into
her consciousness at once, like a slide across a white screen.
Purple and white. The syllabus murders. A series. She was
trying to figure out who was next. *Othello*. Smothering was
next.

She pulled back the sleeves of her nightgown. On her
right forearm, just above the wrist like a grotesque bracelet,
there was a rapidly darkening, circular bruise. And then,
with a rustle of dark wings, the nightmare descended. The
unseen figure grabbed her, pulled her down. "No!" she cried
out. "No!" Someone was trying to kill her! She fought,
kicked, and flailed and struggled, but he was too strong,
grabbed her and threw her down, the foot coming toward
her, the dark exploding into a million stars, then the muffling, choking, smothering . . .

"Are you all right?" Iris said from the doorway. "I thought I heard a shout."

Roz looked up, still trembling. "Oh . . . ah, yes, I was just trying to remember what happened last night," she said.

"Well," Iris snorted, "that doesn't bear much looking into, I'd say. What's done is done. Tell the cops what they want to know and then just put it out of your mind. You'll be right as rain in a day or two." And before Roz could say anything else, Iris was putting on her coat. "I've got to run along now. I've plugged the phone in by your bed, and the doctor says you're to stay there all day. Here are some more papers; you can take this opportunity to get them out of the way. Nothing like a day in bed for playing catch-up. I'm envious." Iris placed the stack of student essays on the bed next to Roz. "I've left some chicken soup and sandwich makings in the kitch, and I see you've got some freeze-dried stuff on the shelf you can boil up in an emergency. If you need anything, just give me a call." With a nod, she buttoned up her sensible wool coat, turned, and strode briskly away. Roz heard the front door close firmly, the bolt snapping automatically into place.

Now what am I going to do? Roz thought with a sense of panic. The syllabus murderer strikes again, and this time it's me. She passed a chilly hand over her face. But why me? In the theory she had developed, what had linked all the other victims together was Alison Nelson and the revenge motif. But she had nothing to do with Alison, or with the others. So why had the killer attacked her? She pondered this question for several minutes.

Suppose it wasn't revenge after all. Suppose she was wrong, and there was another motive. Then the possibilities were endless. How about Iris LeBeau? Suppose being passed over repeatedly for the chair made all her anger and resentment finally surface after all these years, so she had gone quietly berserk, knocking off all the men who had gotten in her way? Roz smiled wanly to herself. Of course it was preposterous. Well, then, how about Knight, Pierce, Kelley and Feeney, or any combination thereof, finally driven mad by Franklin's windy oratory, Manciple's sneering condescension? Even more preposterous. Disgruntled students up in arms about the abolishing of fraternities? That was what the police thought. Student pranks. Pranks, my eye. Parsons, Franklin, Huberd, Shipman, Manciple, and now me— not exactly your run-of-the-mill pie-in-the-face routine, but criminal assault involving grievous bodily harm. Or worse.

All right, get serious, Roz, she told herself. It all fit— *Othello*, smothering; clearly in method at least, it was a continuation of the series. But, she wondered again, why me?

Then another thought occurred to her. Her suspicions, however reluctantly, had focused on Thor as the killer, the avenger. But if the syllabus killer had attacked her—and who else would it be?—then Thor was in the clear. She distinctly remembered seeing his bald head gleaming in the firelight as he ran off toward the Chapel, just before she was attacked. So it had to be somebody else. She lay back against the pillows and shut her eyes; her head buzzed slightly. She had always known it couldn't be Thor...but who then? Who...And then she was asleep.

The next moment, it seemed, the phone was ringing. She picked it up groggily, heard Chasse's voice inquire politely, "How's your head?"

"Not great," she answered.

"Oh, gee, that's too bad," the detective answered. "I was going to send somebody over to take your statement. But if you're feeling punk..."

Roz hesitated. She wasn't feeling *that* punk, but she had the sense that she had been onto something before she dropped off, and she needed more time. "Is tomorrow okay?" she said, making her voice sound just the tiniest bit feeble.

"Okay, no problem," Chasse agreed cheerfully. "I'll be sending a man along tomorrow afternoon at two, okay? Stay cool." And he hung up.

Roz stared at the phone for several moments. She could hardly stay cool; someone had tried to kill her. Her head was achy, and a wave of nausea passed over her. She reached for a few dry crackers Iris had considerately placed beside her bed, along with the bucket, and munched them thoughtfully. She had the sense her mind was going around in circles. She had to get it off this for a while. Remembering Iris's advice, she picked up the stack of papers and looked at them. There were two sets, one from Franklin's class on Milton, the other from Manciple's. All right, then, a little *Samson Agonistes* never hurt anyone, eyeless in Gaza, at the mill with slaves...

Sure enough, the English professor's stand-by compulsive activity worked, and she soon found herself sitting up in bed, enjoying her enforced leisure. Iris was right; it was a chance to catch her breath. The papers distracted her from the present moment and its problems; before long she was completely occupied with the students' struggles to understand the material, with varying degrees of success. Anyway, it was good preparation for teaching *Paradise Lost*, which she would have to start next week, come hell or high water. She finished Franklin's set about noon, recorded the grades, and put Manciple's papers aside, then made her way gingerly into the kitchen to investigate the possibilities for lunch. Iris had left everything ready; all she had to do was turn on the burner. She finished the soup and sandwich, brewed herself a cup of tea, and went to sit in the living room. She was just contemplating getting dressed when the doorbell rang.

"Hi there," Luke Runyon said cheerily when she opened the door. "How's your head?"

Luke put down his teacup, leaned forward thoughtfully, elbows on knees, hands loosely clasped and dangling between, staring at the floor. After a moment he looked up at Roz. "Now, about this cockamamie theory of yours..." He held up a hand as Roz opened her mouth to protest. "No, hear me out, because I've been thinking about it." He sat back, arms along the couch. "Okay, let's consider the incidents so far. We know the police are still officially calling them accidents, and I don't know as they have much choice. Franklin's grappa was adulterated, but there's no way in hell of ever finding out by whom, or even when. As for Manciple..." Luke shook his head, then shrugged. "The theory there is that he was too far out. No, literally," he responded to Roz's odd look. "He had been carefully instructed how to jump down to avoid any danger. But he got carried away with his own enthusiasm, histrionics, whatever you call it, and leaped too far back, right off the edge of the platform, and took the whole thing down with him." Luke shrugged. "Anyway, there were no signs of tampering, as far as anyone could see in that pile of lumber. So where does that leave your theory?"

Roz watched Luke, trying to evaluate his tone. Was he, like Iris, trying to talk her out of her theory by going back to the simplest explanation? It certainly sounded like it. But she was not about to give up so easily.

"Someone could have given him a shove," she said. "Or broken his neck for him after he fell," she added, remembering the swarm of Ninjas that had invaded the theater. One quick chop or twist... but of course they hadn't been real Ninjas, just kids in costume.

Luke sighed, placed his palms flat on his thighs. "Well, the fact is, there was no one there to do it. Only Rick

Squires, who hardly knew Manciple and had no reason to kill him. And Thor, who did." Once again he acknowledged her protesting look by holding up his hand. "Now then, to get back to this idea of yours. I've been thinking about it, and it doesn't sound so crazy after all."

"Gee, thanks," Roz snorted.

"I'll ignore the sarcasm," Luke said. "Just listen. Most crimes, even practical jokes that misfire, generally have a motive, don't they? It satisfies people's ideas of the order of things, cause and effect, the Great Scheme, and so on. So..." Luke leaned forward, eying her narrowly. "Remember that we're trying to convince the police. So, what we've got to make them see is that these are not accidents or student pranks, as they, bless their naive hearts, believe. You've established a possible connection which seems to reach beyond coincidence with this syllabus business..."

Roz nodded.

"...So what we have to establish next is a motive for all of them. And..." he added triumphantly, "who among us has the best, possibly the only, motive for doing grievous bodily harm to Parsons, Franklin, Manciple et al.?"

Suddenly it dawned on her who he was driving at: Thor. She opened her mouth to speak.

"Oh, I know," Luke went on. "That was over a year ago, and they all seemed to be getting on just fine. 'Let bygones be bygones; all is forgiven.' But haven't we heard of biding one's time? Do you suppose Thor really ever got over what they did—or what he believed they did—to that poor girl? Particularly if he thought their actions, one way or another, were the immediate cause of her death? Suppose Thor has spent all this time stewing, waiting to see what the police came up with, waiting for justice to be done. After all this time, a person might tend to get a bit impatient." He paused. "Did you know that the anniversary of Alison Nelson's death is this week? November thirteenth, to be exact?" Roz shook her head. "And what, in ancient Scandinavian tradition, is the usual way of dealing with someone's unavenged death? Known in those old sagas of yours as *wergild*, I believe. In this day and age, what with women's lib and all, it would count for women as well. What we've got here, if you ask me, is an honest-to-God vendetta, or—as it's called where I come from—vigilante justice." He paused again, waiting for his words to have their full effect. "My best guess is that the Viking's gone quietly berserk and taken matters into his own hands. And don't think Chasse won't see it too, once we tell him all this. Don't let that hick-kid-from-the-wilds-of-Maine routine fool you; he's one smart cop. And he's still got his eye on Thor; you mark my words."

"But it can't be Thor," Roz said.

"Why not?"

"Because I saw him running across the Quad right before the killer attacked me."

Luke gaped at her. "Who said you were attacked? I thought it was an accident."

"Ha," she replied. "Where have we heard that before?" Quietly she told him all she remembered about being pulled down, knocked against the plinth, the face in the mask trying to smother her.

Luke listened intently. When she was finished, he said: "So who do you think it was?"

"Well, it wasn't a student with a cream pie, I can tell you that."

"Roz, be serious. Why would the syllabus murderer want to hurt or kill you? You had nothing to do with Alison Nelson."

Roz shrugged. Why indeed? What was the usual reason in cases like these? "Maybe whoever it is thinks I know something."

"But what?"

"Damned if I know." Even as she said it she realized how ridiculously trite the whole thing sounded. But Luke didn't seem to think so. He sat forward eagerly.

"Did you mention your syllabus idea to Thor?"

Roz shook her head. "That's one thing I do know. It can't have been Thor; we'll have to think of someone else. I think I'll start reading through *The Norton Anthology*. Find out what's in the middle."

Luke stared at her. "What for?"

"Maybe it's a clue," Roz answered curtly, unable to keep the impatience out of her voice. She was beginning to get tired. "Anyway, that was the book found on Alison Nelson's lap, open to 'somewhere in the middle,' according to Iris." Across from her, she saw Luke flush at her cross tone. Obviously he had taken the hint, for he stood up abruptly.

"I've got to be going. Is there anything I can get you before I go? More tea and toast? A little Scotch? After all, 'malt does more than Milton can/To justify God's ways to man.'"

Roz shook her head. "Don't be funny." What she really wanted was a pizza, loaded. But she didn't tell Luke that; he might not leave. Luke bent down, gave her a brief peck on the cheek. "You take it easy now," he said, holding up his hand in his habitual gesture. "Peace."

But Roz was still to have no peace. As soon as he had gone out the door, the phone rang, poor Griselda Franklin, asking in a quavery voice how she was feeling, wanting to talk about all the terrible tragedies lately, the whole place jinxed, it seemed. And the phone continued to ring the rest of the day, Emily Shipman, Madelayne Huberd, Julia Knight, Feeney and Kelley and several other colleagues, Rick Squires, the well-wishers, the merely curious, even Judy Laster, calling from Boston to find out

what the dickens was going on. They had a long conversation, Judy filling her in on heretofore unsuspected
further foibles of the faculty, which made Roz laugh so
hard her head throbbed.

The only person who didn't call was Thor.

CHAPTER
16

Promptly at 2:00 the next afternoon, Sunday, the doorbell rang. Chasse's man, no doubt. Roz, who was feeling much better but still a little lightheaded, shuffled over, opened the door without undoing the chain, and peered through the crack. It was not Chasse's man; it was a uniformed policewoman, notebook in hand.

The policeperson, a nice young woman named Tapicier, shut her notebook with a snap. Through her patient prodding—"Just tell me everything, Professor Howard; don't worry about whether you think it really happened or not"— Roz had managed to dredge up all her recollections, both real and what she had taken to be nightmare, taking Chasse at his word that the police would sort everything out.

Apparently they already had. "Thanks, that's just fine," Tapicier said. "I'll get this typed up and bring it back for you to sign." She stood up briskly. "You'll be interested to know that a witness came forward this morning who saw the attack, and is prepared to swear that your attacker was one of the ones who disrupted the play; you know, the guys in the black suits? We think he's been harassing women all over the campus. The students are calling him the Grabber.

Actually, there may be more than one. These fraternity kids..."

Roz stared at her, mouth agape. Attacked by the Grabber? She had never even considered the possibility. She smote her brow, remembering just in time to avoid the large patch over her left temple. Of course, how could she be so stupid, jumping to conclusions like that? She remembered Dori's description, even down to the mark on her wrist. It all fit, the black mask, the technique, not to mention the occasion....

"Yep," Patrolwoman Tapicier averred. "We're pretty positive that's who it was. Don't worry," she said sympathetically, peering closely at Roz. "We'll get him."

Roz simply nodded, still bemused. If this was true, and she had been attacked by the Grabber, not the killer, it changed everything. The attack on her had had nothing to do with Alison or the syllabus murders, or whatever knowledge she, Roz, did or didn't have. Once again she had leaped to conclusions.

"This will be ready for you to sign tomorrow or the next day. If you're feeling well enough, you could come to the station." She looked at Roz's bandaged head. "Or I could come back."

"No, that's all right; I'll go there," Roz said absently. Tapicier nodded, packed up her notebook, and left.

Roz sat with her head in her hands. So it had not been the killer who had attacked her after all, unless the killer was the Grabber, and that seemed highly unlikely. So much for *Othello* and smothering. She was going to have to rethink some of her conclusions, go back over everything, if she wanted to convince the police to take any action at all. It was back to square one. She should do what she had said she was going to, and find out what was in the middle of *The Norton Anthology,* see if it made any sense out of all this mess.

The very thought made her head ache. She stood up and staggered back into the bedroom, feeling suddenly quite woozy. She got into bed and lay back against the pillows. I can't do it right now, she thought, feeling her mind spin around and around in an aimless jumble. But I've got to do something; I can't just lie here and listen to my head spin. She glanced around the room. There was the stack of papers from Manciple reproaching her from the bedside table, still largely unread. They would do. She picked the top one off the stack. It was on Bacon's *Essays*. Sighing, she settled farther back into the pillows and began to read.

Roz put down the copy of *Brighton Rock* she'd started reading in desperation Monday afternoon after finishing the Manciple papers. She never wanted to see a student paper again, and the same went for *The Norton Anthology,* which most of them had copiously quoted, footnotes included. But she had done her duty and read them all. The doctor had advised her not to teach that morning, so Feeney and Kelley had obligingly taught the last classes on *Othello* and *King Lear* for her, which was good, considering the turmoil her mind was still in over the latest developments in the Manciple case, not to mention the attack on her. She read the last few lines of the book over again—Pinkie snatched over the cliff, burning with acid, as though he had never been, just retribution for the murder of poor Fred. Now *there* was an ingenious crime for you; the police had ruled it death by natural causes when all the time poor Fred had been choked to death by a stick of rock candy crammed down his throat, which had then melted away, leaving no trace. Only the bruises on his arms where they had held him. Very ingenious indeed. And there she was, off again, thinking about her so-called syllabus murderer.

She had been trying her best to put the whole thing out of her mind, which is what Chasse had told her to do when

she had called him early that morning to find out more about
the investigation. He had verbally patted her on the head,
and told her to take it easy. They could talk later. She felt
patronized, dismissed. But now that her head no longer felt
like a split melon, all her—and Manciple's, *and* Franklin's—papers were graded, no class until Wednesday, and
she'd listened to just about all the baroque harpsichord music
she could stand, she felt compelled to do something. Nobody
else seemed to be. Chasse had had nothing to say about the
attack on her, and she hadn't heard from the policewoman;
not only had they discounted her evidence, if you could call
it that, but they were dragging their feet on the assault as
well. Maybe everyone had concluded after all that it was
merely a misguided student trying to give her a pie in the
face, not the Grabber. There had certainly seemed to be—
still was, if they were including the attack on her—a
concerted attempt by the administration and the police
to put the best face on things, this an accident, that a prank,
suspects released with reduced charges or no charges
at all. The police were getting nowhere. So what were they
thinking?

Sighing, she gave in, let her mind run back over the
events of the last several weeks. Here she had evidence that
strongly suggested the deaths, the assorted attacks and
assaults were the deliberate work of a methodical killer,
with a clear motive.

But the police didn't seem to want to believe her. So it
was up to her to find out who the killer was. Here she was,
sitting all by herself on square one.

So where was square one? That was easy. It was the death
of Alison Nelson. But how much did she really know about
it? Oh, she'd heard a lot from various sources, but that had
all been hearsay. In the scholarly world, which, after all,
was her world, square one meant starting with the best
primary sources available. She thought for a moment, con-

sidering her options. In this case, that meant the morgue.

Roz felt the bandage on her head. It was mushy from what she hoped was some kind of medication and not her own life's blood. When she pressed carefully but firmly, the bump underneath seemed to have subsided, was not too tender to the touch. She went into the bathroom and peeled the dressing back. A wound resembling a moderately skinned knee surrounded by a rim of black and blue stared at her. Not as bad as she had thought. She searched through her medicine chest for the box of sticking plasters Alan had given her as a joke farewell present after she had admired the size, color, and flexibility of English Band-Aids, which were made of some kind of soft elastic fabric, instead of that awful flesh-colored masking tape that usually passed for a bandage around here. She rummaged through, found a large round one just the right size, and plastered it on, then fluffed her hair, which she was wearing down because it hurt to pull it back, around it. Much better, almost inconspicuous; people wouldn't stop and stare at her on the street.

All right, how was she going to get downtown? The college jitney was out; she didn't want a bunch of students gawking at her, wondering what she was up to. Luke Runyon? But no, she didn't want him asking questions, either. Besides, there had been entirely too much Luke Runyon of late, sandy-brown hair and crinkly eyes disturbingly superimposed over the mahogany mane and clever faunlike features of Alan Stewart. With a guilty twinge she realized she hadn't written him in over a week. But things had been happening so fast, and, anyway, he wasn't even there. She'd start a letter as soon as she got back.

She picked up the phone and ordered a taxi, then got dressed while she was waiting. She had the rest of today and all day tomorrow to do what she had to do, and more time later if she needed it.

The taxi pulled up under her window, honked. Grabbing

her down vest and windbreaker—it was getting alarmingly
cold, snow-weather cold, not to mention dark, and still
barely the third week in November—she hurried outside.

The driver looked at her inquiringly as she slid into the
back seat. The morgue it was.

"Please take me to the *Morning Courier* office," she said.

CHAPTER
17

*T*he driver stopped in front of a large brick building in the middle of downtown. "They never sleep," he said inconsequentially as he reached over the front seat and opened the door for her. Sure enough, lights were blazing in all four stories. It was a morning newspaper, after all; no doubt they were just getting started at six o'clock in the evening. She looked around the interior of the cab; there was no meter. Obviously everything had a flat rate; there probably weren't that many places you could go in Southwark, Maine. She looked inquiringly at the driver. "Buck," he said, and Roz handed him two; she might need him again later. There probably weren't that many taxis in Southwark, Maine, either.

She wasn't sure what she would find when she ventured inside the building. She suspected that the typesetting machines, Addressographs, even typewriters, all the old mechanical paraphernalia of newspaper offices that in the old days had given them that satisfying clatter of activity and smell of ink and hot lead, had in this modern day been replaced by computers, microfiche and film-and-dot, photo-offset and printer-ready copy. This made her nostalgic, riding up in the self-service elevator, for the dark, musty

basement of the newspaper office she had haunted in high
school in upstate New York, digging through the racks of
old papers, the envelopes of clippings for her first literary
research paper, a comparison between the plot of *An American Tragedy* and the real-life murder on which it was so
closely based, the Chester Gillette case. The actual incidents
had taken place not far from her hometown, and there was
a great deal of local coverage, right up to Gillette's landmark
execution in the electric chair at Auburn Prison, the nation's
first. She had been so swept away by the whole process
that even now she traced the beginning of her life as a scholar
back to the moment of seeing Gillette's picture on the front
page of the July 1906 edition of the Syracuse *Post Standard*.

But she wouldn't find anything like that here. She wasn't
sure what she would find, even if they did let her in. The
door of the elevator slid open and she stepped out, desperately trying to remember the name of the reporter
she had spoken to earlier. Names are fate, she'd thought,
Braine the neurosurgeon, Neriad the swimmer. Gag-none
the reporter. That was it. In a pinch she could always ask
for him.

She didn't need to. Her entry was unquestioned, and ten
minutes later she was comfortably ensconced in what was
no longer called the "morgue," but the "library"—"Too morbid, not to say confusing, what with 'Quincy' and the police
shows and all," the woman who had shown her where everything was had remarked—relieved to find that things had
not changed so much after all. Oh, there were computer
terminals all over the newsroom, either clicking or patiently
humming to themselves, but there were also battered old
typewriters, "in case the computer goes down, which it does
a lot," she was informed by her guide, and microfilm view-
ers in the morgue—sorry, the library—but also racks and
stacks of newspapers, and file drawers full of Manila folders

holding clippings indexed and cross-indexed by name and by subject.

"Our busy time is starting now," the nice gray-haired woman said, "so I'll just leave you to it, but if you need any help..." She ducked out before saying what then, but Roz wasn't worried. She felt perfectly at home right where she was. She bent down, pulled open the drawer marked N–P and searched through the folders until she came to the one marked "Nelson, Alison." She took out the folder, replaced it with an Out marker, walked over to the big oak table against the wall, sat down and began to read.

An hour later, Roz put down the file of clippings. She had read them over and over, looking for clues, any new information that might shed some light on the recent events she had found herself so unwillingly involved in. With a stretch that made her forehead throb, she leaned back in the heavy old-fashioned oak swivel chair, like the morgue a comfortable remnant of the days before chrome, plastic, and microfiche, and brooded over what she had learned.

Which was not much more than she already knew. The fact was, there was rather less to the Alison Nelson case than had met the eye, or, more precisely, the ear. The few clippings in the file, no more than half a dozen, made it clear how much of what Roz had heard was truly hearsay, gossip, rumor, and speculation. Her sources were varied, Luke, Thor, and Iris LeBeau being the main ones, and what they all seemed to have in common was a broad extrapolation from the facts of the matter as recorded in the Southwark *Morning Courier* to the interpretation of their significance.

The facts were clear enough. The earliest headline, run across the bottom of the front page on November 15 of the previous year, read simply: CANTERBURY COED FOUND DEAD NEAR CAMPUS. The story described the discovery of the body by an early morning jogger, who had noticed her sitting there on his morning run up the hill and thought nothing of it, except that it was cold and she wasn't wearing her jacket. But as she was still there when he ran back past half an hour later, staring fixedly in the same direction, apparently not breathing, her complexion oddly pale and blue-tinged, he stopped to investigate, saw she was dead, and ran home to call the police. They had contacted campus security, the various deans, the state police, all of whom had converged on the scene at once. They had found her in the stone hut, dressed in only a flannel shirt and jeans, an open book on her lap, her body stiff with cold and death.

PROFESSORS QUESTIONED IN DEATH OF COED was the next banner, and the story detailed the investigation then taking place. No names were mentioned, and no foul play suggested. "We don't suspect anybody," Detective Chasse was quoted as saying. "We're just trying to determine the facts, get some background on the young lady." Chasse, as polite and evasive then as now. On an inside page, but prominently blocked in the middle, still worthy of lurid attention if not space on the front page: DRUGS A POSSIBLE FACTOR IN DEATH OF COED. This story gave the results of the autopsy, death apparently from hypothermia caused by loss of consciousness and subsequent exposure to below-freezing temperatures. Lab tests had showed traces of illegal drugs, and there had been a note in her pocket referring to "enough stuff to turn on." The girl had last been seen by her friends downtown, who had naturally denied any knowledge of drug use or availability, even though the police had confiscated from said friends' apartment an Alice B. Toklas cookbook, a suspiciously large bottle labeled "Oregano" and several strange-looking brownies. The brownies had been found to contain *Cannabis sativa*—pot, to the layperson—but not in sufficient quantity to have caused death unless one had eaten several dozen, but where there were pot brownies there was also likely to be pot à la carte, as well as other mind-altering drugs currently in fashion with the young— mushroom caps, hashish, and synthetic LSD.

But none of these had been present in sufficient amounts to cause death, or even unconsciousness. Another possibility was that the pot might have been contaminated with the more toxic drug paraquat, commonly used as a weed-killer, or even PCP, the favorite among youths yearning to see their unsuspecting friends go crazy. This was occasion for a dire warning about the dangers of ingesting even the most innocuous-seeming recreational substances. But Detective Chasse's best guess was that the girl had ingested a small amount of LSD or PCP, which, because she was not a habitual user, had had more than the usual effect. Her friends had characterized her as very depressed; "Really bummed, zoned out and spacey, like she was in another world, you know? Like she had heavy stuff coming down" was one acquaintance's description. But then she had seemed to perk up, more like her old energetic self, so no one was worried when she left to walk back to campus about 11:00 P.M.

She was not seen again until her body was found the next morning. The night had been foggy, with rain changing to sleet, then freezing on the trees and ground. She had been wearing her jacket when she left, but not when she was found, and this was seen as a contributing cause of death, since it would have hastened the loss of body heat and subsequent confusion, coma, and death. The theory was that she had become drowsy and disoriented because of the drug, taken her jacket off and sat down, the book falling open on her lap, and then fallen into a deep sleep, from which she had never awakened. In the fog no one had seen her, until it was too late.

Even though the owners of the pot-laden brownies had been issued a summons, this was not seen as significant; in this state, possession of marijuana was a misdemeanor, and no one was saying the friends were implicated in her death. "No charges are contemplated at this time," the story concluded. There was no mention of suicide except by implication—why else in the world would anyone in her right mind have deliberately removed her jacket and sat down in the cold to freeze? Perhaps under pressure from the college and possibly the girl's family, the death had been characterized, publicly at least, as an unfortunate accident.

The last story was a follow-up a week later about drug and alcohol crackdowns at the college, the institution of a student-run but college-financed jitney service to ply between the campus and the downtown area, and the installation of several more streetlights along the dark stretch of road that led past the stone shelter up to the campus.

And that was that, except for a small classified ad pasted onto a piece of Manila paper, with an editor's query penciled around it, "Should we look into this?" The ad was dated one month after the Nelson death, and read: "Anyone who might have seen anything suspicious in the area of upper College Hill the night of November 13, any information you might have regarding that time kept strictly confidential. Reply MC box 26n."

Roz fought her way out of the recalcitrantly back-leaning chair and walked over to the file cabinet, replaced the Nelson folder, pulled out the file marked "Parsons," and stood there with her arms folded, contemplating the rest of the drawers. She opened L–M, found no file for Manciple. Nor was there one on Franklin in D–F. But in the drawer above there was a thick packet of clippings in several folders marked "Canterbury College—faculty and staff." The most recent was well over two weeks ago, however, and none of them concerned Manciple's murder; she would have to look up those stories in the uncut back issues. As she suspected, the stories on Franklin and the others were relatively sparse and inconclusive. She already knew the college had a fairly good

hush-hush mechanism, being the town's major employer
and chief intellectual enterprise.

The Parsons story was much as Luke had told it to her,
with no mention of any rumors, ritual mutilation, arm ripped
off, just your run-of-the-mill accident in the woods, with a
special feature article running alongside on safety measures—never go in the woods, operate heavy machines,
chain saws, splitters, etc. etc. alone—regrettable, a tragedy
of carelessness, as detailed in a relatively lugubrious edi-
torial the next day. There the file ended; no more had been
written about it since; certainly no reporters had sniffed out
a possible connection, either with Alison Nelson or the
Franklin incident, at least up until a week ago.

Roz replaced the files, shut the drawers, and looked up
at the clock on the wall. Ten P.M. She wasn't tired, having
slept or read most of the day, but her head ached slightly,
and her stomach was feeling mildly queasy. Enough for
today, even if she hadn't gotten much of anywhere. She
could come back tomorrow, look up the back issues on
Manciple, see how that had been treated, look up what they
had to say about the riot on Friday, her own attack...

But wait a minute. She passed a hand over her eyes. Thor
had been released from custody in the Manciple case only
on Friday. There probably would have been some coverage
of that, maybe a review and follow-up. The riot had been
on Friday, but probably had happened too late for anything
much about it to appear in the Saturday-morning edition.
There was no Sunday paper, so they would be playing catch-
up, all the follow-up still coming out, still possibly logged
into those computer terminals humming away out there.
There would have been coverage Monday, today, at least
of the riot, but someone was bound to be still working on
the follow-up. She stuck her head out the door, looking for
the gray-haired woman.

The place was a madhouse, terminals beeping, typewriters chattering, the thunder of heavy-laden rolling stock overhead, telephones squalling. Why it had come to be called "putting the paper to bed," she would never know; there was certainly nothing restful about this. Young men and women in shirt sleeves in various stages of coming undone (both the shirt sleeves and themselves) ran up and down through the maze of desks and shoulder-height partitions, bumping into each other, waving wads of fanfolded print-out with the telltale margins full of holes. The gray-haired woman was nowhere in sight. Watching the scene speculatively, she wondered which of the many figures, sitting, standing, or flying, was Gagnon.

Several minutes later, having wandered casually out into the newsroom as though she belonged there and said to the first person who ran into her, "Where's Gagnon?" she was standing over the shoulder of a swarthy, dark-haired young man with an improbably Etruscan profile, watching the latest on the Manciple story scroll by.

"College spokesperson Yeoman said Monday that a full investigation into safety measures in college dramatic productions was underway in the wake of the unfortunate accident involving Professor Winston Manciple. No charges are contemplated at this time, Detective Jeff Chasse of the Southwark Police informed reporters late Saturday night, though investigation is continuing to determine if there are any charges to be brought. 'What we're talking here is possible involuntary manslaughter at the most,' Chasse commented at the close of a news conference on Saturday. 'Somebody not taking enough care with dangerous machinery, like running your car into the rear end of a Pinto, accidently like, and blammo. I mean, you got to lay the blame somewhere, but it isn't necessarily a crime.'" Roz contemplated the last quotation, Chasse being, at least in her estimation, uncharacteristically forthcoming, even loquacious, all about nothing. It sounded like he was either stuck for something to say or else covering something up.

It all looked a little suspicious to her, even smacked of a smoke screen. News conference, indeed. As if in answer to her thoughts, Gagnon said over his shoulder, "We haven't heard the end of this one, mark my words. Chasse's up to something. He isn't usually that philosophical."

"Can you bring up the earlier stories?" Roz asked.

"Nah, they've been killed. As soon as they go to press they're automatically deleted from these files to make room for more. You'd have to look them up in the daily issues themselves. Want me to get you some copies? They'll have them down in Classified."

While she was waiting for Gagnon to come back with the papers, Roz wandered back to the library, where the gray-haired woman was now checking through the file drawers, to thank her for her help.

"Oh, don't mention it. We're always glad to help anyone find the information they need." She paused, bending over a drawer, and reached for the Out marker that Roz had forgotten to remove.

"I'm sorry," Roz said quickly. "That was careless of me."

"That's all right; people do it all the time." She paused. "The Nelson case," she said thoughtfully. "That was so sad, such an unfortunate incident. Every once in a while I get someone in asking about it. Why, there was that nice young man a while ago, wanting to go over everything." She looked up at Roz. "Maybe you know him. I'm quite sure he was a Canterbury student. Tall fellow with black curly hair, nice-looking, very polite?"

"I think I know who you mean," Roz said, smiling to herself. Rick certainly didn't let any grass grow under that disreputable footwear of his. A born scholar if she'd ever seen one; with that peculiar blend of curiosity and compulsiveness, he'd probably started working on the Nelson

connection right after she'd mentioned it to him, the day
after Manciple's death. He hadn't said anything about it to
her the night of the riot, but then she'd been pretty well out
of it.

The woman nodded. "He didn't give his name; not that
he was rude about it. Don't know if he found out what he
needed; he never said." Then she added, "But that was
almost two months ago and he hasn't come back, so..."

Roz stared at her, feeling dazed. Two months ago? But
hadn't it been only last week that Rick had gazed at her
with his innocent blue eyes and said, "Alison Nelson? Never
heard of her."

"Here're your papers, Miss Howard," Gagnon's voice
said from behind her. Roz turned. "Hey, are you all right?"
the reporter asked, looking concerned.

"I'm fine," Roz said calmly. "But could you call me a
cab? I think I'd better go."

CHAPTER
18

All right, so Rick had lied when he told her he had never heard of Alison Nelson, Roz thought to herself the next morning. But why? What did it mean that he had? She had finally fallen asleep somewhere around 2:00 A.M. after several restless hours of going round and round these questions, trying not to let her imagination run away with her. Now she was writing everything down—sometimes in black and white things made more sense, seemed more concrete—in a letter to Alan, using him as her audience, trying to imagine what he might fix on as significant, the questions he might ask in that rough but gentle Scots-burred voice. . . .

She put the pen down, sat back and stared at the paper. "What this means is that there is a connection of some sort between him and Alison Nelson that he doesn't want known around here." And as clearly as if he had spoken in her ear, she could hear Alan saying, with that pointed, ironic grin, "Ah, fair Rosamund, I think we need more information."

More information. That meant more questions. For instance, if Rick wasn't just another student, what else was he doing here? Gathering information about Alison Nelson, obviously, but to what end? Reluctantly she acknowledged the horrifying thought: All the recent injuries and deaths were linked to Alison Nelson, and to the syllabus for the class Roz had taken over from Parsons. And Rick was in that class.

"I'd like to see the records for Patrick Squires," she said to the clerk behind the counter at the Registrar's Office.

The clerk looked askance at her, taking in the worn jeans, Icelandic sweater with down vest over it, the rubber-bottomed hiking boots, and said crisply, "Sorry. We don't give out student records to other students."

Roz grinned, feeling as though she were in disguise. The pigtails probably didn't help much, either. She reached in her knapsack, took out her faculty card. "Thanks for the compliment, but I'm Roz Howard. I work here," she said. "English department. He's a student of mine."

The young man flushed, muttered an apology, and ducked below the counter. Roz heard a drawer roll out, papers shuffling. The young man reappeared with a Manila folder in his hand. "Not much here. He's a transfer. You'll have to get the entry records from the Dean of Students' Office across the hall."

Following a similar contretemps with the Dean of Students' secretary—after this she would have to remember to dress more like a grownup—Roz sat herself down in an empty conference room to read over Rick Squires's records.

Place of birth and hometown, Aberdeen, South Dakota. Hm. Transferred from Pomona as a senior exchange; that sounded vaguely familiar. Grade point average, as she would have expected, hovering around 3.5, Phi Bete material. An Economics major at Pomona, changed to English on transfer to Canterbury.

Okay, Pomona. Why did that ring a bell? She racked her brain, hoping the crack on the head hadn't affected much more than her memory of Friday night. Hadn't Alison Nelson gone to Pomona? After a quick glance at the autobiographical statement—but of course there would be nothing revealing there, and sure enough there wasn't—she closed the folder and crossed back to the Registrar's Office.

"Do you have Alison Nelson's record?"

The clerk stared blankly at her. Yours not to reason why, Roz thought impatiently. "Is it still available?" she prodded.

"Is she a student here?"

It was Roz's turn to stare. Could it be he hadn't heard about Alison Nelson's death? But perhaps this incredible naiveté might work to her advantage. "No," she remarked casually. "Not since last year."

"Then it would be in the computer. These are only current records." The clerk gestured at the file drawers from which he had extracted Rick's record. He walked over and sat down at a small terminal with an attached keyboard. "Just give me a minute to turn on, okay?" He flicked a switch, and in seconds the machine was purring quietly. Roz stood watching curiously from the doorway. She was surprised to see a computer here at Canterbury at all, much less one obviously in such constant use. Tabard Hall might be a relic of the age of dinosaurs, but here in the administration building twentieth-century technology had arrived. She wondered idly how many other terminals there were scattered around campus, and whether students had access to them. Could Rick, for instance, have gotten into Alison's records somehow? Probably not; surely there were access codes to prevent that kind of thing.

Meanwhile, the young man was tapping out a brief message, which Roz, standing behind him and peering over his shoulder, was amused to see was a simple "Hello."

"What class was she?"

"She would have been a junior, I think," Roz said. The

clerk tapped a few more keys, and, just like the machines at the *Courier,* lines of letters began to appear on the screen. The wonders of modern technology.

"Do you know how to use the system?"

"Not really," Roz confessed.

"Well, we're already logged on, and all you need to know is how to call up the information. I've already done that, so it'll just roll by. This button lets you go backward, and this one here stops the document from scrolling if you want to read it. This one lets you go forward at your own speed." He stood up, and Roz sat down in front of the screen. "I'll be right over there if you need help."

Roz sat down at the terminal. Alison Nelson's grades were rolling by, A's and B's, a lot of courses, English and Art. No surprises there. But what was it she was looking for? Her hand hovered, then carefully, with one finger, she hit the button that made the lines go backward.

All the way to the beginning. Alison Nelson, born Aberdeen, South Dakota. Transferred from Pomona as a junior. Roz stared at the screen, her heart sinking. This was no coincidence. How many people were likely to grow up in Aberdeen, South Dakota, enter Pomona and then transfer to Canterbury College in Southwark, Maine, in the same two-year period? Rick had followed Alison here.

And then what?

Roz let her hands fall to her lap and sat there staring at the screen. There it was, floating in black and white on the terminal, the connection she'd been looking for. Things were starting to look pretty bad for Rick Squires.

She sighed. What was she going to do now?

The obvious answer was to call Chasse. She could just hear him, too, inquiring so politely, with that tone of elaborate patience: "Ah, Ms. Howard, how nice to hear from you again. Oh, you've found out something else? And what exactly *is* this latest discovery of yours?" In other words, what crackpot notion have you come up with this time? Then he would question her and want to know her evidence, her reasoning. And it would be clear she hadn't done her homework; all she had was this tentative connection between Rick and Alison Nelson. Well, maybe not so tentative; nevertheless, perhaps she was being a bit premature. Rick as the murderer was hardly better than Thor as the murderer; she liked them both. Maybe that was her trouble; she liked everybody. And he was her student; didn't she owe it to him to see if it all fit before she blew the whistle on him?

Hardly aware of what she was doing, she stood up, shouldered her bookbag, nodded vaguely to the clerk, and left the office.

Back at her apartment, she fixed herself a sandwich, then sat down and started once again from scratch, with Alison Nelson, sitting so primly propped in the little halfway house, *The Norton Anthology* open in her lap. Roz had told Luke half-seriously it might be a clue. All right then, there was only one way to find out. She went into her study, picked up her *Norton Anthology,* held the volume on its fat spine and let it drop open in the middle. She looked down at the heading: John Webster, *The Duchess of Malfi.*

Roz stared at the open book in stunned disbelief. She flipped a few pages over, read the lines in front of her, murmured them aloud. "'Tis weakness,/Too much to think what should have been done./I go, I know not whither." These were Julia's lines, spoken just before her death by poison.

Stricken, Roz looked up at the syllabuses she had tacked on the wall. There, on both Manciple's and Parsons's for the week of November 16, almost a year to the day after Alison Nelson's death, was one of the works she had eliminated from her syllabus: *The Duchess of Malfi.*

She had been completely wrong about the syllabus murders.

For the next several hours she pored over the text of the play, then the rest of *The Norton Anthology,* comparing syllabuses, dates, events, going back over all her previous conclusions about the murders. It was nearly midnight when she finished, exhausted and depressed but certain. There was no longer any doubt in her mind that the killings had been done to avenge Alison Nelson, and that Rick Squires was the syllabus murderer.

Quickly she went through her new conclusions again, rehearsing what she would tell the police. Rick had known Alison Nelson; she had been either his hometown girl or a very close friend; the exact connection hardly mattered. Anyway, the police could find that out easily enough. He had come east to find out what had happened to her, had discovered the circumstances of her death, had no doubt heard through the grapevine the kind of academic terrorism she'd been the victim of: Parsons threatening to fail her, Franklin and Manciple refusing her appeal, Luke unwilling to help, and Thor unable. Alison Nelson had killed herself in despair over her situation; *The Norton Anthology,* open to the assigned reading for the week she was to be thrown out of the course, had been her suicide note, the final statement of her plight, the story of a woman trying to make her own way, undone by the treachery of men. Young, idealistic, no doubt in love, Rick had cracked under this knowledge and determined on revenge. He had signed up late for Roz's class—it was still Parsons's then—and those damned literary masterpieces lined up one after another had given him the idea of how to carry out his justice all too poetically.

So there it was, a clear motive for revenge, and method as well. Not simply revenge, but justice, an eye for an eye, or so it would seem to the more rigidly conceived morality of youth.

It all made perfect sense. Rick had had the motive, the means, and the opportunity, particularly in the case of Manciple. He had been there behind the scenes at the fateful moment.

And he had not taken his text from Roz's syllabus at all. The plan was even more ingenious and involuted than she had thought. It smacked, ultimately, of an obsession. Rick the avenger, brooding over this unnecessary waste, cruel death, had taken his text and methods from the guilty ones themselves, from their syllabus, and from their book. There it was, on the same page, the Cardinal's vindictive taunt: "... thy curiosity/Hath undone thee: thou'rt poison'd with that book;/Because I knew thou couldst not keep my counsel,/I have bound thee to't by death." Really, she had to admire his ingenuity, awful as it was. The irony was inescapable. And it all fit. Except for her, of course. She still had no idea why Rick had attacked her in the Quad, smothering her like Desdemona. Perhaps it had been a warning. An attempt to frighten her off. But it hadn't worked.

Roz put her pen down and closed the volume. Now what? It was late, too late to call the police. She would need all her wits about her when she talked to Chasse. She yawned until her jaw cracked. Time for a good night's sleep.

She shuffled into her bedroom, got undressed and into bed, sank back against the pillows, and turned out the light. But sleep eluded her. Her mind kept circling back over and over, names and dates, Chaucer, Shakespeare, Marlowe, Webster, Milton... around and around. When and where and how and why. And now who. Rick. Oh, Rick.

She forced herself to think about the victims, Franklin et al. merely injured, the worst offenders, Parsons and Manciple, dead. The justice, if that was what you called it, was carefully meted out to each in accordance with his involve-

ment in hounding the poor girl to death. Had any of the
victims known? Had Manciple, falling to his death like
Faustus, perceived the drift? But for the killer it would
hardly matter; the intellectual triumph was clear. Such hatred,
Roz thought, so terrifyingly methodical, so complete.

But was it complete? Did Rick consider his revenge
accomplished now? Or would he go on to complete the
syllabus? Would Rick the killer, smelling blood, feeling the
power of ending lives, find himself, as so many did, unable
to stop?

Suddenly a new thought struck her, sending her bolt
upright. She had finally realized what her subconscious had
been trying to tell her, both in dream and in fragmented
memory. If it had been Manciple's and Parsons's syllabus
after all, then she had been wrong about who was next and
how. The attack on her in the Quad had not been part of it.
Why, *Othello* wasn't even in *The Norton Anthology,* never
mind the syllabus. She could forget Desdemona smothered,
and Othello dead by his own hand. That wasn't the text
at all.

So what *was* next? And who? With a sinking sensation,
she remembered that Thor had been the girl's adviser. And
Alison had worked part time in the Dean's office. "Why
didst not thou pity her?" says Ferdinand of the doomed
Duchess of Malfi, "what/An excellent honest man mightst
thou have been,/If thou hadst borne her to some sanctuary!/
Or, bold in a good cause, oppos'd thyself/With thy advancèd
sword above thy head,/Between her innocence and my
revenge!" That could be an apt reproach to Thor. Or Luke.

"And my poor fool is hanged." *King Lear.* Luke hanged
in effigy from the Chapel balcony. That left Thor. So what
came next on the syllabus? Francis Bacon's *Essays,* but
there was no means of murder there, unless it was boring
someone to death. Roz laughed in spite of herself, as much
from tension as anything else. Then she grew serious again.

The next work was *Paradise Lost*. Hellfire and brimstone. A long day's dying, to augment our pain. Tombs of fire and ice. The foundry. Thor. She had to warn him.

Roz picked up the phone and dialed Thor's number, listened to ring after ring. No answer. She replaced the receiver, feeling the beginnings of panic. She picked the phone up again, started to dial the police.

She hesitated. What would she tell them? That there was a crazed killer on the loose? Chasse wouldn't be there, and no one else would even know what she was talking about. Maybe he wouldn't, either, but at least he would listen. All right, call him at home. Quickly she flipped through the phone book. There must be fifty Chasses, but no number for Jeffrey. Damn, it must be unlisted. Now what? Roz jumped up and began to pace around the room. She had to do something.

Luke. She would call Luke. He would know what to do, and anyway, she had to warn him too, just in case the mock hanging was only a dress rehearsal. After all, there were lots of other kinds of killing in *King Lear*. She sat down on the bed and dialed his number.

"Whazzat?" a sleepy voice answered. Roz looked belatedly at the clock; it was three o'clock in the morning.

"Luke, I'm sorry," she began, "but it's important—"

"Roz? Is that you?" Luke interrupted. "Don't tell me. You want me to come over."

Roz ignored this; it was clear from his tone he was teasing. "Luke, I know who the syllabus murderer is."

There was a long silence on the phone, then a grunt, as of someone rolling over in bed. But when he finally spoke, Luke sounded fully awake. "Okay. Who is it?"

"Rick Squires," she answered. "He's from her hometown."

"Hmmm. Coincidence maybe?"

"Afraid not. He's been doing research on the case at the

local paper. He's got everything, Luke. Motive, means, opportunity. It all fits..." and she proceeded to tell him everything, ending with her concern about him and Thor. "If anything happened to either of you after this...I had to call and warn you...."

"Why, Roz, I'm flattered," Luke drawled.

"...But I couldn't get Thor. His phone doesn't answer. Luke, I'm really worried."

"Hey, take it easy, okay? I doubt he'd be in the foundry at this hour. Anyway, I'm sure the Viking can take care of himself. Have you called the police?"

"No," Roz blurted. "No one but Chasse will know what I'm talking about, and his phone's unlisted."

"Listen, I've got Chasse's home number right here. Why don't you let me call him? I'll do it right now and get things started. He's used to hearing from me at this hour anyway, and—sorry, but it's true—they're more likely to take it seriously coming from me. I'll have Chasse get in touch with you first thing in the morning. Okay?"

"Okay," Roz said, feeling almost limp with relief. Luke had taken charge, and for once she was grateful.

"Good." There was a brief pause. Then, in a husky, urgent voice, Luke said: "Roz, take care. You know how I feel about you."

Roz was glad he wasn't there to see her blush. "I will," she said in as even a voice as she could muster. "Good night. And thanks," she added belatedly. But Luke had already hung up.

Shivering now, Roz lay back in bed, drew the covers up to her chin. Nothing had changed, really; only now she knew the answer to the question who. And it was out of her hands.

She closed her eyes, and fell into an exhausted sleep.

CHAPTER

19

*I*t feels cold enough for snow, Roz thought the next morning as she made her way across the Quad to her first class. She shivered, but not from the cold. She had spent much of the previous night wondering what would happen to Rick now that he was in the hands of the police. The evidence seemed damning; he had lied to her about knowing Alison Nelson, and he had the motive—revenge—even the opportunity, particularly in Manciple's case. So it was over, the killer caught, and there would be no more "accidents." Chasse hadn't called her yet, but she assumed he would at some point. Or maybe he hadn't had to. Maybe Rick, once apprehended, realizing the weight of the evidence against him, had simply confessed.

She had called Thor's house this morning and once again gotten no answer, but when she had tried his office in the museum, though he didn't seem to be in at the moment, the secretary had reported seeing him "around here just a minute ago." So Thor was safe and in the clear, both as villain and as victim.

Roz squinted up at the pewter-colored sky, blinked her eyes. It did look like snow. Sure enough, while she was teaching Manciple's class great fluffy flakes began to drop

out of the sky, and by the end of it, the ground was dusted
with white. Standing at the window in the Faculty Lounge
between classes, she watched the snow come down. It was
so beautiful, covering and muffling all. She wished that she
could muffle her own thoughts, which kept coming back to
Rick, now reposing downtown in jail.

But Rick was not in jail. When she entered her classroom
the next period, there he was in his usual place, propped
against the back wall, looking as innocent as ever.

Class was something of a trial. Even though she did not
look directly at him, she was distracted by Rick's presence.
Why hadn't he been arrested? Maybe the police didn't believe
the evidence? Didn't they know they had a killer on the
loose? Avoiding his eyes, she saw him tilt his chair forward
suddenly, his glance fixed on her. She had the feeling that
he knew she knew. What were the police waiting for? Hadn't
Luke called them? Or were there warrants and things that
took time?

Well, there was nothing she could do now. She had to
go through with the class, even with Rick's shadowy menace
in the back of the room. At least she knew where he was,
and he could hardly try anything in here. She found herself
thinking of the night of the riot, the night she had gotten
her head bashed. Rick had attacked her, which meant that
all along Rick had also been the Grabber, a perfect cover
for his other activities. Then, to throw everyone off, he had
pretended to find her, taken her home. But why? To find
out how much she suspected about the murders, his connection with Alison Nelson? But she had passed out on him
before he could learn anything.

She became aware that the whole class was staring at her.
Of course they were! She had been standing there for several
minutes, saying nothing; probably they all thought she had
suffered brain damage from her knock on the head. She had

to get hold of herself. Hurriedly she walked around the desk, flopped open her copy of *The Norton Anthology*. The text of *The Duchess of Malfi* stared up at her. She flipped the pages over to *Paradise Lost*.

"Milton," she announced in a firm voice. "Page fourteen ten."

There were some groans among the audience, which she ignored; though she herself found it hard to love, there was no doubt in her mind that *Paradise Lost* was a necessary part of any educated person's background. To justify the ways of God to man, the answers, at least in Milton's mind, to the age-old riddle of how an all-powerful, all-benevolent, all-knowing God could allow evil to exist. Fixed fate, free will, foreknowledge absolute. It was a challenge, she thought, and so is this class, if I can just get through it. Then, if Luke hasn't called the police, I will.

She took a deep breath, and began by summarizing Milton's explanation of God's Great Plan, the doctrine of the Fortunate Fall, so they could keep the plot in mind while they were reading. "Think of it as fantasy," she said. "A kind of theological Dungeons and Dragons version of the Old Testament." Now that she had their somewhat startled attention, she quickly drew a time line across the board, like a stretched-out yardstick, with steps down at the beginning, up at the end, and slash marks indicating the fall of Adam, the First and Second Comings, the Rule of the Just, the Apocalypse, and the final institution of the New Heaven and Earth.

She was going over the main events of the plot when she noticed Oblonsky, of "you gotta get dressed for 'em all" fame, sitting in his usual seat in the front row, his eyes growing wider and wider and his expression more and more skeptical.

"Felix who?" he interrupted as she tapped a piece of chalk at the point on the line where Adam fell, plunging mankind

into the dark days of post-Lapsarian sin, corruption, and
death. Glaring at several titterers in the background, Roz
proceeded to explain carefully once again, running her now
considerably more blunted chalk along the line that ran its
up-and-down course the length of the blackboard illustrating
the progress of God's Great Plan (as conceived by Milton,
that is, and she had to admit, as she did every time, it made
a lot of sense, metaphysically speaking), how Adam's original sin would ultimately lead to a higher plane of existence
(here she chalked up a higher plane than the one at the far
end of the board where she'd started), a perfect Paradise,
where evil no longer existed, where all souls entered into
a state of eternal bliss.

Oblonsky's jaw dropped. She looked at him with a sense
of pedagogical satisfaction. Between them, she and Milton
had gotten to him; he really understood. If there was ever
a face transformed by revelation, his was it.

"But . . . but . . ." he stammered, as his expression trans-
mogrified into one of absolute horror. "How can it be
perfect?" he finally burst out. "There's no room for
advancement!"

Roz started to laugh and couldn't stop. Tears came to her
eyes and rolled down her cheeks as she became helpless
with laughter, along with everybody else except the ultimate
pragmatist, Oblonsky. Even Rick was laughing. Finally Roz
dismissed the class, after admitting in a choked voice that
he had a point there.

She was still wiping her eyes when Rick stopped at her
desk. "How are you feeling?" he asked.

Roz could hardly believe her ears. She stared at him,
appraising his ever-innocent, rosy-cheeked, blue-eyed, open
Irish face. Surely he must be able to tell she knew? Searching
his face for signs of disingenuousness, she replied evenly,
"I'm doing fine, Rick, thank you." And thank you for the
kick in the head—and the heart—as well.

Rick's glance fell to the desk top; he reached out and idly fingered Roz's copy of *The Norton Anthology*. It seemed he was about to say something. Roz waited. What was there to say? Surely he wasn't going to confess? The characteristic flush spread across his cheekbones as he studied the frayed dust jacket with the ruffed and bejeweled Queen Elizabeth staring suspiciously and coldly outward. Then the flush subsided, leaving him unusually pale. He looked up, and Roz thought she saw a flicker of panic in those so innocently ingenuous eyes. "Listen, Miss Howard, I've got to talk to you, but I've got to go to my seminar right now. Can I come over later this afternoon?"

"Of course, Rick," she said in a neutral tone. Right. Appointments with murderers. She'd see him in jail first. But she kept up the pretense. "At my office, shall we say four?"

Rick nodded, gave her one more hunted look, then fled down the corridor, lumpy rucksack dangling dispiritedly from one shoulder.

Roz watched him disappear down the corridor, wondering how you could be a cold-blooded killer and still worry about cutting class. Or was he just keeping up appearances to the bitter end? She went into the Faculty Lounge and called Luke's office. His secretary answered, and informed Roz that he had gone downtown on an important errand. Try as she might, Roz couldn't get any more out of her; but at least she knew he was all right. Then she called Chasse's office, only to find he wasn't there, either. *His* secretary informed her he was in conference, whatever that meant, and wouldn't be coming back until later. Roz hung up the phone, feeling slightly reassured. No doubt Luke had gone downtown to see Chasse, and they were now in conference together, deciding what to do about Rick. She wondered what the hitch was. Oh, well, Rick was stuck in his seminar for two and a half hours and he didn't know yet she had rumbled him; the world would be safe enough until 3:00, if the police didn't come and get him before then.

Anyway, it was out of her hands. Shaking her head, she went across the Quad to the College Hangout in search of lunch, even though she wasn't the least bit hungry.

It was nearly one o'clock by the time she started back to her office. The sky was lowering, a heavy gray quilt spread across the horizon, shaking down snow. At least six inches had fallen; Roz looked down at the recently plowed walks in amazement. Going past the Chapel with its slightly scorched cornice, she realized with a start that in thinking so much about Rick, she had forgotten all about Thor. She wanted to tell him what had happened, let him know everything was over. She went to the office first to drop off her books and papers, and found a note from Thor himself in her mailbox in the English office, asking her to come over to his workshop at the museum at 3:30. She tried to call him to say she'd be there, but there was no answer at his extension. Didn't the man ever answer his phone? She hung up, disappointed; she had wanted to tell him right away, before he heard the story from anyone else. Oh, well, she would see him in a couple of hours, and meanwhile she had work to do.

She spent the intervening time finishing her letter to Alan, bringing him up to date on what she had learned about Rick. She wished she could talk to him, but there was no chance of reaching him out in the middle of the desert somewhere, lurching around on a camel, or worse, so she sealed her letter and put it in the mail, then read over the first two books of *Paradise Lost*. As always, and usually to her own later disbelief, she became totally immersed in Milton's version of the universe. When she looked up, she was startled to see that it was nearly three-thirty, and for a moment she could not recall what it was she had to do at that hour. Overwhelmed by Milton's language, Milton's world, Moloch, Belial, Beelzebub, not to mention Lucifer, Son of the Morning, she had forgotten all about Canterbury College, students and professors, syllabuses and suspicion and sudden death, everything in fact except the life of the mind as evidenced in Milton's words. That was the beauty of literature, of the written word; it existed, created a world elsewhere, another country that one could enter freely and at will. She felt as though she'd been skimming along on a smooth surface, happily, unmindful of the current issues troubling her. But now here it was, the dark shape just below the surface, the rock that trips us back into reality.

But even so she felt refreshed, more in control of her own experience, juxtaposed against the world's long experience in time, in which the events here at the college took on a smaller dimension of importance. It would all work out in the end; justice would be done, order restored.

She stood there for a moment, gazing out the window at the impossibly large and fluffy snowflakes that were still drifting down, floating lazily through the air like huge wads of down; a foot deep on the ground. And not even winter yet. She thought of Thor and his penchant for winter camping. This would certainly give him an early start. And maybe she would join him after all.

Affixing a note to her door giving her whereabouts and when she would be back, Roz put on her heavy coat and locked her office door. On the way out she passed Iris's office, and that made her think she ought to tell her about how things had turned out. The door was ajar, but there was no Iris. She must have stepped out, Roz thought, so she scribbled a brief note and left it on Iris's desk, then said good night to George, who nodded briskly as she typed away madly, red hair and fingernails flying. Then, *Norton Anthology* tucked under one arm, Roz marched down the stairs and out the door of Tabard Hall, across the Quad to the Art Museum.

This far north, she had found, the end of daylight savings took some getting used to. The loss of that hour meant that in mid-November it was pitch-black not much later than 4:30, and the hour before that was the difficult time of dusk, when it was still too light for street lamps, yet dark enough to make one stumble around in the half-light under the mistaken impression one could see. She nodded to the receptionist in the lobby, to the burly female security guard in an impressive navy-blue leather flak jacket, blue police shirt, gabardine pants, and holstered gun, making her rounds jiggling doors and peering in dark corners, her night stick swinging from a chain on her belt. Roz smiled, thinking of Iris. We women have to stick together. "I'm just going down to the foundry for a minute to see Mr. Grettirsdottir," she said to the guard, who looked at her curiously. She nodded back and went in search of Thor.

The rest of the Art Museum was quite dully illuminated. Obviously no one had bothered to turn on all the lights as yet. She flipped a switch or two as she went, to light her way down the stairs and through the maze of corridors that led to Thor's domain. The security guard was right behind her; she could hear her footsteps coming down the stairs, keys rattling, night stick bumping.

Even from quite far away, or what she thought was far away, she heard the roar and thunder of the foundry furnace, and was glad to think that Thor was back at work. All this suspicion, this disruption of his life must have been difficult. But the end was in sight, with Rick undoubtedly in custody by now, thanks to Luke and Chasse.

Thor's workshop, next to but not connected to the foundry, opened off the lower corridor. The roar of the furnace sounded louder and louder in her ears as she made her way down

the last few steps and pushed the fire door open. They ought
to hand out earplugs at the desk, Roz thought; the thing
makes such an unearthly racket. The lights at the end of
the hall were out, which was annoying but not unusual.
All the college light switches had energy-saving reminders
in the form of signs declaring "Please Save the Juice! Turn
Me Off When Not in Use!" around them, and some of them
had self-timers, but this one was just plain not working, she
decided after flipping it on and off several times. Oh, well,
she could feel her way down the hall to Thor's workshop
and turn the lights on there.

But that was odd, now she thought of it. If he had asked
her to meet him, why wasn't he already here, with the lights
on, waiting? The only light visible right now was the ruddy
glare at the end of the hall, the red flickering from the roaring
blast furnace, hardly more than darkness made visible. Even
in the foundry there seemed to be no other light. She stopped
momentarily, an uneasy feeling prickling her neck, backed
up and tried the hall light switch one more time. No luck.
But never mind, she told herself sternly; it was probably
something perfectly simple, a blown fuse, a tripped relay.
She considered going to see if she could find a custodian,
but she was nearly there, and the guard was right behind
her. Wasn't she? Roz turned to peer down the dark hallway,
and was relieved to see the sturdy figure passing by the fire
door. She looked back the other way. A long shadow stretched
up El Greco-like against the wall of the foundry; she could
see it through the open door. He was here after all, lights
or no lights. Running her hand along the rough concrete
block of the corridor, Roz headed again toward the open
door of the foundry.

"Thor?" she called. There was no answer; but of course
over the deafening roar of the furnace he couldn't hear her,
particularly if he was wearing his usual Darth Vader getup
to protect his face and head from the high heat. The light

flickered across the open door, reminding her of the bonfire the other night, only this fire was infinitely hotter, an unthinkable two thousand-plus degrees, so that coming within even several feet was enough to singe the hair and scorch the flesh. Anything closer meant instant cremation. That was why Thor always wore that welder's helmet with the isinglass window, huge asbestos gloves, and even flameproof overalls.

The noise increased as she drew nearer, and, stuffing *The Norton Anthology* in one deep pocket, she put her hands over her ears to shut it out as she stepped through the doorway. She could see him there, head enclosed in the helmet, bending over the fire pit. "Hi, Thor!" she shouted over the din.

Then all hell broke loose.

CHAPTER
20

*I*t was all noise and motion, the round circle of the blast furnace a white-hot pool of molten flame leaping and fuming over its rim, the air over it blurred and shimmering with heat, the sound of jet engines roaring in her ears, so loud that even through her fists balled over her ears she could hardly bear it, and the crucible swinging overhead on the track, white hot as well, gyrating like some hellish wrecking ball, the long hooded shadow on the wall now flat, now taking on shape and motion, whirling, and coming toward her.

She could not see clearly. Looking at the white-hot pool of light, she had temporarily blinded herself, and now the moted atmosphere, smelling of superheated air, scorched sand, and molten metal, was only sound and motion, and a black shape, darkly visible, was moving toward her. "Thor?" she shouted again. The figure came on, without a word of greeting. She blinked, and blinked again, gazed in horror as the figure slowly removed the welder's helmet, revealing, not a face with humanly recognizable features, but only two implacably staring eyes, the rest covered by a black executioner's mask.

She screamed, but could not even hear her own voice

above the din. She turned and tried to run, but her legs
pumped uselessly, as in a nightmare. As she turned, she
screamed again, her voice cracking with the strain, even
though she knew she would never be heard above the noise
of the blast furnace. The masked figure loomed over her,
grabbed her, pinning her arms to her sides from the back,
the gloved hand clapped over her mouth, the harsh stiff
asbestos gloves she had last seen when Thor poured out her
twigs. No, Rick, don't kill me! she tried to mouth against
the rough material crushing her lips against her teeth; you
don't understand; even as the figure, hard and muscular
against her flailing body, manhandled her toward the thun-
dering pit, dragged her bodily across the concrete floor,
closer and closer, the glowing crucible swaying overhead,
only a slap of the hand and the molten steel would come
pouring down on him, on her...

   Then, her mind dissociating itself from the struggling,
terrified body, suddenly objective about what seemed inevitable, she wondered what would happen next. Would he
put her straight into the pit, feetfirst? Going limp for an
instant, she coolly contemplated the first bite of fire, of two-
thousand-degree heat, shriveling her flesh and bones in an
instant of searing pain, as she turned into no more than a
warm curl of ash, a few pebbles of bone. What a way to
go, she thought, with all due respect to Milton, but really,
isn't this just a trifle premature? Why, we've just started
Paradise Lost.

   Well, she thought, tensing her muscles, she wasn't going
to go without a fight. She dug in her heels, felt even through
her heavy socks—her boots having been dragged off somehow in the struggle—the flesh abrading across the rough
cement. She flailed with her hands, trying to keep herself
from being turned upside down; she was damned if she was
going to go headfirst. The executioner picked her up bodily
from the floor; desperately she scrabbled with her hands,

her feet, trying to find something to grab onto, as he turned her upside down like a baton. *The Norton Anthology* fell out of her pocket with a crash, distracting her assailant momentarily. Relaxing his hold slightly, he kicked the book viciously. It spun away, pages fluttering, and dropped into the burning vat, a hole in one. There was a brief hiss, a puff of vapor. I'm next, Roz thought, and shut her eyes.

Was that a shout she heard over the roar of the furnace in her ears? Dizzy now, all the blood rushing down to her head, nevertheless she sensed a hesitation, a further flagging of Rick's attention. Then suddenly she felt a lurch, a thud. Here we go! she thought as she felt herself flung bodily across the scorched and roaring air. . . . Alan, I'm so sorry I won't be coming back to you. Then she crashed into unconsciousness.

After all, she thought, how odd, but it was improbably cool, this being burned to a crisp in seconds. No doubt the sensory faculties, overloaded beyond any rational possibility of taking it all in, in terms of pain, would convert it to perhaps its opposite, and therefore fire became ice. That was no doubt why her feet were cold.

But had she in fact been totally incinerated? Could this remnant of thinking consciousness reside in what was for all intents and purposes a live coal? It seemed that there were fingers and, more important, toes and feet still in the circle of her senses. An illusion, like the pain and twitches felt by amputees in absent limbs? She twitched her almost certainly long since vaporized toes. They felt convincingly solid; she could even feel the gritty texture of her socks across the soles of her feet.

She opened her eyes and looked up from where she was sitting, in the angle of the floor and wall. Dust—or was it smoke?—rose in clouds and filled her nostrils, stung her eyes. Disoriented, she tried to get her bearings in this room

full of odd shapes and angles, Thor's partially built constructions like children's discarded Junglegyms, barrels
stacked to the ceiling. She started to get up, but a wave of
dizziness made her sink back against the wall. Overhead
the crucible swung to and fro, dark as a clinker except for
the hot sulfurous yellow glow at its very center. Mesmerized
by the glow, she stared at the swaying crucible for a moment.
Then, her eyes still unaccustomed to the dimness, she peered
across the room at the blast furnace, still roaring and filling
the room with its mammoth, intolerable noise, the pool of
white light seeming to pulsate brighter and hotter, and
watched in horror as a figure materialized out of the dusty,
scorched air, silhouetted against the glow, looking down
into the pit.

Excuse me, but isn't this where I came in? she thought
with an odd sense of *déjà vu*. But she couldn't just squat
here like a sitting duck, waiting for the killer to have another
go once he'd got his incinerator tuned up to his liking. But
what to do? She couldn't seem to think fast enough. She
started to scoot backward on her hands and knees. If she
could only get out of sight, she could hide herself in the
giant Tinker-Toy graveyard.

But it was too late.

He had heard her moving. Black against the fiery glow
of the furnace, the killer turned, paused for a moment as if
to contemplate her, then moved slowly but purposefully in
her direction. He had taken off the mask; it dangled from
his hand. In the gloom she made out Rick's angelic face,
besmirched with soot, his brow furrowed, staring at her
with a perplexed expression, as if trying to guess what she
was going to do next. Lucifer, Son of the Morning. It was
a matter of seconds now, and there was no escape; he was
between her and the door. If she was going to get out of
here in one piece, she needed a weapon to bash him with.

She felt around her, remembering her last sight of the

place in daylight, junk everywhere; there must be something bashworthy close to hand. And sure enough, here was what felt like a crowbar conveniently lying next to her on the floor. She clutched it to her, eyes on the figure slouching toward her, stood up, and edged along the wall until her shoulder bumped something. A switch plate. The lights! She could flip on the lights and dazzle him, then, while he was temporarily blinded, run past him out the door and scream for help. She slid her hand up, eyes still on Rick, hit the switch . . . and watched in amazement as the huge dolly overhead lurched into motion, began to swing along the track with a purposeful whine, lowering of its own accord the heavy crucible, swaying and slopping over the slag-colored sides lavalike beads of molten metal that fell to the floor one after another spattering off sparks like an upside-down miniature Fourth of July. Rick whirled, stared transfixed at the molten juggernaut bearing down on him, while Roz tensed herself to run.

Then something—someone—hurtled through the door and leaped across the room, flying through the air feet first, accompanied by a high-pitched cry, and struck her attacker square amidships with bare toes as stiff and pointed as spears. Roz stared as Rick went down without a sound, laid out flat on the cement floor, while the guard—who else could it be; but what had she done with her blue suit?— dropped to her feet like a cat, and stood up lightly, hands on hips, looking down at him. Then she turned to look at Roz.

"Are you all right?" said the clipped, stern voice of Iris LeBeau.

Then all the fire alarms in the building went off.

CHAPTER

21

"I'm fine," Roz yelled over the din of clanging bells and blatting buzzers. "I think." She was still staring dumfounded at Iris, who was standing in her stocking feet looking down thoughtfully at the prostrate figure of Rick Squires. Roz dropped the crowbar—but it wasn't a crowbar, she saw to her dismay; it was one of Thor's discarded twigs, the little whorls and pores distinct, the peels of bark razor-sharp along the length—to the floor with a clang, and seeing that the crucible was still lurching drunkenly along the track, reached up and banged down the switch. The crucible stopped. Far off she heard the sound of fire engines braying, coming closer, no doubt with Feeney and Kelley at the helm.

Rick was still lying on his face, one arm flung out. "Is he dead?" Roz asked.

"I shouldn't think so," Iris said. "I didn't hit him that hard. Only enough to drop him. He must have hit his head. I think he's out cold." Roz knelt down, grabbed him by the shoulders to roll him over. He moved only slightly; what she had hold of were the straps of a rucksack. She looked down sadly at his face, no longer rosy-cheeked and fair, but smoke-streaked and unconscious. The black mask was still clutched limply in one hand.

Just then all the fire alarms fell silent, and in the ensuing silence Roz realized that the blast furnace was no longer roaring. Already it had cooled to a sulky orange, and was percolating away quietly to itself in the floor.

"Everyone all right in here?" someone shouted, and Roz turned to see the female guard, her eyes wide, standing in the doorway. "I thought I heard something."

"Your hair's a little singed, got a bump on the back of the head, elbow abrasions, and your socks are a dead loss, but you'll do," the young doctor told her. It was the same one who had examined her before; this must be a one-ambulance town. "I'd say the other guy definitely got the worst of it," he added with a note of admiration in his voice. The paramedic was still trying to revive Rick; he was now sitting up with a dazed look on his face while a uniformed policeman read him his rights. The doctor paused for a moment, regarded Roz quizzically. "Say, aren't you the concussion and abrasion from last Friday?"

Roz nodded. The doctor shook his head. "You've been pretty busy lately, haven't you?" He looked over his shoulder at Rick. "Okay, guys, you can take him now." The paramedic and a policeman between them hauled Rick to his feet, handcuffed him, propped him up between them, and staggered out. He shot Roz one brief, perplexed glance as they hustled him out the door. Obviously he still didn't know what had hit him. Iris and Roz followed the little parade at a safe distance behind; the doctor brought up the rear, whistling cheerfully.

The Fire Department was conducting a thorough search of the entire building, just in case there were any other casualties. The general opinion was that the superheated blast furnace had finally set off the alarms, and as soon as the guard had tripped the safety switch just inside the door, the system had reset itself. In the lobby the police were questioning the receptionist, but of course she had seen and heard nothing until the alarm system went off. Roz told the uniformed policeman about the message purportedly from Thor; he dutifully noted it down. The receptionist remarked that she had not seen Professor Grettirsdottir around at all this afternoon. She had seen him go downstairs at lunchtime, but he had not come back up. The fire chief shook his head. "We've searched the whole building, Cliff. Everyone's out."

Roz walked outside to the little group huddled near the fire truck, as if gathering warmth from its stroking light, its bright metal sides. She searched among the faces, but there was no sign of Thor.

"Detective Chasse will be in touch shortly, ma'am," the uniformed policeman told her. "He'll want a sworn statement, but that can probably wait until tomorrow. Would you like us to take you home?"

She shook her head. "No, thanks. I'll be fine," she said vaguely, her head buzzing. It was over; she was safe, thanks to Iris. But where was Thor?

"You can come home with me if you want," she heard Iris say as if from far away. "My truck's right in this parking lot."

So she let herself be led away by the firm hand of Iris LeBeau.

"I started with tai-chi; the doctor said the exercises would be good for my back," Iris explained as she handed Roz a tumbler full of bourbon, neat, in the living room of her house just down the hill from the campus. "Then, I thought as long as I was doing the martial-arts bit I'd see what else they had to offer. I figured a knowledge of exotic self-defense couldn't hurt, what with all the muggings and rapes and crimes against women—suppose that little aerosol can of Mace lost its fizz, lying there in the bottom of your pocketbook, then where would you be?—so I tried out some of the others. What you saw was tae kwon-do. Korean kung-fu."

"But . . . but how did you know? I mean, what were you doing in the museum?"

"Looking at paintings," Iris said imperturbably. "I saw you go downstairs. It didn't strike me as a particularly good idea at the time, but I figured you knew what you were doing. But then, when you didn't come back up within a few minutes, I decided I'd investigate. Better safe than sorry."

Roz stared at her hands, clutched around the glass, feeling rather foolish. Iris stood up briskly. "Oh, well, it's over now. And it did serve some purpose; the killer is caught. And don't waste your sympathy; the kid was going to put you right down the furnace before you could blab around any more about him, and try to make it look as though Thor did it. He's been trying to pin it all on Thor right along. I don't see how he ever thought he'd get away with it. But there's not much doubt about who did it now. Caught in the act."

Roz shook her head. No, not much doubt at all. She put her glass down on the coffee table and stood up. "I should go. Iris, I . . ."

"Don't mention it. Sure you don't want to stay here?"

"No, thanks. I'll be fine."

So Iris drove her back to her apartment, waited in the purring little truck until Roz went inside, shot the bolt, put up the chain, and waved out the window that she was safe. With a jaunty beep, Iris drove her little pickup truck off through the heavily falling snow.

The phone rang. It was Jeff Chasse, telling her that he

would need a sworn statement from her in the morning, and he would send a squad car to pick her up, that is, if she didn't mind. And, by the way, Mr. Grettirsdottir was still unaccounted for, so if she heard from him, would she please have him call the station? Roz didn't mind, and yes, she would. If she heard. Good-bye.

Feeling very wobbly, Roz sat down on the sofa in the shabby living room of her temporary quarters. Suddenly she had a terrible apprehension that not only had Rick tried to do away with her, but *had* done away with Thor already. The shadow wavering on the wall, the figure in the welder's helmet bending over the furnace . . . that innocent face, those sincere blue eyes; no one would suspect until it was too late. One push and . . .

Otherwise, where *was* Thor? She wanted to tell him everything was all right now. Her eyes roved over to the collection of cast metal birch twigs in the umbrella stand by the door. Her eyes fixed on them, she began to shake and, finally, to cry.

CHAPTER

22

When Roz awoke the next morning, it was to a veritable winter wonderland of snow-encrusted landscape, at least a foot on the ground, several inches coating the tree branches and every other moderately level surface. It was very lovely. The trees were filigreed with white, the evergreens shrouded, their branches sweeping the ground. After she had dressed and eaten breakfast, she went to stand by the window, her arms clasped over one another. She stared out the window at the snow. Suddenly she felt very cold. If it had not been for Iris LeBeau, she would now be a pile of ash and bone at the bottom of the pit, as white and insubstantial as the snow.

She stood at the window contemplating the scene with mixed emotions, thinking at once how lovely it all was, how quiet and muffled and serene, and wishing she could run outside, run far away and forget everything, even for an hour. If she had a pair of cross-country skis, she could just step out the door...

Her thoughts were interrupted by the arrival of an unfamiliar car outside her door. Then she realized that it was an unmarked police car, Chasse thoughtfully appreciating the fact that the arrival of a squad car at her door at nine o'clock in the morning would cause quite a stir in the dorm. A burly cop in a plain overcoat was getting out; quickly she put on her down jacket and went outside.

Chasse was waiting for her at the station. They walked down the hall to a small room where a police stenographer was waiting, with what appeared to be an old-fashioned adding machine poised in his lap. Chasse and Roz sat down opposite each other. "Just tell me everything that you remember about yesterday," Chasse said gently. Roz began to talk, starting with her finding of the note; the stenographer began to tap rapidly and inconspicuously on his machine. At first the clicking sound distracted her, but as she got further and further into the story, she forgot all about the little room, and the tapping, and even Jeff Chasse. She was back in the foundry, fighting for her life.

"That's fine," Chasse said when she was finished. "You're a good witness." He motioned to the other officer, who stood up, machine and all, nodded, and left the room. "It'll take a few minutes to get that typed up, and then you can sign it, and that'll be that—for the moment, anyway. Any questions?"

Roz shook her head. She felt limp, empty-headed, drained. The police were convinced at last, the killer caught. It was over. They knew who had tried to kill her, who had done away with Manciple, with Parsons, had nearly killed the professors three, terrorizing coeds into the bargain. . . . Yet there was still the sense of something tugging at the edge of her memory, a shadowy loose end dangling just out of sight that she couldn't quite put her finger on. Everything had happened so fast. She couldn't recover it. Not that it really mattered now.

Then Chasse asked unexpectedly, "Are you absolutely sure it was the Squires kid who attacked you?"

The stooping faceless figure, swooping down on her. Was

she absolutely sure? Fixed fate, free will, foreknowledge absolute. There were no absolutes in this life. But then he had pulled off the mask. She nodded. "Everything happened so fast. . . ."

"I can appreciate that," Chasse said. "Of course he's denying everything. We had trouble getting a warrant first off—you've got to admit, it all sounded pretty implausible—and then we couldn't find him to pick him up, thought he'd split for sure, but he claims he was in class until three, then went to pick up his mail and found a note from Thor asking him to come over there. He called for Thor, got no answer, walked in, saw you on the floor there, was just about to help you up and, pow! Yeah, I know it's a likely story. But we're working on him. I'm pretty sure we'll get a confession sooner or later. He looks good for it. Real good. Motive, opportunity—it all goes back to Alison Nelson, as you already know. I suppose you could call it revenge, vigilante justice, the idea being that someone had to pay for that girl's death. When the law didn't come through in a reasonable time, he found out who was responsible, or who he thought might be responsible, and took matters into his own hands. And then you came along, snapping at his heels. . . ." Chasse shrugged, spreading his hands wide in an eloquent gesture.

"I still can't believe it, Rick a homicidal maniac," Roz said. "And he really blamed them all for Alison's death?"

"Not without good reason."

Startled, Roz stared at Chasse. "What do you mean?"

Chasse took a deep breath, leaned back against the cracked leather chair, and rubbed his eyes, then stretched. "The whole thing's so damned complicated, it's *all* hard to believe. First we've got Nelson's death, then Parsons's accident, then those professors letting off a little steam, then Manciple, another accident. A riot or two thrown in, a gang of hoodlums dressed in weird outfits, a sexual pervert. . .

and then *you* come along with that business with your whatdycallit . . . ?" He looked at her interrogatively.

"Syllabus," she replied. So he *had* been paying attention.

"Syllabus, right. And all of a sudden it's a series, just like something out of Agatha Christie. Anyway, the kid did it. After all, what are the chances of having more than one homicidal maniac operating in a place this size at any given time? And I'm not so sure he's a maniac, either. Wild as it is, it all makes sense, the idea of frontier justice not so farfetched. One of those guys certainly deserved it." Chasse paused, took a deep breath. "I probably shouldn't be telling you this, but there was a lot more to the Nelson case than was ever made public. We never had enough hard evidence to go on, but the fact is, there were some things there that just didn't jibe."

"Like what?"

"Post-mortem lividity, for one thing. That's when the blood pools in certain parts of the body after death, looks like bruises, and it indicates how the body was positioned at the time of or immediately after death."

"And?"

"The Nelson girl was lying down on her side when she died, and for at least an hour after. But she was sitting up when she was found. Dead bodies don't sit up by themselves," he added unnecessarily.

Roz blinked at him, trying to take in the implications of what he was saying. "Somebody put her there?"

Chasse nodded.

"You mean she was murdered?"

Chasse held up a hand and cocked his head in a cautionary gesture. "We can't say. All we can say is that she was moved after death. Whether she was killed, and if she was, *how* she was killed and by whom are unanswerable questions at this point, and I'm afraid always will be. We investigated our brains out over that one. The only chance now is for the killer to make a mistake and reveal something only he—or she—could know. That's why we kept all this business, particularly the part about the down, secret."

"Down?" Roz's mind went scampering. Down doobee-doobee-down, downy-puff, Down East... what in the world was he talking about?

Chasse shrugged. "There wasn't a mark on her. The only odd thing was that the autopsy showed particles of down in her throat and lungs."

"I don't understand."

"The official explanation was that she had fallen unconscious on her jacket and breathed in some of the down before she died. Down is down, right?"

Roz nodded. "Right."

Chasse held up an admonitory finger. "Wrong. That's what I thought until I asked the lab if the down definitely came from the girl's jacket. Pretty obvious, right?" He leaned forward. "Do you have any idea how many different kinds of down there are? There's white European down, gray duck down, prime Northern goose down, eiderdown, and Bauer down, for Pete's sake. And that's just for starters. The girl's jacket was from out West, Eddie Bauer's, and one lab guy thought the down was L. L. Bean's, something about the percentage of feathers, but the other lab techs disagreed. So the lab says, find us some more down articles, and we'll see if we can get you a better match. Do you have any idea how many down vests and jackets and sleeping bags—never mind the pillows and comforters—there are in a place this far north, winter six months of the year, L. L. Bean right down the road, Orvis next door in Vermont, not to mention all the other mail-order outfits, Yak Works, Lands' End, Great Pacific Whatever? Who ever thought there were that many downy birds in the world?" Chasse leaned closer, added conspiratorially, "Personally, I think they're cloning it. The ducks, I mean. I would if I were a duck."

Roz smiled in spite of herself.

Chasse sat back. "So I guess we'll never know. Anyway, that's where it was left last fall, death by misadventure or suicide. But the Squires kid never believed it for a minute, and after the family sent for the autopsy report and the results of the inquest, apparently at his request, of course the fat was in the fire. The kid's no dope; he knew she'd been murdered. He told us all this last night, trying to explain what he was doing here. He and the family had insisted right along that the drug theory wouldn't wash; apparently the girl was hypersensitive to most drugs, used to get wired on half a cup of coffee, patent cough medicine gave her visions, and they insisted she'd never touch the stuff, too risky, no matter what the note said. As for the suicide theory, the kid had just talked to her about all her problems, she sounded fine, and everything was going to work out. She was going to see this Thor guy . . ." Chasse looked at Roz. "You okay?"

"Yes. I just was wondering about . . ."

"Yeah, right," Chasse interrupted. "Well, to make a long story short, I think the kid was certain all along the girl was killed by somebody here, and it finally got to him, brooding on it out there on the other side of the country, not able to do anything, knowing the killer was going to get away with murder. Just twisted him all up inside. But why he had to be so"—Chasse stopped, momentarily at a loss for words— "so *literary* about it all, I'll never know." Chasse sat back, with the air of someone who has said his piece. "I mean, I know we found a book on her lap, but just the same . . ."

"Poetic justice," Roz murmured.

"Yeah, I guess."

Roz sat across from him, mulling over what he'd told her. But if Alison Nelson was murdered, why had the killer put the open book in her lap? To throw everyone off the scent? Luke had thought it was meant to be a suicide declaration, a reproach to the cold-hearted academics who had brought her to this pass. "Thou'rt poison'd with that book." The family had discounted the accidental overdose theory, but there had been the note found in her pocket, written in her hand, something about drugs. What exactly had it said? Had the killer given her the drugs? Rick had known, with good reason, that Alison had been murdered. He had had his revenge. But who had really killed Alison Nelson? Did Rick think he knew? "About my syllabus..." she began. "You mentioned Agatha Christie."

Chasse nodded, regarding her curiously.

"I was just thinking. Series murders usually are meant to cover up the real target, throw people off the scent as far as the true motive goes, aren't they? I was just wondering whether Rick really knew who killed her."

Chasse shrugged. "How could he miss? He starts with Parsons, goes right down the line, makes it look like someone's out to wipe out English professors. Make it look like the work of a maniac, and get off on grounds of insanity. Who was it who said, 'if this be madness, then there be method in it'? Of course," he added in response to Roz's surprised look, "they also happened to be English professors connected with Alison Nelson. But maybe he did know— or thought he did—who was the main event."

"So who *was* the main event?"

"It would have to be either Parsons or Manciple, the two who were actually killed, wouldn't it? I'd say the real target was Manciple."

Roz thought a moment. "But why would Manciple kill Alison Nelson?"

"Maybe she just got in his hair. I hear he had a nasty disposition. Or maybe there was some sexual thing..."

"Or maybe it was an accident..."

Chasse stared at the ceiling. "Anyway, he sure got his." Roz, remembering the scene from *The Rover,* briefly closed her eyes. Blunt the lecher, the lascivious demeaner of women. "And I will beat thee and rob thee, strip thee naked and hang thee out the window by thy heels...." Poetic justice indeed. Rick the avenger. It all fit.

"It's crazy," Chasse said mildly, "but I still think it's possible the kid really did just go quietly berserk once he got here, and started knocking off anybody who could possibly have done her in. Revenge, pure and simple. There's no accounting for crazies."

There it was again, Occam's razor. The simplest answer, after all. But Chasse had said earlier that he didn't think Rick was crazy. Was he still holding something back? "Do you believe that?" she asked.

"Maybe," Chasse said cryptically. "Maybe not." He looked down at his watch. "Whoops, I gotta go. The doctors say Franklin's coming out of his coma any time now, and we're hoping he'll be able to shed some more light on this mess. I'm not counting on it, though." He stood up, hands in his pockets. "Listen, you've been a really big help."

Roz stood up, turned around to put on her jacket, then remembered she hadn't asked him about the note. She did so now. "You can see it," Chasse said, "but I guarantee you it won't help." He went away, came back shortly with a copy, a dusty gray reproduction of a piece of paper torn off at an angle, reading simply, "Thanks but I've got all I need to turn on ... [torn through]" and "another session with old PCP ..." She had to admit, as Chasse had warned, it did nothing more to clarify the circumstances of the girl's death.

"One more thing," she asked as they were on their way out the door. "Have you heard any more about Thor Gret—"

Chasse turned in the doorway, regarding her with such a serious expression that the words froze in her throat.

"I was hoping you wouldn't ask." He paused, as if choosing his words carefully. "I'm afraid I have some bad news for you. When the blast furnace cooled down enough, about five o'clock this morning, I had my men sift through the ashes."

Roz stared at him, feeling the cold creep up from her feet. Fire and ice, fire and ice. The hooded figure bending over the hellish furnace.

"They found pieces of bone, chemical traces of burned flesh and hair. They haven't been able to tell much about them yet, but they can tell from preliminary studies of the cell structure that"—he hesitated, then said quickly, his eyes on her face—"they were the bones of a long-legged creature."

He caught her as she fell.

C H A P T E R

23

*R*oz sat on the couch in her apartment, her eyes hot and swollen from crying. She had been remembering Thor, the last time she had seen him, his bald head bobbing across the Quad in the direction of the Chapel, shining in the ruddy light of the bonfire. She couldn't believe that he was dead.

But maybe they were wrong. Maybe those weren't Thor's bones in the furnace after all. Maybe they were other bones, say, from his lunch; such a convenient incinerator, wouldn't it be logical just to toss your garbage, assorted burnable trash, old steak bones ...? Her heart soared, then sank. Thor was a vegetarian. She put her head in her hands again. If only she had acted sooner, called the police and insisted they take Rick in as soon as she suspected ...

She jumped when the doorbell rang. Slowly she went to open it. Luke Runyon was standing there. Without a word, he stepped forward and wrapped his arms around her, murmured into her hair: "My dear, I just heard. How awful for you."

Roz was conscious only of broad shoulders, comfortable chest, strong arms that held her gently, the faint smell of tanned leather and freshly applied aftershave. She tilted her head back to look at him. His hair was tousled, as though he'd been running; his usually well-tended mustache was in a state of disarray, his face tense with concern.

"Oh, Luke," she said. "Oh, Luke," and started to cry again.

"Now, now," he said. "Just go ahead and cry, let it all out."

Roz obliged, weeping fresh tears into the front of his shirt, clutching the supple material of his coat. His arms went around her again loosely, in a comforting embrace; she felt his mustache lightly graze her cheek. She sank forward, sobbing, into an unspecified interval of total self-indulgence.

"I shouldn't have done that," she said some moments later, pushing him away gently but firmly.

Luke released her. "Why not? Crying's good for you. If it weren't for that old bit about hating to see a strong man cry, I'd probably be doing it myself." Luke shrugged. "Old habits die hard."

Roz stepped back and wiped her eyes. Strong men indeed. Well, she could stiffen her upper lip with the best of them. In a tone as brisk as she could muster (slightly undercut by a still-trembling voice and a loud hiccup) she asked: "What brings you here?"

"I wanted to make sure you were all right." He stood in the doorway, shifting his weight in his boots, looking concerned.

"Oh, come on in and sit down," Roz said with more asperity than she felt. She went to put on some coffee and splash cold water on her face.

"We tried to get him sooner, you know. I called Chasse right after I talked to you," he told her when she had brought him a cup and had sat down across from him, on the sagging couch. "I told him everything, but then he had to go wake up a judge to get a warrant, and by the time we got to the kid's place he'd already left for the college. We decided it would be better not to take him out of your class—too disruptive, and we want to keep this as quiet as possible. Anyway, they were supposed to keep an eye on him, but I got called away to an emergency meeting, and the next thing I knew they'd lost him, and you know what happened after that. Interesting meeting, by the way. The Committee on Faculty Personnel Policy's all bent out of shape because we've lost two tenured professors in a matter of months, and now Art Franklin's decided to retire early. He woke up yesterday, and the first thing he said was that he was throwing in the towel. Said this was no longer any profession for a gentleman."

"Did he . . . ?"

Luke shook his head. "None of them knows how the kid could have spiked the grappa. All they know is it wasn't one of them." Luke sat back in the chair. "Phew! I've just been out straight. Hey," he said, sitting forward and studying her face. "You *are* all right, aren't you?"

Abruptly Roz stood up, walked over to the window, stood contemplating the snowy landscape. "He loved the winters here, you know. This morning, when I got up, before I knew, and saw the snow, I wanted to go out in it, just to get out and get away, go skiing or something. . . . To forget. And I keep thinking of that poor girl, sitting there dead with the book on her lap. 'Now you shall/Never utter it; thy curiosity/Hath undone thee: thou'rt poison'd with that book. . . . I have bound thee to't by death.' Oh, Luke, it's so true for all of them, and so sad."

There was a long silence. Roz pressed her hot face against the cool glass, the image of Alison Nelson sharp as ice in her imagination. Then the silence was interrupted by a loud beep-beep. Roz looked up, startled. Luke was reaching into his jacket pocket, looking annoyed. "It never lets up," he said as he pressed a button on what appeared to be a small walkie-talkie. Of course; his beeper, so his office could reach him in case of an emergency, just like a doctor. "Where's your phone?" he asked, standing up and glancing around the room.

"Over there."

Luke strode to the phone, picked it up and dialed. Roz turned back to the window, trying not to listen. But his murmurings were almost completely monosyllabic. She wondered idly what the trouble was now. As if there weren't enough already.

She heard the sound of the phone being hung up. Luke came to stand beside her, put his arm around her shoulder. They stared out the window together. "The Squires boy just confessed. To everything."

Roz turned. "Thor?"

Slowly Luke nodded. Roz shut her eyes; then once again hid her face against Luke's broad chest.

"Let's go," he said softly some minutes later.

Roz lifted her head. "Go where?"

"Skiing. You mentioned it before. I think it's a good idea." He paused. "It's over, Roz. Life must go on. Look at all that beautiful snow out there." He gestured at the trees, the expanse of white. It was lovely, serene, unbroken.

She hesitated, then shook her head. "I don't have any skis."

"You can use Alice's; you're about her size. She left them behind when she took off with the boys," he added, that same note of bitterness briefly edging his voice as it always did when he mentioned his wife, "along with just about everything else." Then he smiled his disarming smile at her. "Let's do it; it'll be good for both of us to get out. I could use the exercise; it's been a hell of a week. Hell of a semester, as far as that goes. Get your stuff on, and I'll drive you down to my house. It's right by the entrance to the Arboretum."

As it turned out, he would not take no for an answer.
And maybe it was a good idea. She could mourn Thor—
and Rick, or, rather, the idea of Rick—just as well on skis
in the quiet woods as moping around her apartment. Maybe
better. And Luke even had skis for her to use; she wouldn't
have to bother borrowing a pair from CROC, the student
recreational organization. Hers were still back in Poughkeepsie, along with most of her ski clothes. She rummaged
through her closet and slipped into the best she could find
in the way of winter outdoor recreation wear—silk long
johns, blue jeans, turtleneck, flannel shirt, down vest, and
windbreaker—and went back into the living room.

"Nice," Luke commented. "You look like you just put
on ten pounds. Very becoming. What a swell wife you'd
make. For somebody," he added quickly. "Well, don't just
stand there, let's go."

They drove down the hill to Luke's house, which Roz was
surprised to see was not only directly across the street from
the Arboretum, but also next door to Iris LeBeau's. And
Art Franklin's house was right around the corner. Luke
hadn't been kidding when he talked about everyone living
in everybody else's pocket. Sure enough, as she got out of
the car, she noticed a shadowy figure looking out one of
the windows of Iris's house next door. She waved; the figure
waved back, then disappeared.

She stood to one side while Luke lifted the door of the
two-car garage and pointed out several pairs of skis in grad-
uated sizes; Alice apparently had left the boys' skis behind
as well. There was something pathetic about the family of
skis lined up there, with no family to use them. And two
cars, or, rather, a car and a pickup, the big brown one she
had seen before, for just one person. She glanced sympathetically at Luke. "Not much use for these in Florida," he
said. "Went back to her parents." He opened the inside door;

beyond, Roz saw a modern, very neat kitchen. He rummaged around in a bin next to the door, handed Roz a pair of square-toed cross-country boots. "Here, these should fit. Every woman I've ever known is a size seven and a half." Roz flushed. That was her shoe size, but she was not sure she liked being lumped together with every woman Luke had ever known. Luke motioned to her, oblivious. "Come on in while I change."

"No thanks, Luke. I'll just try these." She put on the boots, then took the second longest pair of skis down from the rack. Luke disappeared inside, reemerging several minutes later in a dark blue elasticized ski suit that molded to what was revealed as a very muscular, strong body. "You look like you belong in the Olympics," Roz commented as she looked him up and down. "That's quite a suit."

Luke smiled. "You don't look so bad yourself," he answered. Just then the phone rang. Giving her an exasperated look, Luke slammed back inside. She heard him pick up the phone, then silence. He reappeared in the doorway, his hand over the mouthpiece of the phone.

"It's my office again. Why don't you start without me? I'll catch up." He hesitated. "Unless you'd rather not go alone."

Standing there, contemplating Luke in his tight, very masculine blue outfit, Roz suddenly felt a surge of annoyance. Strains of a nursery song popped into her head: "If you go out in the woods today/You'd better not go alone. . . ." Who did he think she was, anyway? A child? No, a frightened woman. And she thought they'd gotten past that. She smiled sweetly at him. "That's fine, Luke. I'll just go along, and you catch up—if you can."

And without a backward glance, she shouldered the skis and poles and marched across the street.

CHAPTER

24

*T*he entrance to the Arboretum was a level clearing off which several paths disappeared into the woods. The skis Roz had were of the no-wax variety with fish-scale bottoms, slower in the long run, she knew from experience, but not bad for the occasional early outing when conditions were uncertain, as they were bound to be this afternoon. But if this cold weather settled in for good, she could always send for her own skis. Or she might even spring for a new pair, since those old army skis of her late father's hardly owed her anything. They were getting pretty beat up, but she had a sentimental attachment to them.

She clamped the skis onto her boots—actually, Alice's—and glided over to the large aerial photograph posted by the side of the clearing. Six—or was it nine?—miles of trails. A person could stay out all day. Even days at a time. She studied the map, trying to memorize the configuration of trails in case she got lost. But how could she? It was perfectly simple; the trails flowed down from the top of the hill like rivulets of marshmallow sauce on a chocolate-ice-cream sundae, the water tower like a huge cherry on top, around and down and over and through, but always back to civilization. This entrance was midway down the hill, the beginning of the main trail, which seemed to start out downhill—she assumed that was what the crosshatching meant, arrows pointing down, anyway—for a couple of miles, then ran back up, circled around the power line, the water tower, and came out at the top of the hill behind the President's house. It looked like a good run down that broad slope at the end, nice and fast, if you liked that sort of thing. And Roz did. There were lots of side trails going off into the woods, but one of the nice things about cross-country skiing was that you couldn't get lost; there were always your own tracks leading back the way you came. Unless, of course, there was a blizzard. Roz looked up at the sky. It was as clear and pale blue and brittle-looking as a porcelain bowl. Then she thought of Luke. Think you can keep up? she imagined him saying. Watch me, she thought.

She thumped her skis in the powdery snow, slid them back and forth vigorously, pushed her poles in hard, and took off, humming perversely to herself: "If you go out in the woods today/You'd better not go alone...." But she was alone; the snow in front of her was as untouched and virgin as the moment it had fallen, not even an old rut or two to show that someone had gone before. And that was another thing about cross-country skiing: you could always tell where you'd been, *and* if anybody had been there before you. She was alone. Until—*unless*, she corrected herself—Luke could catch up.

"The Teddy Bears' Picnic" was a charming song, but as far as serious skiing was concerned, she herself preferred "Waltzing Matilda," so as she strode briskly along the path into the woods, she began to sing, softly at first, then more loudly, the rhythm picking up along with her exhilaration, until shortly Roz forgot all about her annoyance with Luke. The woods, to quote a more appropriate source, were lovely, dark and deep, the snow in front of her unbroken, as she thumped farther and farther on, swooping downhill with a

minimum of drag, running on the straightaway, the whap-
whap rhythm of her skis the only sound.

Deeper and deeper, up and down she went, pushing into
what seemed to be the next best thing to forest primeval,
great bent and naked-looking paper birches interspersed with
huge pine trees looming over the path, their branches swinging low with their burden of snow, the only sound provided
by the thud and swish of her own skis and the occasional
small explosion of white as piles of snow suddenly cascaded
down one of the shrouded branches with a firm thump-
thump-thump as she passed, only to swing back upward,
causing a further avalanche from adjacent weighted branches.
Roz swung along, oblivious of everything, letting her mind
wander aimlessly back and forth, thinking of nothing in
particular, until it fixed benignly on her class the day before,
and she remembered with a smile Oblonsky's shocked face,
and then Milton's prophetic description, long before the
discovery of Antarctica, of a land of ice, came back to
her—being a quick study, over the years she had in spite
of herself memorized great chunks of Milton, among other
things—"Beyond this flood a frozen continent/Lies dark
and wild, beat with perpetual storms/Of whirlwind and dire
hail, which on firm land/Thaws not, but gathers heap, and
ruin seems/Of ancient pile; all else deep snow and ice,/A
gulf profound as that Serbonian bog/Betwixt Damiata and
Mount Casius old,/Where armies whole have sunk: the
parching air/Burns frore, and cold performs the effect of
fire...."

And there it was again, the memory of yesterday, of Thor
and the furnace. She shuddered, trying to shake the recollection off. Desperately she tried to put her mind onto memories of a rather more personal and pleasant nature than
Milton's mighty lines and what they inevitably reminded
her of. Luke was right. It was over. Life must go on. There

must be no regrets; she had done the right thing; she had done her best.

Gradually she became aware of two things. One was that Luke had *not* caught up, nor was he anywhere in sight, as far back as she could make out looking over her shoulder in the dimming light. She had no idea how far she had come or on what trail; mindlessly humming happy tunes, she had finally and mercifully been overcome by the sheer momentum of breaking her own trail in the trackless snow. The second was that off in the distance, very faint, but growing more distinct, she heard the sound of dogs. Not just one dog but several, yelping and barking rhythmically the way a pack of dogs does when it is hot on the trail of something, a deer or some other poor hunted animal.

She stopped in her tracks and listened. There was no other sound, not even the plop of snow falling from the trees, just the distant yelping, coming closer. But packs of dogs loose, running in the Arboretum? Hadn't she read something about enforced leash laws, dogs shot for running deer around here?

But that was out in the country, surely not here, where, unless she had completely lost her bearings, she was not at all far from houses and town, just over that hill . . .

Suddenly her skis stuttered under her. She looked down and saw that the track was no longer smooth, but rough and bumpy. Puzzled, she began to pick her way along with short cautious strokes, shoving herself with her poles, careful to keep the tips of her skis from dipping into the holes. There were many paw prints now, large splayed ones with the imprints of claws. She felt a chill creeping over her. Wolves? A bear? Shivering convulsively, she stared at the mess of tracks, the sound of barking and yelping sounding in her ears again. Could it be closer? Did bears yelp? Somewhere

a twig snapped like a pistol shot, and she felt herself go
tense. This is ridiculous, she thought as her neck prickled
under the layers of clothes. She picked up one foot and
pirouetted around, laid the other ski in the track, and started
back the way she had come.

She had not gone far before she realized that something
had obliterated her tracks. She had followed them back for
a half-mile or so to a kind of woodsy crossroads. But all
around the snow was roughened, tumbled about, both by
animals and by someone on foot. She couldn't tell which
way she had come. Someone had certainly been here after
she had. Was it hunting season? But surely there was no
hunting in the Arboretum; it must be poachers, with their
dogs. Not entranced by the idea of running into such rural
lowlife, she decided she had better find her way out. But
where was that? She cast along the other trails for some
while, but they all looked the same. But never mind, she
wasn't lost, she told herself; these trails had to lead back
to civilization somewhere. So she picked a trail that wound
uphill, remembering that they all came together in a point
at the top. Then with any luck she could find her bearings
and get back to where she had started.

But what she saw, as she stomped quickly up over the
hill, was not houses and civilization, but yet another hill,
winding up and up. I must be on the upper loop, heading
for the power lines, she thought. At least I hope that's where
I am. She scanned the darkening sky above the line of trees
for wires and poles. The sound of yelping was growing
louder again, had the distinct hysterical sound of dogs on
a chase, a sound she recognized only from reluctantly
watched parts of movies delineating fox hunts and other
blood sports, of which *Tom Jones* was the one that came
most readily to mind. Here was the same noisy baying and
yelping, and in spite of herself she thought of the deer, the
lithe, terrified animal, its thin spearlike legs striking down

deep into the snow over which the dogs, with their broad splayed paws, could run with ease, the deer running breathless, frantic, until the dogs caught up, the first one lunged, and caught and pulled. . . .

She realized that she too was running breathless, pumping her skis swiftly, faster and faster, as if the dogs were chasing her. Unwilling to break stride, she glanced down to see if she was in fact on a deer track, the narrow V-shaped beaten path so distinct across the shoulders of country roads, the two-pronged hooves driven deep . . . but no. The snow ahead of her lay pristine and unbroken. And behind, the dogs sounded closer. She realized she was afraid. She was alone and lost. The dogs were hot on her trail. She looked behind her, looked all around, saw nothing, at least not yet. Well, you can't just stand here and wait for them to swoop down on you and . . . and . . .

She struggled to keep from panicking. After all, she couldn't be that far from help; if only she could get her bearings, not get lost and go round and round endlessly in a loop, she could probably ski safely right into the President's backyard, down the broad fast slope to safety.

She listened intently. The sound still seemed to be coming from behind, and that meant the only thing to do was to go ahead. She took a few tentative glides forward. The trail at this point seemed to run level for as far as she could see; that was a blessing. There was not a moment to lose. Digging her poles in hard, double-poling, she struck out almost like a speed skater, kicking hard from side to side, as fast as she could go.

Several minutes later, she crossed the power line. The problem was, she could not tell which direction to go from here, since everything seemed to be on a level. More ominous, the yelping noise had stopped, not simply faded away as though she were outdistancing its perpetrators, but abruptly, as though someone had ordered it to stop. She tried not to imagine what for. Sweat trickled down her neck and under her arms; she panted for breath, slowed down, but did not stop. Wasn't there some way, by the look of the wires or something, that you could tell which way civilization was? She looked up, her breath rasping in her chest. It was hopeless; the lines all looked the same to her. All right then, no more pride, time to call for help. Damn Luke. Why hadn't he caught up with her? Of course, if she hadn't been proud and stupid enough to take off on her own ... But no time for pride now.

She stopped in her tracks, put her mittened hands around her mouth like a megaphone, and yelled, "Luke!" Her voice echoed back to her. "Hey, Luke!" She shouted several times, in all directions. "Somebody! Help!" She waited, ears pricked, for an answering cry.

None came. In fact, there was total silence in the woods, not even the sound of the dogs.

And then, as she stood chilled and shivering in the declining light, she saw in the distance a dark figure coming toward her. Luke. He must have heard her. Anyway, the figure was making straight for her. Faint with relief, she poled hard, skied off to meet him. At least she assumed it was Luke Runyon; even squinting and staring hard she could not make out his face; something dark was drawn over it, his hat, probably, but surely that was the dark ski suit he had been wearing, his figure black against the snow. She stopped, panting for breath, and rested on her ski poles, watching the figure grow larger, the face still indistinct.

But what was that covering his head, some sort of balaclava? Conscious of a growing chill, she watched the figure toiling closer, seeming somehow larger, bulkier in the dim light. Was Luke that stocky, his movements that labored?

Roz tensed. And it was not the skin-tight suit Luke had been wearing; this was looser, baggier, and black, not navy blue. She watched the ungainly, upright figure trudging up the hill. It did not resemble Luke at all. Closer and closer, the shadowy image looming in her mind. . . .

A black mask with only one slit for the eyes, burning eyes, white-rimmed, the foundry, and, before that, the night of the riot, breath panting in her ears, and blackness as something heavy closed over her head, covering her face so she couldn't breathe, in her nostrils, hard against her mouth. And then the hard foot smashing against her temple, and blackness dropping like a trap door to nothingness . . .

Feet shuffling, bare feet, stocking feet, booted feet. Head to foot, head to toe. The Ninja movie. Ninjas had feet with toes. Her attacker had had feet with heels. High heels. It all fit. The house so near, overlooking the gazebo. Shoes with heels. The jealousy, the resentment, years of being put down, passed over for the chairmanship. Satan, Iago, the Pardoner, Grendel, they had all felt themselves impaired. And so had the killer. Not Rick after all. Rick, like Thor, had been framed.

Paralyzed, she watched the tall, erect figure moving inexorably toward her, now no more than a dozen yards away. The figure stopped too, and from behind the dark knitted skier's mask came a low chuckle.

"'Cover her face; mine eyes dazzle; she died young,'" the figure said, voice muffled by the mask, unrecognizable. But the taunt was clear.

Roz stared in horror directly into the burning eyes, the crazy eyes. She had been wrong, all of them had been wrong. Only one homicidal maniac at any given time. Who had killed Alison Nelson, had killed them all? Frozen in her tracks, Roz whispered, "It was you all the time."

"I knew you'd realize it sooner or later," the voice hissed, muffled through the mouthless balaclava so like a Ninja hood. But the police had the hood now, picked up in the foundry. "And you such a smart girl, as well as young and pretty, and so very very persistent, always asking questions, always poking your nose in. What a waste. I knew when you started talking about that damned play." The figure paused, elbows resting casually on ski poles. "It was a risk, leaving her like that, but I had to get back at her somehow, the little bitch. She was in my way. She was going to tell them everything, the harmless little pranks in the dorms, about my liking young students, young girl students. Oh, she never seemed to mind, at least not at first, but then she changed, was going to tell. Make my life 'an open book.' It would have been the end of my career...." The figure began to shuffle forward.

"Oh, that's terrible," Roz blurted, backing up slowly, the fish scales of her no-wax skis inhibiting her motion. Then, forcing her voice into the level tone of disinterested sympathy, she said. "But how did it happen? It must have been an accident."

Once again the figure held up. "Of course it was an accident. She came to my house, stopped by on her way up the hill. I could tell right away she was on something, the silly idiot. All her high and mighty talk about never touching the stuff—she was higher than a kite. She'd talked to her boyfriend, the one they think did it, thanks to you—when all the time I was trying to make them think that Thor ... But no, what was I saying? She came raging in at midnight, saying it was all my fault, and she was going to tell them if I didn't do something, get her reinstated, and she was going back to the Squires boy, that I was dirty and perverted ... She was screaming at me so loud I thought the neighbors would hear for sure, and then the doorbell rang, and I stuffed her in my closet, the cedar closet with all the winter clothes, to stop her shouting, because if anybody found her there, what would they think? And she was crazy, violent. I could hardly control her, and I took my down quilt and stuffed it in on top of her, and all the pillows, so she couldn't move, and I locked her in, and went to answer the door. . . ."

"Who was it?" Roz inquired, her eyes fixed on the masked face, now unmoving, staring off into space. Keeping her upper body turned toward the figure, slowly, almost imperceptibly, she began to work her skis around so they were pointing sideways.

"Griselda Franklin," the figure spat out in disgust. "Old busybody. She'd seen the lights go on, heard noises, thought there was something wrong. She came barging right in. I told her I had the flu. She wanted to fuss over me, but I sent her home. Then I went to get the girl, and . . . she was dead. Smothered. You understand, it would have been the end of my career, and I'd worked so hard for so little, to have it all ruined, even though it was an accident, not my fault; I had to get rid of her, her and her damned book for the course she'd failed, waving it in my face, saying it was all my fault, so I put her out in the truck and covered her up, then I drove up and down the road a while to make sure no one was around—it was so foggy—and then I sat her in the stone house, in the cold, and put the book in her lap. I gave her the damned book—it was so clever of me—so people would think she'd done it herself. And just in case they didn't get it—but you got it, didn't you? So smart— I put the other note in her pocket, about the computer, and turning on, some work she was doing for me. It fit perfectly. . . ."

Making little innocuous stamping movements, Roz had managed to turn her skis almost downhill. Not far enough yet. Nevertheless, she gripped her poles, really to take off. It was her only chance. One killer had killed them all, Alison too, all the ones who got in the way. And Thor was to take the blame. But Thor had died instead, and it was Rick now. And she was the only one who could tell them where to look . . . whose down. Who pulls me down? Oh, God.

"I don't know why I'm telling you all this," the figure murmured. "But it doesn't matter, because out here in the woods, with no one around..."

Roz watched helplessly as the figure casually switched one ski pole to the other wrist and started to shuffle toward her slowly, like a lion tamer advancing on a mesmerized beast. "But Alison died of exposure," she said, trying to gain time, distract the killer once again. "So it *was* an accident."

"I always wondered about that," the killer said. "She must not have been dead after all. I thought she was, but that was even better. Freezing to death like that, not a mark on her..."

Roz gazed, fascinated, a deer caught in the headlights of an approaching juggernaut, as the figure shrugged itself out of the down vest that covered the bulky upper body. "It worked once; I don't see why it won't work again." The figure came nearer, the down vest held up like a dark cloud...

And suddenly Roz found her volition, whirled around in a thump and spray of snow and skis and, jamming her poles in with all her might, fled across the snow as fast as she could go, through the line of trees, along the narrow trail, not knowing whether it was ahead or back the way she had come, aware only of the pounding of her skis, her heart, indistinguishable from the pounding behind her, the pounding of her pursuer's skis. And as she went, with what breath she could spare, she screamed: "Help, somebody! Help!"

Help me, help me, her skis repeated; if I'm killed no one will ever know about Alison, and Rick, know who the real murderer is....

And then she broke through the trees into an open field, the land falling away abruptly, far away down the hill a house, small against the expanse of unbroken snow. The President's. A sob caught in her throat; no more screaming.

She had to save her breath. If only she could stay on her feet...

She dug the poles in hard and kicked off, tucking her head down in the attitude of a downhill racer, but already she knew it was hopeless, even as she whizzed down the hill, losing momentum as the rough fish scales impeded her skis, and she heard the panting of breath behind her, closing in. Then she was struck from behind, one shoulder glancing at her hip, knocking her right off her feet into a tumbled somersault of snow. And they were rolling over and over, skis and poles and arms and legs every which way until they stopped, and the executioner was bending over her, bringing the down vest down, blackness descending....

CHAPTER
25

She had imagined before what death would be like, black, cold, like an electric shock, then dot dot dot, and had known, waking up in the foundry, that somehow that was not quite right. This was somewhat more convincing, this inability to move her limbs, this soft blackness over her face, stopping her breath.

But surely not the rousing strains of the "Ride of the Valkyries" done in bagpipes, squalling and skirling in her ears, echoing over the hills and valleys. The air lightened, and she looked up to see another figure swooping across the snow toward them, still distant but clearly huge, clad partly in fur, partly in what appeared to be the skins of antelope, the appearance of a horned helmet on the head, flying down the slope at breakneck speed, poles flailing in rhythm with the great strides on enormous skis turned up at the front like dragon boats, the scream of a jet plane landing, skidding, throwing up sprays of snow that came pattering back down, the shush and rush and slow rising thunder of great piles of snow collecting, an avalanche, rolling and breaking like surf over her, hurling cold needles on her face, then clouds of it everywhere around, and grunts and groans and thuds and whacks, then blessed silence, the sudden influx of air and light (comparatively speaking, since really it still only qualified as dusk) as she wiped the slush from her eyelids, lying there in the deep snow on her back— no surely not this bizarre horned and furred apparition, looming over her like some huge water buffalo, terrifying in its largeness, yet somehow not . . .

Because, peering down at her from his great height, underneath what seemed to be the biggest and most authentic-looking Viking helmet she had ever seen but was in fact only a tan baseball cap with two silvery stuffed horns sticking out on either side, were the mild gray eyes, exquisitely benign features, and—even now—unmistakably sweet expression of Thor Grettirsdottir.

She could not believe her eyes, her ears, but there he was, not the least bit dead, looming up in mounds of snow, plucking her up with one huge hand, brushing her off, looking her over, and inquiring gently: "Can you ski down to Bailey's house and call the police while I stay here with whoever this is who tried to kill you?" He motioned to a mound of snow feebly stirring just behind him.

Roz nodded dumbly, still staring at him open-mouthed. Thor, alive! "What . . . what are you doing here?" she finally managed to babble.

"Winter camping. All this snow—I couldn't wait to get out. Left yesterday about noon. Didn't anybody find my message? I left it on the foundry door." He beamed at her, bent over and untied the rawhide bindings of his skis from the great furry mukluks that made his feet look like the legs of a woolly mammoth, kicked them to one side. He turned his attention to the snowbank, now churning up small avalanches of snow as though it were about to erupt. Thor watched the heaving mound thoughtfully for a moment, then trudged over, turned around, and sat down on it. The snowbank jerked and then grunted; from one end two narrow skis popped out, flailed briefly, collapsed into a dispirited

X across the snow. From the other end emerged the dark, bullet-shaped balaclava, two burning eyes in a pale oval framed by the black mask glaring malevolently at her, at Thor.

Thor reached over and pulled off the snow-encrusted mask, revealing the strong chin, the tight-lipped mouth, the stern, darkly enraged visage of—

Luke Runyon.

CHAPTER
26

Somewhat shakily, Roz had skied down to the President's house, the sweet dour strains of "Amazing Grace," rendered as through a bagpipe, lilting softly over the snow behind her. Yes, it had indeed been Luke Runyon. She and Thor had spent the rest of that day and all the next at the police station, answering first Jeff Chasse's, then the state police officers', then lawyers' questions. Two days later, after the prime Northern white duck down of Luke Runyon's L. L. Bean comforter had been discovered to match exactly the down found in Alison Nelson's throat, Luke Runyon had been bound over without bail, charged with first degree murder in the death of Alison Nelson, with other charges pending in the assaults on Roz, Rick Squires, Franklin, Shipman, and Huberd, and the murder of Winston Manciple. Following Iago's example, Luke had steadfastly refused to speak word, but Thor, Rick, and Roz had among them provided enough evidence for an indictment. Rick had described Roz's attacker in the foundry as wearing a black Ninja suit, his evidence corroborated by the record of the minicameras, which had automatically photographed Luke as he slammed through the locked fire doors, setting off the alarms. During the attack on her in the Quad by the putative Grabber, Roz had seen not the usual Ninja bootees, with the distinctive separate big toes, but boots with heels and pointed toes: Luke's cowboy boots. The Ninja suit Luke had used to impersonate the Grabber was found at his house, hanging in his son Larry's closet, and the hood that Rick had picked up at the edge of the furnace proved to be part of the same outfit.

Rick of course had never confessed at all, had insisted on his innocence through many hours of interrogation, claiming that he had come looking for Thor, shouted for him inside the workshop, then in the foundry, picked up what he thought was an old rag, and had just seen Roz huddled behind the Giant's Playpen, when he had been set upon by the flying Iris. With the arrest and charging of Luke, he had been released without a stain upon his honor. What he *was* released with was a pair of crutches, for the roundhouse kick that Iris had administered in the foundry, mistakenly taking him for Roz's attacker, had torn some ligaments in his knee, which had been duly strapped up and was now immobilized. Luke, obviously planning to kill two birds in one stoke (of the furnace), had sent him a note as well, after he had learned from Roz that Rick had known Alison Nelson. So the poor boy had innocently walked in some fifteen minutes early for what he thought was his appointment with Thor because he had a meeting with Roz later, only to be dropped by Iris just as he was going to Roz's aid.

Not to anyone's surprise, the first thing he did on being released was to buy a plane ticket on the first available flight back to South Dakota, so Roz, Rick, Thor, and Iris agreed to gather at Thor's house for a farewell dinner, Thor promising a vegetarian banquet of such gourmet perfection and diversity that it would make converts—or at least fellow travelers—of even the most suspicious of carnivores, or so he said, looking significantly at Roz. Iris laughed and laughed.

"So Luke saw you going into the Arboretum at noontime," Roz said as she sat on a stool in Thor's kitchen watching him peel a very ripe banana. He had already peeled and chopped three apples, a cantaloupe, and a peach, which were now reposing under several inches of pineapple juice in what must surely be the largest and most complicated Cuisinart in creation. Roz wondered idly if Thor had customized it for his own purposes.

"Umm," Thor replied as he reached for a carton of buttermilk. "He asked me what I was doing, so he knew that I was planning to be gone overnight. The conditions were perfect, I couldn't wait, no classes the next day, and so forth. So he went back to the office, fired off those notes to you and Rick, leaving plenty of time to dispose of you, and then have Rick show up to take the rap. He went to the foundry and got rid of my note, and lay in wait for you. But Rick was early, and you"— here he paused, gave Roz, who was experiencing a case of the shudders, a look of mild concern—"were not quite so easy to dispose of as he had planned. He heard Rick call, dropped you and the mask on the floor, and split the quickest way, through the fire exit. Of course, everybody thought it was the furnace that set the alarms off. They didn't believe Rick for a minute when he said there had been somebody else in there."

"And Luke, being so ingenious and flexible, was able to turn everything to his own designs. Just like Iago."

"Right. And now his lips are sealed. But so is his fate. For the Norns." Thor dumped the buttermilk in with the fruit juice, tossed the banana in after it, and flicked a switch. The contents swirled for a split second. "There, that's done," he said.

"What is it?" Roz asked.

"Fruit soup. My grandmother's recipe. Want to hand me those bowls?"

"Fruit soup?"

"Fruit soup. And that's just the beginning."

Thor had cleared another part of the counter and was now mixing up a concoction of cottage cheese, sour cream, eggs, brown sugar, and wheat germ. He added a dash of vanilla extract.

"Is that dessert?" Roz asked.

Thor shook his head.

"Then what is it?"

"Noodle Fugel. It's one of the entrées."

Roz made a small spluttering noise, then bit her lip. Thor looked thoughtfully at her for a moment. "Do you want to see the menu, or would you rather be surprised?"

"I think I'd like to see the menu."

Silently Thor handed her a piece of paper scrawled over with purple Magic Marker. It read:

> Fruit Soup
> Peter Rabbit Salad
> Pasta with choice of sauces:
>   Mondo Fandango, Salsa Yucatano,
>   Soy Vay, Alio-Olio
> Noodle Fugel
> Zucchini Lasagne
> Thousand-and-One Nights Casserole

"Hmm," Roz commented after several moments. "Very interesting. Something for everyone." But there was something missing. After another glance at the list, she realized what it was. "What *is* for dessert?"

Thor shrugged. "Don't know. Rick's bringing it."

Reassured, Roz asked, "Speaking of which, where are Rick and Iris?"

Thor had put aside the Noodle Fugel, and was now crushing a whole garlic. Roz watched as he took down a jar of peanut butter. She got down off the stool and wandered across the kitchen to look out the window. "They went to Franconi's Preowned Auto Store to sell Rick's car. Iris thought she could get him a pretty good deal."

Roz smiled, wishing she could have witnessed the scene; Iris going head to head with a used-car salesman. Just then headlights wheeled into Thor's turnaround. "Here they are," she said. "I'll get the door."

Rick came in first, swinging on his crutches, Iris right behind with what looked like a covered pie plate. Rick grinned at Roz. "Dessert," he announced proudly, shifting his weight onto the good leg and swinging down his rucksack with a clunk. "Dakota Dad's TNT Torte."

Several hours later they had worked their way through all the courses, including Rick's many-layered torte. Roz had to admit the dinner had been a great success, none of the dishes anything like she had expected, or anything like the ersatz meatloaf, the tofu lamb chops she had experienced elsewhere. Thor was explaining to an enthralled Rick the different types of vegetarianism. "I'm a lacto-ovo, which means I eat eggs and cheese and dairy products. But no meat, no poultry, and no fish," Thor concluded.

"What about shellfish?" Roz asked, suddenly recalling the dinner at the Franklins', so long ago now it seemed forever. "The oysters Rockefeller. You ate a couple of huge helpings."

Thor grinned. "I gave Griselda that recipe. It's mock oysters Rockefeller, made from edible seaweed. You know those little knobs that you see on some of the seaweed at the beach; kids call them poppers..."

"Never mind," said Roz. This discussion, interesting as it was, had reminded her of something else. She leaned forward. "Thor, what about the grappa? You stopped me from drinking it. . . ."

"Because you didn't know where it had been. Do you have any idea how they make that stuff? After they drain the wine off of the vintage, they leave the leftover skins and stems and twigs rotting away at the bottom of the barrel or on somebody's dirty concrete floor. Then when this rotten liquid starts oozing out they bottle it up and sell it as grappa." It was Thor's turn to shudder, which he did. "Yuk. It was all right for Franklin and his pals—they knew what they were getting—but you, especially with all the other junk you eat..."

"Speaking of junk," Roz interrupted, "while we're tying up loose ends, what about the bones?"

"What bones?"

"In the furnace. They found bone fragments. For a while we thought they were you..." Roz broke off, feeling chilly again.

"Poached moose," said Thor.

Iris, Rick, and Roz stared at him as if he had taken leave of his senses. "Poached moose?" they cried in unison.

Thor nodded. "The custodian got an illegal moose, and he wasn't about to leave the evidence lying around. Meat is meat, but moose bones are something else, so he asked me if he could put the carcass down the blast furnace." Thor shrugged. "What could I say? Now they know, of course, and Sumner got stuck with a fine, and he's disqualified from next year's moose lottery, but..."

Iris and Roz got up and began to clear the table.

There was still some time left before Rick's flight, so they sat in the living room, on chairs that Thor had made himself, around a rug with the picture of a horned animal in the center, drinking coffee and continuing to tie up loose ends. Several aspects of the case still puzzled Roz.

"What about old Clark Parsons? Isn't that where it all started?" she asked.

"No. Parsons's death was in fact an accident," Thor answered. "But that's what gave Runyon the idea, that and his conversation with you on the plane that day. You told him all about your course, remember?" Thor nodded at Roz.

"So when Manciple started to pressure him, told him that if he didn't lay off Freshman English that Manciple and the rest of the English department would have his job, and if he had any plans to become President, they'd see him in hell first, he went quietly berserk," Iris added. "He wanted more than anything to succeed President Bailey in a year or two, so he could restore this place to what it had been in his time. He'd never approved of admitting women, and when they started going after the fraternities it was the last straw. So of course we were all getting in the way of his ambitions, just like Alison Nelson. And when you've killed once, felt that sense of power over other human beings, there's really no place to stop. . . ."

"Better to reign in hell than serve in heaven," Roz murmured. "But why did he want to kill me?"

"I suspect it was your interest in *The Duchess of Malfi*," Iris said. "Leaving the book open to that one quotation, 'thou'rt poison'd with that book' was a little bit of arrogance that he couldn't resist."

"Like the Pardoner," Roz said. "And then I quoted it to him in my apartment, just before . . ."

" ". . . he set off that little charade with his beeper." Thor nodded. "It was his secret revenge on Alison Nelson for threatening to ruin him, and something he never expected anyone to catch on to. But you guessed, or he thought you did, and that meant he had to get rid of you. And it would fit right in, a whole bunch of dead English professors. Clearly the work of a maniac. Of course Rick would be in the clear, but he planned to go back to his original plan, and make it seem as though I had done it, if not with fire, then with ice." Thor tried, without success, to assume the demeanor of a demented killer.

"Parsons and Franklin and Manciple didn't have a clue about any of this, but Luke suspected, wrongly, that Thor did," Iris said. "So when Manciple threatened to end Luke's career, he figured the whole bunch were in cahoots against him, and decided to take out everybody who had gone against him in one fell swoop. Kill them all, and incriminate Thor."

"And all because Alison confronted him with evidence of his own corruption." Roz was watching Rick, and saw his face go pale. He had been very quiet most of the evening. It was a good thing that he was going back to Pomona to finish school, away from this place where Alison had died.

"And it wasn't just his reputation at stake, either," Iris continued. "If the truth about his affair with Alison came out, especially with Rick here pushing the police to reopen the case, then there was a good chance he would be implicated in her death. He had thought right along that Thor suspected something about Alison's death, even though he knew Thor couldn't prove it, and when Manciple turned up with his clumsy attempt at blackmail—well, he decided it was time to clean the slate."

Rick turned to Thor. "What *did* you know about Luke and Alison?"

"I didn't know she had actually been murdered," Thor answered. "But I never felt right about the explanation of her death. Like you," he went on, "I knew she would never have knowingly taken the drugs, and I didn't think she'd deliberately take her own life." Thor hesitated, then took a deep breath; this was the most difficult part for him. "But what really didn't jibe was that I was *there*. I had gone by the place half a dozen times looking for her after she missed our appointment, even before the fog set in, and I knew that if she had been sitting up and visible, the way she was found, I would have seen her, fog or no fog. If not her, then certainly that red jacket. And I didn't." Thor sat forward, stared at the horned beast in the rug, holding his coffee cup between two huge fingers. "I didn't find her."

"Because she wasn't there then; Luke brought her later," Roz murmured. "But what about the drugs found in her body? And the note?"

"The drugs were in some pot-laced brownies her friends gave her as a joke. Some friends," Rick said bitterly. "They didn't know the pot was contaminated with PCP. It really hit her hard; she went right out of control, decided she'd confront Luke that very night. Otherwise she would never have done anything so foolish. She was pretty incoherent when she called me, but I didn't suspect what was going on. After she hung up, she went straight to his house. She didn't tell me his name, only that it was some professor." Rick shut his eyes briefly. "Somehow they got into a struggle and he smothered her in the closet. They can prove that now since the down matched up. Then he put her in the stone gazebo with a part of a message she'd sent him about some work she was doing for him on the Registrar's computer after hours. . . ."

"'Thanks, but I've got all I need to turn on . . .'" Iris said.

"That's right," Thor said. "She had written to tell him he *needn't* be there; she had all she needed to run his programs. She didn't *want* him there, looking over her shoulder, using that as an excuse to fondle her."

Roz looked from Thor to Iris and back again, puzzled. "But what about the reference to PCP?"

"That was her name for Clark Parsons—Old Pedantic, Confusing, and Pompous, she used to call him—PCP." Rick smiled wanly, adjusted his weight in the chair with his arms, and stuck his injured leg out straight. He picked up what was left of his wine and gulped it down. "That and the book open on her lap were supposed to set the scene for suicide. But nobody ever got the part about the book"— he nodded at Roz—"until you came. They just wrote it off, publicly anyway, as an accidental overdose."

Roz looked at Rick; she really had to admire him. After all he had been through, sitting there talking about it so calmly. But he was tough, resilient; he would be fine. And she would probably never see him again.

"What about the Grabber?" Roz asked. "How did Luke work that?"

"One of the students involved came forward," Thor answered. "Luke had formed his own little secret society of fraternity men to terrorize women on campus, hoping eventually they'd leave. He was always masked when they met, his voice muffled, so they never knew who he was. Their orders would come by phone. He ordered them to disrupt the play as a diversion so he could set up the scenery for Manciple's fall, and he came up with the witness who was ready to swear you were attacked by the Grabber in the Quad. Sometimes he was the Grabber, sometimes one of the others was. There's no doubt that he enjoyed harassing women."

They sat silent for a while, thinking about Alison Nelson, and Luke, and the others, Roz remembering Luke as he had seemed to her, polite and circumspect, thoughtful and chivalrous to a fault. A gentleman of the old school, biding his time. A man who would brook no interference with the fulfillment of his ambitions or his desires. She had turned out to be another damnable woman, just like his wife, like Alison, and, like them, had gotten in the way. Luke had reacted just like Iago, like the Pardoner, like Satan. He had tried to destroy them all, finally, for the sheer fun of it, for the challenge. Like Iago, he had thought he had justification, and also like Iago, he had overreached himself, allowed himself to be pulled along further and further into evil.

"Whoops," said Iris. "Look what time it is."

Rick turned to look at the clock, then struggled to his feet, grabbing his crutches. "I've got to go; my plane leaves in twenty minutes, and it's the last flight out until next week," he said anxiously, addressing the whole company, but looking straight at Roz. Impulsively, she stood up.

"I'll drive you, Rick," she said, adding quickly, "That is, if it's all right with Iris."

"Of course. It'll give me and the big fella here a chance to get started on the dishes." She reached into her bag and tossed Roz the keys.

Southwark's tiny air terminal was hardly more than a shack, with the Moosehead Airlines ticket desk, boarding gate, Rent-a-Wreck, and several soft-drink and coffee machines crowding around the two rows of chairs that constituted the waiting room. Neither of them sat down. Rick stood somewhat awkwardly between his crutches, his weight resting lightly on both feet, while Roz checked his one bag through; he was carrying the ever-present rucksack on his back. The ticket agent demanded the rucksack too. With some difficulty they removed it, Rick twisting and turning, hopping from one foot to another, his face whitening. The rucksack was full of *Norton Anthologies*: Roz had given him several more varieties as going-away presents. Roz plunked it on the scale and glared at the agent. "Sorry, miss, no carry-on baggage allowed on the plane. No room; it's all gotta go in the nose."

Overhead Roz heard the plane roaring in for a landing. It flashed by the darkened window, wheels squeaking. Rick's flight was due to board in five minutes; there was just enough time allowed to get the incoming passengers and their luggage off, the outgoing ones on. Walking back toward Rick, who was looking away from her out the window, Roz felt

a sudden sharp pang; she would never see him again. He
looked in her direction, his cheeks red again, his black hair,
which she was certain he had not had cut since she'd met
him, now tumbling down over his eyes. It made him look
years younger, almost urchinlike. He smiled, and her heart
flopped over in her chest.

"I don't suppose..." he started to say, and Roz waited
for him to finish, with what she hoped was a dispassionate,
impassive, academic look on her face. Then they called his
flight.

Rick looked distractedly around the terminal, then helplessly at Roz. Clearly he did not want to miss this plane.
But, for the moment, he also looked as though he didn't
want to leave.

The baggage was being brought in on a rolling cart that
looked more suitable for a small public library, and the first
of the passengers was stepping off the plane, heading for
the opening in the chain link fence that served as the incoming gate. There wasn't a moment to lose. Even this small
airport had an electronic weapon detector in the shape of
an empty doorjamb all passengers had to depart through,
their luggage sent along a conveyor belt beside it through
an x-ray scanner. The two other passengers had already
gone through.

"Here," Roz said, "I'll do your ticket while you go
through," she said, waving him off in the direction of the
gate. Only one gate out and no gate in; a meager stream of
passengers was walking from the plane toward the opening
in the fence. She snatched the ticket stub back and ran to
help Rick, whose crutches were too wide for the narrow
opening of the detector. She held them while he hobbled
through, then walked around to hand them over, say good-
bye....

"Passengers only beyond this point. Sorry, miss," the
agent said, barring her way. "You can go back around to

say your good-byes, young man, but make it snappy," he remarked to Rick, who looked ruefully at Roz, then shifted his weight and started to hobble back toward her.

She shook her head, held out her hand over the barrier. "That's all right, Rick. We can say good-bye right here." Her mouth was oddly dry. "Have a good flight home. And thanks for everything."

He gazed at her for a moment, his look unfathomable. "Thank *you*," he said finally. In that instant he seemed unspeakably forlorn, so young and vulnerable, she almost leaped over the barrier to throw her arms around him. But there wasn't time, and even if there was . . . Planting a chaste kiss on her hand, she reached forward and patted it onto his fresh cheek. He smiled.

"Last call!" the clerk said sternly.

Rick swung away through the outside door, down the ramp, into the floodlit area where the small plane waited. He turned and waved, mouthed something that looked like "I'll write" before he disappeared into the darkened plane. But Roz knew he wouldn't.

She turned away, walked toward the exit. It was just as well. She walked quickly out of the terminal, and, eyes unused to the dark outside, almost bumped into one of the passengers, a rather large figure in a lined trench coat and an Irish tweed hat pulled down over his face, as he leaned down to pick up a battered suitcase. "Sorry," the figure said in a pleasantly husky, slightly British-sounding voice. But not *quite* British. She stopped short. The figure straightened and turned to look at her, then abruptly took one step forward and wrapped two muffled arms around her. The aura of paint thinner was unmistakable.

After some breathless moments during which Roz was only dimly aware of the sound of a plane taking off and passing overhead, Alan finally released her, said in a puzzled voice, "But how did you know I was coming?" He looked down at her quizzically. "Or are you going? Because if you are, you just missed your plane."

"Neither...both...Oh, I don't know." Roz tried to catch her breath. "Actually, I was seeing Rick Squires off."

"Well, listen, I got your packet, and came as soon as I could. Really, Roz..." As Alan gazed down at her face, she saw terrible suspicion dawn. "Rick Squires has left before the end of term?" He stared at her thoughtfully for a moment. "That means it's over, isn't it?" he said dispassionately. "And I have flown all this way to be at your side, including the last hour on an aircraft the size of a vacuum sweeper painted to look like an elk, only to be too bloody late *again*?"

Gravely Roz shook her head. "As a matter of fact, you're just in time."

And overhead the last plane flight banked its way around a turn, heading west, the pilot taking his bearings from the twin strands of glowing amber streetlights that festooned the darkness all the way up College Hill.

FOR THE BEST IN PAPERBACKS, LOOK FOR THE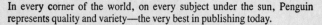

In every corner of the world, on every subject under the sun, Penguin represents quality and variety—the very best in publishing today.

For complete information about books available from Penguin—including Pelicans, Puffins, Peregrines, and Penguin Classics—and how to order them, write to us at the appropriate address below. Please note that for copyright reasons the selection of books varies from country to country.

In the United Kingdom: For a complete list of books available from Penguin in the U.K., please write to *Dept E.P., Penguin Books Ltd, Harmondsworth, Middlesex, UB7 0DA.*

In the United States: For a complete list of books available from Penguin in the U.S., please write to *Dept BA, Penguin*, Box 120, Bergenfield, New Jersey 07621-0120.

In Canada: For a complete list of books available from Penguin in Canada, please write to *Penguin Books Canada Ltd, 10 Alcorn Avenue, Suite 300, Toronto, Ontario, Canada M4V 3B2.*

In Australia: For a complete list of books available from Penguin in Australia, please write to the *Marketing Department, Penguin Books Ltd, P.O. Box 257, Ringwood, Victoria 3134.*

In New Zealand: For a complete list of books available from Penguin in New Zealand, please write to the *Marketing Department, Penguin Books (NZ) Ltd, Private Bag, Takapuna, Auckland 9.*

In India: For a complete list of books available from Penguin, please write to *Penguin Overseas Ltd, 706 Eros Apartments, 56 Nehru Place, New Delhi, 110019.*

In Holland: For a complete list of books available from Penguin in Holland, please write to *Penguin Books Nederland B.V., Postbus 195, NL-1380AD Weesp, Netherlands.*

In Germany: For a complete list of books available from Penguin, please write to *Penguin Books Ltd, Friedrichstrasse 10-12, D-6000 Frankfurt Main I, Federal Republic of Germany.*

In Spain: For a complete list of books available from Penguin in Spain, please write to *Longman, Penguin España, Calle San Nicolas 15, E-28013 Madrid, Spain.*

In Japan: For a complete list of books available from Penguin in Japan, please write to *Longman Penguin Japan Co Ltd, Yamaguchi Building, 2-12-9 Kanda Jimbocho, Chiyoda-Ku, Tokyo 101, Japan.*